A FaeVille Novel

KIERIAN

N. F. SCHMITT

Books by N.F. Schmitt

The Courting Seasons Series

A Kingdom of Promises and Lies

A Queendom of Heartbreak and Deceit – *coming spring 2025*

A Queendom Book 3 – *To be Determined*

A Kingdom Book 4 – *To be Determined*

FaeVille Series

Kierian

Tennyson – *To be Determined*

Erilea – *To be Determined*

Pronounciation Guide

PRONUNCIATION GUIDE

CHARACTERS:

Erilea: Ear-Uh-Lay-Uh

Kierian: Keer-Ree-En

Skyla: Sky-La

Tennyson: Ten-Uh-Son

Al'Kede: Al-Kade-Day

Aerie: Air-Ree

Mytilda: Meh-Til-Duh

Syreni: Sigh-Ren-Knee

Rhoda: Road-Duh

Lorelei: Lore-Uh-Lie

Towns:

Piggs Burough: Pigs Burr-rough

Fairfield: Fair-Field

Chapter One

SKYLA

The last two weeks of my life had been a nightmare. My mind was frazzled, and my eyes had a constant burning ache to them. I desperately needed sleep. I was running on fumes, but this deep within the Fae woods had offered me very little reprieve. My very first night had taught me to not risk dozing off for too long. I had barely escaped with an inch of my life from the Fae beast that had attempted to make a meal of me. When the trees nearby had low enough branches, I would climb them and take quick naps during sunup. The last few days had proven fruitless, as the tree branches were far too tall to climb.

My nerves were beginning to get the best of me. I jumped with every snap of a twig and my vision started playing tricks on me. I began seeing shadows out of the corner of my eyes or a dismantled figure in the distance. I shook my head, hoping the current one I was seeing a hundred yards out was a figment of my imagination. When I looked in the same spot again, it was gone. By this point, I think if my heart ever slowed, it would feel funny to not be running on this much fear.

A warm summer breeze caressed my skin. I welcomed it and secretly begged for more. It was the cusp of summer, and humidity already threatened the air, making the dampness of the woods smell musty. The nights, however, dipped and would turn my shakes from fear into ones from the coolness. My clothing was inadequate for the shifts in temperature. As threadbare as they were, the only decent thing they were able to do was keep me clothed.

My stomach growled, and I glanced at the red berries in the bushes I was passing by. The idea of eating them made me too nervous. There was no telling what side effects they could cause me. Normal berries could leave me with vomiting or hallucinations, but an unknown berry in the Fae woods could have me begging for death. If I took the unknown berries, it would be a risk with the outcome. Shifting the knapsack's weight on my shoulder, I sighed at how light it had become. My food supply probably would last me another day at most.

Making a last-second decision, I picked some of the berries, putting them in my pocket. Come two days from now, when I was desperate and out of options, I would take my chances when I ate them. A squirrel darted in front of my path, and I watched it longingly disappear into the shrubbery. Starting a fire to cook any animals I trapped, meant risking bringing unwanted attention to myself. An involuntary shiver ran through my body from the thought of the nearest unknown creature.

When I first set out on this quest, I had foolishly believed I knew what I would be up against. I had been naïve. After the first week, I had begun questioning if this trip would be worth the cost. Seven days later, the question roared in my eardrums. But turning back now would lead me to absolutely nothing. I no longer had a home to go back to. There was no family waiting for me. I had a couple of friends from the orphanage, but to them I would be nothing more than a distant memory. I would become like all the other children that had aged out, a name with a memory attached and nothing more.

I knew that maybe I had been putting too much stock into a story I had heard many years ago. A traveling wagon had stopped in my pathetic town to sell their wares. The majority of the travelers paid little heed to children, especially orphans. They knew we did not have the coin to buy from them. However, in this traveling group, there was one lady who did pay mind to us. She was beautiful with long black hair and ocean-blue eyes. She would sit us all in a circle and tell wonderful tales of their adventures.

I ought to curse her and myself for the reason I started this journey. The one tale she told was about a Fae warrior who lived in a cottage deep in the Fae woods. There, he brewed potions, remedies, and would grant anyone's deepest, darkest desire. As a child, I never thought it was an odd combination for a warrior to make potions. Now, as I made this trek, I found the notion completely ridiculous. Why did I put myself through this? Oh, I know why because I wanted him to grant my desire to get as far away from Piggs Burough as possible. I wanted to live in a place that was charming, with a life that I could afford and a husband who adored me. I didn't need luxury; I wanted happiness.

The secretly, selfish part of me would fantasize about a Fae Prince whisking me away and giving me everything I desired. He would be tall with broad shoulders and muscular arms, capable of effortlessly swooping me into his arms to carry me away with him. I swooned over the high cheekbones, strong jawline, and pointed nose to look haughtily down upon everyone else. Sometimes, I gave him long black hair; other times, it would be silver starlight. When I was playful, I imagined it was red like my own fiery locks. Oh, how we would giggle at the fortunes of having hair that blazed in the sunlight together.

I sighed to myself, chuckling; instead of my fantasies coming true, I had been tromping through the woods to make my own destiny. This mystery Fae warrior wasn't a prince, but he had to be out there. Maybe this, too, was a bit of folklore I was chasing after. When reality came crashing down, I would know that this adventure was for naught. I reminded myself that I had survived two weeks thus far and that I could keep going. My stomach let out another growl in protest; okay, maybe another two days, depending on the berries weighing down my dress pocket.

The dense woods started allowing patches of light to stream through the tree-top canopy. A flash of bright green caught my notice, and I shoved ferns out of my way to gain a better look. It was green grass. Was this the clearing? Had I made it to the edge of the Fae Woods? I started shoving more fern leaves out of the way, carelessly creating a racket in my path.

Emerging from the woods, my gaze looked out at the grassy knolls. The breeze blew through the grass, causing the blades to look like waves on the hills. My heart leaped as I noticed the single tree on one particular hill. It was tall, gnarled, and old but full of healthy green leaves. Taking a deep breath, I let my eyes fall upon the house that, in my heart, I knew would be there.

The cottage was quaint. It was simple, with little windows and flower boxes nestled beneath them. It was painted cream with intricate white trim around the doors, windows, and roof edging. I questioned if the Fae painted or if they used magic from the witches.

I had to remind myself that just because this cottage's appearance was identical to the description I had heard from that traveling lady. That it did not mean this was the very same cottage I had been searching for. As my heart raced with excitement, I decided there would be only one way to find out. I hauled my knapsack over my shoulders and made my way to its front door.

I noticed the closer I crossed the distance to the cottage, the variety of plants surrounding it had been meticulously planted. There were dozens of herbs growing throughout, and the planter boxes under the windows held more herb varieties. Off to the side of the cottage, away from the singular oak tree, were three honey hives, and I edged away from them. Fae bees could be quite ornery when messed with.

The grass turned into old, worn stone steps leading me to the front door. I did not hear any rustling inside, and taking a deep breath, I knocked on the door three times.

Chapter Two

KIERIAN

I glanced at my door, not certain I had heard correctly. No one has knocked on my door in decades. Rarely did another Fae, aside from Tennyson, come this far for me. It was the way I preferred it. I would make the trip to various towns to sell my healing remedies and then retreat back for months on end. I only left when I needed to replenish my supplies again. Annoyance and curiosity swirled through me at who could be on the other side seeking my attention. I looked down at the new healing salve that I was in the middle of mixing. I had been attempting to perfect this particular mixture for a while. I looked back at the door, debating on ignoring whoever was on the other side or staying to mix. If I left this healing salve to sit for too long, the batch would be ruined, and I would need to start over. I looked up at the ceiling of my home to see if I would glean any answers from it.

A meow brought my attention back to the door. The lavender cat that lived with me, against my will, sat at the door. Her tail swished back and forth as she eyed me expectantly. I set down the mortar and pestle I had been holding. Closing my eyes, I pinched the bridge of my nose as my brows furrowed in frustration. I would not take orders from this cat.

She meowed impatiently this time and with my heightened Fae senses, I heard her tail swish against my wooden floors. There would be no winning against her. I let out a huff of frustration as I opened my eyes to cross the room to my front door and where the cat sat.

I did not sense danger or ill intent on the other side of my door. Instead, there was a lingering sense of hope and despair. Traces of female came through, but that didn't ease my mind. Females were far more cunning in a fight; for all I knew, this one was masking her true intentions with despair, and I could be attacked the moment I opened the door. The cat meowed again, looking at me expectantly. I released a breath of irritation, and with curiosity, I opened the door to the surprise waiting for me.

Of all the things standing before me, a human woman was not at the top of my list. The nearest human village was not an easy feat from here. I questioned how long she had survived in the Fae woods and how she had found herself within them. I did not see a weapon on her and doubted the knapsack on her back provided any. I widened my senses to the perimeter of my valley. When I came up empty, I understood why hope, despair, and now fear rolled off of her. She was completely alone. I relaxed; she was not dangerous to me.

As she studied me, I roamed my eyes over her. The first thing I noticed was her fiery red hair. It looked ablaze in the sunlight, even with the broken twigs and leaves stuck within it. Her bright green eyes were held full of curiosity. Freckles splashed across her cheeks and button nose. She had naturally pouty lips, and momentarily, I wondered what they would feel like to be pressed against my own.

Mentally, I shook the notion from my head; I did not need to bring that kind of distraction into my life.

I moved my eyes down to her clothing; they were in a desperate state. The dingy orange dress and brown leggings were ripped in various places. They were thin enough that the barrier left little to the imagination from the amount of skin I could see through the articles of clothing. She huffed in tiny gasps as she began catching her breath. I wondered if from her desperation when she saw my cottage, hope swelled within her and she ran up the hill to knock on my door.

Maybe she was one of the gullible females who had heard Fae could make wishes come true. Humans never got the story straight about what creatures granted wishes. The fluffy lavender-gray tail caught my attention as the cat began to intertwine between this human girl's legs. She glanced down at the particular-colored feline, and I noted how her knees slightly bent momentarily before straightening again. She was trying to withhold herself from petting the creature that was vying for her attention. Peculiar, usually, the cat did not pay heed of attention to anyone.

I realized I had dallied too long in my thoughts over this strange human girl. I was afraid she would be fairly disappointed in me, and I needed to resume mixing the ingredients. I did not have excess time to give her unless I wanted the potency of the salve to diminish, and then I would need to sell it at a lower cost on top of starting a new batch.

I tilted my head to the side, taking her in. She braced one of her hands on my door frame, steadying herself. I simply did not have time for this. I turned, closing the door behind me, but it didn't click shut. Irritably, I glanced over my shoulder to see her scuffed, muddy boot wedged in between the door and the frame. I followed the boot up her leg to her red, scowling face. I quirked my eyebrow at her, waiting for an explanation as to why she would hinder me from closing my own door.

"You're. . . you're Fae," she bluntly stated.

I stared at her, becoming bored by the entire situation.

"My name's Skyla," she rushed out. Her breathing became easier as she was no longer huffing anymore. She stood there, not saying anything more, and I wasn't certain as to what she was waiting for. I needed to get back to mixing.

"If you could please remove your boot, I need to return to my work," I briskly stated. Opening, and slightly closing the door on her boot harder to get the point across. She flinched from the slight pain it caused but did not remove the offending footwear from my house.

"You're supposed to state your name," she responded.

I blinked at her from the audacity that she dared to have. With my barefoot, I softly tapped her boot out of my door, closing it. The lock clicked shut in her face. The cat could find its own way back in, as it usually did. The red-haired human began pounding on the door in an attempt to gain my attention as I could hear her shouting in frustration. I put a silencing bubble around the interior of my house and blocked her out. Turning, I returned to my kitchen to resume making my salves. I sighed with relief that despite the time she had taken up, it had not ruined the potency of this batch.

Chapter Three

SKYLA

I stood there in momentary shock; I could not believe the audacity. My hope quickly turned to anger as I started pounding my fist against his door. In the back of my mind, I knew I was at his mercy, but I had thought he would have at least let me in. He was nothing like I imagined; he had brown hair that went past his shoulders, and on the left side, a white streak ran through his hair. His brown eyes were like warm honey in the sunlight. Similar to the other Fae I had seen in the past, he wore clothing in the shades of nature. He had loose brown pants on and a green tunic. Like most Fae, he was tall, and his features were more angular.

When the side of my hand began to throb, I stopped beating on his door. If he hadn't come back to open it up now, he probably wouldn't anytime soon. I let out a shriek of frustration; huffing, I looked down at my second-hand used shoes. I wanted to kick his door, but I knew with the minimal protection my footwear gave me, my toes would feel more pain than my anger found relief.

I huffed again as I remembered the oak tree and caught sight of it out of the corner of my eye. I glared at his front door again before stomping over to the tree. At least it provided me with shade as I took my seat below it. I narrowed my eyes at the cottage; all the excitement I had felt moments prior turned sour. I knew my daydreams had gone wild; what had I been expecting? For him to welcome me in with open arms?

I ought to be grateful that he was unlike the Fae beasts lurking in the woods. Fear slid through me as I turned my attention from the cottage to gauge how close the woods were to me. I looked up at the tree's lowest limb and knew I couldn't climb it. I would need to take my chances of it still being daylight and in the middle of an open clearing so that nothing would attack me here.

At least the Fae people were not supposed to be dangerous to humans like myself. Even with the Fae Wars ending three hundred years ago, there were still humans that claimed a Fae had snatched up an unsuspecting female maiden or a newborn baby had been swapped in the dead of the night. I knew there were still cases when a Fae or human would break the law and kill one another, but it was not something I worried about too often.

My eyelids were becoming heavy as my body slumped against the tree. I fought to stay awake in this vulnerable location, but it was a losing battle. My blinks became slower and longer until my head nestled into my shoulder, and the world faded.

Chapter Four

KIERIAN

Hours later, I stepped outside of my house and was surprised to find the red-haired human still in my yard. I had completely dismissed her from the front of my mind. She was curled up under the old oak tree on my hill with her eyes closed. From where I stood, I was under the impression she was asleep, given how slack her face was and the tiny bit of drool coming from her mouth. With how much time had passed by, one would assume she would have traveled back the way she had come from.

Hmm. I dismissed my thoughts and continued on my way past her, venturing into the woods to pick up a few more ingredients. I had run short on witch hazel and needed a few more branches along with elderberry. Following the deer path to where I needed to go, the nagging curiosity of wondering why she was in my part of the woods kept coming back to me. I kept shooing the thoughts from my mind. It was inconsequential. She would be gone from this life soon enough, and then she would just be a part of the collection of memories that randomly surfaced for me. I probably would wonder what had happened to her after leaving my woods, but that would be all the attention I would give the memory of her.

An hour later, I was traveling back with my ingredients. I noted the red-haired human was still asleep under the tree. I sniffed the air and could not detect rain or any predators nearby. Sleeping on the ground was not the most intelligent thing to be doing this deep in the woods. I glanced at her, questioning how humans had survived this long making these kinds of careless mistakes. But I knew, in the end, it was not my concern. Sighing to myself, I walked back into my cottage, allowing natural selection to take its course.

Chapter Five

KIERIAN

Bang. Bang. Bang. Came from my front door in the dead of the night. Groggily, I crawled out of my bed. Who would be banging on my door at this ungodly hour? I casted my senses to the other side of the door, ensuring it was not a threat to me. Sensing minimal ill intent, I half shifted into my other form, grabbing my dagger just in case. With my free hand, I gripped the door handle and partially opened the door. I glanced down to find the red-haired girl glaring up at me until her eyes widened. A look of startlement flashed across her face.

"You have antlers," she blurted out.

"Do you always say the first thing that comes to your mind?" I asked, irritated by her disturbing my sleep. Her gaze left my antlers and trailed down my naked body.

"You're naked!" She squeaked, backing up but not taking her eyes from my manhood. I crossed my arms over my muscular chest, making sure the dagger still in hand didn't slice me. Standing naked before her did not unnerve me the same way it did her. Her face almost matched the color of her hair from the shade it had turned in the moonlight.

"Why are you naked?" She asked, still not looking away. I twitched my cock a fraction, and her eyes widened as she gulped and brought her attention back up to my face. I had to hide the small sense of satisfaction I felt. She looked everywhere on my face but would not meet my eyes. I watched in amusement as she fought, from looking back down at my naked body to looking up at my antlers.

"Are you really not going to answer me on anything?" She asked. I could tell she wanted to sound annoyed, but it came out as a nervous giggle. I watched her, assessing the female before me. As a human, she posed no threat to me; she was thin on the cusp of being malnourished. Her clothes, I realized, were not only ripped from her travels through the woods but were threadbare. It was the beginning of summer, which did not pose a problem for her, but I wondered what she did in cold weather. The sack she had at her feet did not give me much comfort in warmer clothing attire.

"Can you at least let me in?" She glanced behind her warily, and I followed her gaze as she looked back at me. "Please?" Her naturally pouting lip protruded a bit, reminding me how earlier I wondered what it would feel like against mine. Desire coursed through me momentarily. I did not need this kind of distraction. Her eyes flickered to meet mine, then my mouth up to my antlers, and then, if I had to guess, settled on my pointed Fae ears.

"Why?" I asked, curious about her reasons.

"Because it's getting dark, and it's scary out there." She glanced back over her shoulder nervously.

"I only have one bed," I stated blandly, *one bed that I wouldn't mind having my fun in with you.* I inhaled sharply; maybe I had been alone for too long.

"That's fine! I'll sleep on the floor." She rushed out as she tried to push past me on the left, but I stepped over to block her way. I felt the rough material of her dress brush against my cock, and a low grumble rumbled from the back of my throat. Her eyes widened, and she stepped back. My already hardening cock from the thoughts of her now stood fully erect with the subtle touch it had felt. My gaze trailed down her body, taking in the soft roundness of her breasts and the curves of her hips. My mouth becoming dry. When was the last time I had laid with a female?

"Please?" a whine entering her voice. I trailed my eyes up and down her twice before letting out a sigh.

"Fine." I uncrossed my arms, letting the dagger hang loosely in my left hand at my side. I moved, allowing her to walk past me. She glanced down at my dagger, but then again, maybe she was watching my hardened cock. I twitched it again, and she squeaked, walking faster past me. Enjoying the view of her backside, I smirked to myself. This would be fun.

I watched as she paused in the middle of my one-room cottage, taking in my whole home in one single glance. I felt my hackles rise that she may judge the simplicity of my living conditions. Closing the door quietly behind us. I stood there waiting and watching her.

Chapter Six

SKYLA

I was highly aware of the naked, aroused Fae male standing behind me as I took in his home. It was both simple and complex, depending on where I looked. The walls were a light pastel green with knotty wooden floors of various shades of oak. I glanced up at the open rafters that were lit by Fae lights; I wondered if they glowed all the time or only when the Fae male deemed it so. I had never seen Fae lights in person before and found there to be a whimsical, magical charm about them. I trailed my gaze back down to take in the rest of the room.

On my right side was his cot with a simple dark blue blanket strewn aside, probably from me interrupting his sleep. I didn't mean to, but when I awoke in the dark at the base of the tree, I had become frightened. It had been weeks since being out in the open like that. I had become accustomed to the dense, thick woods. Fear had slid through me at the thought of walking back to the edge of the woods to find a tree to climb. Instead, I had chosen to wake him up and beg for hospitality.

Moving my vision to the left, I noted a simple light wood, handmade table with two sturdy-looking chairs. Next to the dining furniture, starting at the floor, red and gray stones layered on one another. They built themselves up to hold a slate slab for a countertop filled with jars of various ingredients and herbs. Lavender and other drying plants hung from the ceiling amongst the tucked in kitchen behind the bar nook. There were bowls of various sizes on the counter behind the bar and glass jars filled with liquid substances that I could not determine from this distance. An unlit fireplace was nestled next to the kitchen with a black kettle hanging over top of it.

"I can sleep in the corner here between the door and the fireplace," I offered, trying to indicate I would stay out of his way as best as possible. He remained silent, and I braced myself. Turning back around to face him, I forced myself to look only at his darkened brown eyes and not his hard cock or the antlers on top of his head. He was a deer Fae shifter of some sort. It made more sense to his brown hair with the white streak running through it. I did not know how to handle him being naked or aroused. It wasn't like I had not accidentally seen a male cock before, but it had never been this up close either. I gulped, waiting for him to say anything.

I felt my body warming as he broke eye contact and trailed his eyes up and down my body again. Despite my clothing, he made me feel vulnerable. A flush ran through me, and I wanted to take a step back. I wondered if my chances of survival would be better outside this cottage than inside.

"Alright." My voice came out shaky. "I'll just go over there." I lamely pointed at the corner I had stated I would sleep in. I turned, and it felt like my legs were made of liquid as I walked to the corner. I only hoped they didn't give out from under me. I noticed how fast my heart was racing and the reaction he gave me. I braced my hand on the wall and slowly sank to the ground, sitting cross-legged as I looked back at him.

He stared at me for a moment and then turned, and I watched his muscular buttocks walk away. I never realized Fae males were so beautifully sculpted underneath all their clothing. A small part of me was grateful he had not demanded my body as payment. But the other part of me wondered what it would be like.

Something about him told me he knew his way around a female body. Fae lived for hundreds of years; he surely had to have had his fair share of lovers. Glancing back around the room, I could not find any indication of a female on the premises; maybe he was lonely. I watched as he crawled into bed. He looked back at me, and I yipped as I pulled my knapsack into my lap. I hugged it close to my chest as if it could protect me from him. He watched me and then grabbed his blue blanket into his fist and pulled it over him, turning his back to me.

I let out a sigh and set my knapsack to my side, intending to use it as a pillow as I laid down on my left side and looked at him. The Fae lights blinked out, cloaking the room in almost complete darkness if it were not for the moonlight streaming in through the window onto the wooden floors.

I could not see him in the shadows as the moonlight did not reach there, but I could hear him breathing. I let out another sigh and rolled onto my back with my hands on my stomach. Sleep came easier to me than I had intended. I believed it was because I felt safe tucked away and not sleeping underneath the open sky.

Chapter Seven

KIERIAN

I woke up irritated and did not understand why. I had a hard-on I needed to take care of. Rarely did I have to deal with these anymore, and I rolled onto my back to begin stroking myself with my left hand. A feminine scent caught my nose, and I looked over, remembering the red-haired female still curled up, sleeping in the corner. Now, I understood why I needed release. I had been breathing in her scent all night long. I had caught the scent of her arousal last night but had dismissed it.

Instead, I imagined her pouty lips wrapped around my hard cock. Her tongue playing with the head before she took me fully into her mouth. I pumped my hand up and down faster, feeling my orgasm building. I fantasized about her crawling up my body, her long red hair trailing along my chest as she positioned herself with my head at her entrance, and then she slammed down onto me, and I was enveloped in the warmth of her wet, tight pussy. I came as hot spurts of my cum shot onto my chest. I grabbed a nearby cloth on the ground and cleaned myself up. Unfortunately for myself, it did not cure my hard-on. *Fucking hell.*

I forced myself out of bed, grabbing my tawny pants to wear. I decided not to throw on my shirt just yet. I looked back at the sleeping girl and wondered again what had brought her here. Padding over to the kitchen, I grabbed a cast iron skillet and eggs.

Chapter Eight

SKYLA

The smell of bacon woke me. I was not a stranger to sleeping on a hard floor, but after sleeping in trees upright for two weeks, my muscles protested as I moved to sit up. I felt the kink in my neck from the lumpy knapsack. My mind felt clearer and not as frazzled anymore. I glanced over at the Fae male, who was shirtless as he cooked breakfast. The kitchen bar top blocked my view from the lower half of his body, and it made me wonder if he was still naked. Heat rushed through me, and I shook my head from the indecent thoughts that were beginning to enter.

Gingerly, I stood up and walked over to the bar to get a better look at the food he was preparing. If he were entirely naked, I would have to deal with how I reacted to him.

"Morning. What are you making?" I asked, starting the conversation. He looked over at me, and I noted that he no longer had antlers on top of his head. I glanced at the pan, saw the eggs cooking in it, and, to my relief, caught sight of his pants. It did not go unnoticed how his cock strained against the fabric. I pulled back a bit so as not to be caught looking.

"Breakfast," he replied in his low voice.

"Riveting." I rolled my eyes and said, "You never did tell me your name." His eyes flicked to mine momentarily, and I noticed the irritation in them, and then he focused back on cooking the eggs. He tilted the pan onto a ceramic plate, letting some of the eggs slide onto it, before moving the top plate off the one it was sitting on. The remaining eggs went on the bottom plate. I watched as he put the skillet off to the side, and then, from a covered plate, he procured already-cooked bacon. My mouth started watering. I hope I was not reading into this and would be disappointed if this second plate was not for me. He divided the bacon in half on the two plates. I watched as he grabbed a knife with a jar of what I could only guess was marmalade by the dark berry color and chunks of fruit in it. Lastly, he brought forth a basket of bread. Without saying a word, he handed me one of the plates of food.

"Thank you," I said quietly as we both headed toward the table along the wall with the two chairs. I sat with my back to his bed and ignored the fork he offered, instead grabbing a piece of bread from the basket that he placed in between us. I reached for the marmalade jar and started lathering some onto the bread. When satisfied, I put the knife back in the jar, and moving back to my plate, eased a sunny-side-up egg onto my bread. I took a bite and reveled as strawberry marmalade flavor burst across my tongue, mixed with egg yolk. It was delicious. I paused as I realized the Fae male was watching me instead of eating his breakfast. I swallowed and tilted my head to the side.

"Yes?"

"Do they not have food where you're from?" His gaze lingered over my body, and I felt myself becoming self-conscious. I was aware of how my bones jutted out at certain places and how my dress fell off my shoulders. It was too big for me to begin with, and I had to cinch it with a belt. My only saving grace was the tattered brown leggings I wore beneath it.

"They do," I replied slowly, readying myself on the defense.

"Hmm." He sat back in his chair, assessing me still. I felt the irritation growing in me as I waited for the insult I was positive would come next from his mouth. He dropped his gaze back to his plate and continued to eat. I sat there confused; I was unprepared to be proven wrong. Tediously, I took another bite of the messy egg sandwich I had created while eyeing him warily. The annoyance left me as minutes passed by, and he still did not make an insulting comment.

"Kierian." He commented quietly, and I sat up straighter.

"What?" I wasn't sure what he had said.

"You asked my name; it's Kierian," he answered, his attention leaving his breakfast plate as he set his eating utensil down to look at me. He propped his elbows on the table and folded his hands together to rest his chin on them.

"Kierian," I repeated, testing his name on my lips. A small part of me had believed he was never going to reveal his name to me. Kierian held my stare, and it felt as if he could see right through me. A mental shiver ran through my body. "I'm Skyla."

"So, you have told me already," he commented dryly. I sat there awkwardly as we looked at one another. If I had to guess, he did not feel even remotely awkward about this situation. He sat there across from me, cool and collected, assessing me.

"Do you commune with humans often?" I asked nervously. I wanted to break the tension I was feeling. I only hoped asking questions would be a positive start. Aside from Kierian raising an eyebrow, nothing else about him moved. He sat there still as a statue.

"No."

"Then why me?" I pushed, feeling as if I was pulling teeth. He was like most Fae, a creature of few words. The Fae were too much like cats, silent and always observing. They looked innocent enough, harmless even, but like a cat, they were still a predator deep down, and in this food chain, I was prey.

"Because you are the first human in a very long time that has graced my doorstep," he replied matter-of-factly. Even as he blinked, he did not look away, and I shifted uncomfortably in my seat from his unrelenting stare.

"How long are we talking?" I was desperate to keep the conversation going, and my curiosity was getting the better of me. Kierian cocked his head to the side, and I watched as his white strands of hair moved with the motion. He looked up at the ceiling as he mulled it over. I was quite surprised he didn't already have an answer to give me, but I felt a small sense of relief from him finally taking his gaze off of me. I picked up a slice of bacon to eat while I waited for his response.

"Two hundred years, give or take." He returned to staring at me; he didn't even twitch as I almost started choking on the bacon. Despite knowing Fae lived for hundreds of years, the idea of hearing it out loud by one still startled me.

"How old are you?" I blurted out before I could stop myself. His expression became unamused at my impoliteness, and I gritted my teeth. I should have been more composed than that.

"It is rude to ask one's age; is it not human?" He tried to hide the amusement from his voice, but I still could hear it through the bored tone he attempted. It occurred to me that he was trying very hard to mask everything about himself. He did not want me to know his thoughts or reactions to anything.

"You know my name, Fae," I countered with a smirk. The corner of his lip twitched, but it did not raise to the smile I speculated he was hiding away. *Interesting.*

"How did you know about my cottage . . . Skyla," he said my name carefully, and a warmth of happiness spread through me.

"There was a woman when I was younger that visited my village and told me of various Fae stories," I began, taking a deep breath as I continued. "She mentioned there was a cottage in the woods on a grassy knoll and that the Fae male within would grant me a wish." I knew how foolish it sounded to say it out loud, and I regretted it the moment I noticed the way his jaw tightened.

"Do you happen to know the woman's name?" He gritted out.

"Yeah." I squirmed in my chair. "Her name was Syreni?" I was uncertain if I should have told him her name or not. My only consolation was this had happened decades ago when I had been a child. The woman was long gone now.

"Dammit," He growled. His hands came down to clench the edge of the table. "That sea bitch is still telling that rumor." Anger flared in his brown eyes, turning almost to a murky red-black. I jerked back into my chair. I wasn't ready for him to display this much emotion.

"You know her?" I inquired, hesitantly. My voice came out higher pitched and a bit shakier than I had intended.

"Yeah, I know her." He rolled his eyes, crossing his arms over his chest as he leaned back into his chair. "She loves to torment me. I thought for certain she had stopped telling that story two hundred years ago, but *apparently*, she decided to start it back up again with you now here at my cottage." He pursed his lips, but it didn't feel as if he was annoyed with me as much as he was irritated with the storyteller from my past.

I relaxed as I picked up my utensil to continue eating the food on my plate. I had thought the woman was human, but to now know she was one of the Fae astounded me. I wondered who she was to him. Perhaps a lover or just a friend? My thoughts were interrupted by Kierian.

"I can't grant wishes; I'm not that kind of Fae. Unluckily enough for you, your trip was a wasted trek."

My shoulders slumped, and the food no longer had much taste appeal. I knew my childish daydreams would disappoint me someday. The trouble I now faced would be heading back to a village that had nothing to offer me—that is, if I survived the long trip back.

"Can I stay here?" I asked abruptly, not even thinking. I felt the tears threatening to form as they pricked the back of my eyes. Warmth cascaded over my body as the emotions surged through me. There was fear that he would reject my request, mixed with the disheartening heartbreak that my childhood dreams were all a lie.

"Why?" His gaze looked me over, his mask slipping back into place. It didn't conceal the curiosity and amusement I found in his eyes that were no longer murky. I glanced about the cottage, trying to find my answer. It was evident by the single bed that he was a male who was used to living alone. The living area was tidy but simple, and I wondered if another had ever lived with him. Aside from the kitchen, which was abundant in drying herbs hanging from the ceiling, nothing else about the cottage gave an indication of life. For how bare everything else was, he could have recently moved in, and I would never have known the difference. There was not a single decoration or anything to go off of to gain an understanding of who Kierian was. His home was empty and void of all emotion and life other than the kitchen.

"Because I have nowhere else to go." I felt the raw pain in my throat as I forced my voice not to crack. I looked down at my lap, letting my head hang at the truth before I whispered out, "And because I'm afraid to travel back through the Fae Woods."

"What about your human village?" He did not hesitate to ask.

I blinked back the tears, trying to keep it together.

"There is nothing there for me." The words were strained, and I was ready to move off of this topic. I looked up at him, trying to give my best look of determination. "I promise to stay out of your way and will try to help out as best as possible." It was the only thing I could offer in exchange for staying here.

"You'll help me with anything, I ask?" His voice lowered as his head tilted slightly to the side. His eyes trailed over me slowly, and I had an inkling as to what he was referring to; I gulped nervously.

"I'm inexperienced, but yes." My heart picked up speed, and I wasn't positive if it was from excitement or fear at what I was offering him.

"Inexperienced?" His brows furrowed as he sat back in his chair, crossing his arms once again.

"I'm a virgin." My cheeks warmed as I let my words fall on the table between us.

Chapter Nine

KIERIAN

My ears roared at her confession. This female sitting before me was a virgin. When was the last time I had been with a rutting virgin? I had been asking if she would go collect herbs in the Fae woods, a task that stole too much of my time. Instead, she was offering herself up to me—a ripe virgin for the picking. I forced my body to stay locked in position, trying to keep my control in check. She was watching my every move. Her skin pinkened when she said 'virgin,' and her eyes danced between lust and worry.

"Do you not want a virgin?" She asked as she shifted in her seat. I tracked the way she licked her bottom lip before pulling it in with her teeth. I detected the worry in her voice and clenched my jaw tightly until it began to hurt. Containing my composure was difficult as arousal coursed through me, and I breathed heavily through my nose. I needed to reign in this urge as I felt my hard cock straining against my pants.

"It's not that I don't want a virgin," I replied with great restraint through gritted teeth. I needed to get myself under control.

"Then what is it?" She asked as her teeth let go of her bottom lip. Her tongue darted back out to swipe over the indents left behind. What would it be like if I left my teeth marks on her? I took deep breaths in through my nose and back out. I had no desire to desecrate a virgin unless she willingly wanted it, free of payment. She blinked at me with those innocent green eyes, and I knew I was either going to take her virginity right here and now, or I would need to retreat from my own home.

"I need fresh air," I stated. The wooden chair screeched harshly against my floor as I stood up abruptly. Her gaze fell on my protruding rigid member tucked away in my pants.

"I could take care of that," she offered nervously, her teeth biting her bottom lip again. For half a second, I considered it and shook my head, blinking the indecent thoughts from my mind. I did not utter a word as I crossed my house and yanked open my front door, the wood buckling from the force. The door was still closing behind me as I shifted into my full stag form and sprinted away, trying to run her out of my system.

<h1 style="text-align:center">Chapter Ten</h1>

SKYLA

I sat there stunned. I watched as Kierian shifted and now, a white-tailed deer bounded away from me. I didn't take my eyes off the retreating whitetail until the door slammed shut, cutting off my view. After witnessing his antlers yesterday, it made sense that he was a Fae deer shifter. My gaze fell upon our unfinished breakfast. I suppose I could clean this up while he was away. Maybe he would let me stay if I could prove to him that I was useful. I had not meant to make it awkward, but I was willing to do anything if it meant Kierian said yes to me staying.

I thought I had been reading all the signs right that Kierian was having a physical attraction to me. It wounded my pride that he hadn't chosen to act on my offer. I had not anticipated being rejected to hurt this much. Then again, we had only met yesterday; maybe The Fae had different courtships than humans? Lamely, I picked up both plates and looked around the kitchen. I tried to figure out how I was to clean them. I did not see any water pump in sight. There was a sink but not a spout.

"How am I supposed to clean these plates?" I asked out loud, and with a quiet chime, they were magically cleaned. I had to catch myself from dropping them. "Fae magic," I breathed. My imagination ran wild at the possibilities if I was able to stay here. Manual labor would become a thing of the past if I had Fae magic cleaning up everything after me. I glanced around the cottage again. Maybe that was why it was immaculate; the Fae magic kept it so. My thoughts became distracted as I felt fluffy fur brush against my legs.

"Meow." I looked down and found the fluffy lilac gray cat at my feet. She then began to intertwine between my legs, rubbing up against me.

"Hello again," I said in greeting. I set the two plates on the bar top by me and squatted down to pick her up. Yesterday, she disappeared when Kierian shut the door in our faces, and I wondered where she had run off to. I was glad she was okay, but I feared the creatures in the Fae woods would have eaten her alive. "What is your name?" I asked the cat, knowing it was silly. I would not receive a response.

Mytilda, a deep feminine voice, said in my head. I squeaked, dropping the cat as I fell on my ass, staring at her. *Careful human.* She growled; her tail went ramrod straight up in the air as she walked away from me. I watched as she disappeared under Kierian's bed. That cat had just communicated to me in my mind. Did that mean it could read my thoughts? Were all Fae creatures able to communicate telepathically? Could Kierian read my thoughts? I clapped my hands to my cheeks, feeling how warm they were from embarrassment. *Oh no.*

It was then I noticed the pain in my body from falling so hard. My whole backside felt jolted, and a warm, hot pain was throbbing in my arms and wrists from catching myself. I groaned, flopping back on the clean, smooth wood floor as I stared up at the Fae lights. Pain still throbbed in my lower back as I laid there waiting for it to recede.

The front door opened, and I braced myself for Kierian's return. I closed my eyes and took a deep breath before forcing myself to sit back upright, ignoring the dull throb. I opened my eyes and froze; it was not Kierian. Instead, a different Fae male dressed in complete black and armed to the teeth with weapons casually walked in. He froze mid-step when his eyes landed on me.

"And who might you be, Petal?" He purred with curiosity, tilting his head to the side. He gave me a wicked, cocky smirk where I only saw his right fang. I had thought Kierian gave off predatory vibes, but the energy emanating from this male made me completely petrified for my life.

He had black glossy hair that looked almost like an oil slick with the way the Fae lights shined on his head, catching tones of green, blue, and purple. His brown eyes were the darkest I had ever seen, to the point of being black. Black leather straps crossed every which way over his pants and tunic, securing his weapons into place. This male was a walking warrior of death, and I had the unfortunate privilege of being trapped in this single-room house with him.

"I asked, who are you? Are you mute, perhaps?" He raised his eyebrows, still wearing that cocky lop-sided smile that turned into a full one that now I saw both of his front fangs.

"S-S-Skyla," I stuttered out. I dared not to move an inch, his eyes not breaking contact. I thought he shifted slightly, but it could have been a trick from the light.

"Pleasure to meet you, Skyla; where is my brother?" The death warrior asked.

"You just missed him; he went out." My voice shook. I was grateful to still be seated on the ground. I was certain that if I were standing, my legs would give out from beneath me as my body trembled. He eyed me speculatively and then sniffed the air.

"It smells like . . . arousal in here," he commented, and my eyes widened as my heart hammered in my chest. I glanced about the room; I had nowhere to go and nothing to grab for a weapon.

"I'm surprised my brother would take a *human* for a lover, but then again, when the fruit is ripe for the picking." His eyes lazily trailed over my body. He shifted his body into a relaxed stance, and the energy in the room became less threatening, but it did not calm me. I watched as he brought his hands up in front of him. Taking his attention from me, he started to pick his sharp black nails.

"It's peculiar; once upon a time, I used to pick the likes of your kind from my talons." His gaze flicked to me. "But then again, that was when it was acceptable to murder humans. Ah, the Fae Wars, how I miss them." An evil gleam appeared in his black eyes, and I gulped. This male had been around during the Fae Wars, making him over three hundred years old.

"W-Who are you?" I stammered out. He blinked, coming back to the present. I wondered how many humans he had murdered and whether he remembered any of them.

"You're a bold one, aren't you?" he purred. "Name's Tennyson." He glanced around the room again and settled his gaze back on me. Raising his eyebrow again, he said, "I don't mind sharing with my brother. If you are up for it, Petal?"

I shook my head, blinking rapidly. His brashness didn't faze me as I was used to that kind of talk in Piggs Burough. However, his willingness to have sex eliminated the notion from my mind that Fae had a courting style. Tennyson broke out in laughter.

"Petal, you are too predictable, and you're not my taste anyway." He crossed the room and offered me his hand. I looked at it and then him. Impatiently, he wiggled his fingers as if to say to get a move on.

Taking a breath for encouragement, I reached up and accepted his hand. He pulled me up, and then I was standing close enough to him that I was able to see the blood specks mixed in with the stitching on his leathers. I took a step back as he immediately dropped my hand. He turned and walked to the table, pulling out the same chair I had sat at for breakfast.

"My name is Skyla." It was the only response I could think of as he kept calling me that nickname.

"Yes, but you are fragile like a flower petal." He picked up a drying dandelion that had fallen from the ceiling, crushing it between his hands. He let the pieces fall between us onto the floor. "Petal fits you better," he replied. I took a step back; he no longer blocked the door, and I could leave this cottage. I glanced at the door and tried to calculate how quickly I could get to it. I did not have Fae speed, but maybe luck would be on my side.

"Sit down, Petal, and talk to me a bit," ordered Tennyson as if he sensed my intentions. I dragged my gaze from the door to the empty chair across from him.

"Petal," he warned, and reluctantly, I took the few steps to the chair. Pulling it out, I tried to sit as far away from him as possible. His predatory energy engulfed me, sending all my senses on overdrive. Every fiber of my being screamed to run. He smiled, showing off his fangs as his eyes assessed me hungrily. I gulped, fear sliding through me.

Chapter Eleven

KIERIAN

I stood panting at the edge of my clearing, gazing up at my home and where the red-haired female still lingered. *Skyla.* I had run in my stag form until I was past the point of my lungs burning. Even now, my muscles shook from the strain I had put them through. Cold water dripped from my hair and body from when I had jumped into the stream nearby. It had cooled me down that I should be able to look at her without acting on the lucrative thoughts that played in my mind.

Even as I stood there, I was uncertain why she had this effect on me. She was a stranger who had shown up at my door yesterday. Consequently, as a human, she should be a nobody to me. It was a matter of personal morals and pride in respecting her virtue. There had only been one other who had me feel this way. *No. Don't think about her.*

I shook my head, dismissing the memories that were trying to surface. I wasn't entirely certain what I would make of this matter or what I would do with Skyla. She asked to stay, but I had become accustomed to living in solitude. Kicking her out would mean imminent death. A human life was trivial compared to a Fae's life. A breeze caressed my face, and it was then that I caught his scent. *No.*

My legs screamed in protest as I took off in a sprint. I ignored the raw pain as I pushed my body to cross the distance in the meadow. In the blink of an eye, I pulled open my front door. Ice filled my veins as I prepared myself, afraid of what I would find on the other side. What I found, instead, was far from what I had anticipated.

Skyla was arguing with Tennyson, calling him a cheater as they were playing cards at my kitchen table. Tennyson was laughing, denying her accusations. I lowered my defenses a fraction, analyzing every detail to affirm that I was not making a mistake in what I witnessed.

"Am I interrupting anything?" I asked, making my presence known. The pair looked up at me. Skyla's face was red and scrunched up in anger. Meanwhile, Tennyson remained relaxed, with delight dancing in his eyes.

"He's cheating at cards!" Skyla yelled as she shot my brother a glare and then looked back at me for help.

"I am not. She made a simple mathematical calculation and will not let it go." Tennyson sniffed. More of my defense relaxed as I took a few more tentative steps into my home.

"Tennyson," I began, "you do cheat, and that is why I no longer play cards with you." In my search, I could not find any injuries on Skyla. I looked at my brother, raising my eyebrow as I tried to figure out what game he was truly playing at. Aside from fucking humans, I had never witnessed Tennyson be in any form friendly to one. Curiosity made me wonder why Skyla's blood and organs were not decorating every inch of my cottage at this very moment.

"How insulting of you to state that, Brother," Tennyson commented dryly.

Ignoring his comment, I asked instead, "Why are you here?" The only time Tennyson visited me anymore was when he wanted something. Usually, it involved a remedy to heal some injury he had received. The injuries always came with an interesting story that was never his fault, according to him.

"Can I not come to check in on my brother?" He leaned back in his chair. "And imagine my surprise to find Petal here; what a delight this girl is." He complimented, smiling at Skyla. I wondered if he had been drinking, but I could not detect any alcohol on him.

"Petal?" I asked.

"It's what he calls me." Skyla rolled her eyes. "I gave up on correcting him." I stared at them both, questioning if I had bumped my head and was dreaming. The human girl who had shown up at my doorstep yesterday was showing more personality around my bloodthirsty, human-hating brother, who, in turn, was lounging at my table playing cards with the said human.

"I think I need to go back for another run," I said slowly. Maybe I would wake up from the dream I was certain I was having.

"Why so much running, brother? Can't get all your sexual frustrations out on this little vixen?" Tennyson jabbed, and I stiffened. Skyla shifted in her seat as she looked down at the cards on the table between them. Her face was already flushed from her anger at Tennyson. The only sign of embarrassment was the pinkness that graced her arms.

"Oh, you haven't had sex with each other yet," Tennyson commented. I blinked at him, not allowing him to see past my mask of emotions. He could figure out the truth to anything in a matter of seconds. At one point, it had mystified me how he did it, but now I no longer cared.

"*Tennyson!*" Skyla whined his name.

He laughed, throwing the cards he still held in his hand down on the table.

"She just arrived yesterday," I replied, briskly. I wished he would leave immediately. I did not like how casual she was with him. I feared he was lulling her into a sense of safety, and then I would need to have the cottage cleaned later from her limbs.

"Humans don't last long; probably should get the deed done," Tennyson chided. Skyla glanced at me, and when I caught her eye, she jumped slightly and quickly looked away. Tennyson stood up, and I held my ground, watching his movements.

"I will get out of your hair or maybe your bed." He glanced at my bed and smiled with a waggle of his eyebrows. He reached out using our familiar greeting and departing gesture. We grabbed each other's forearms and gave a simple curt nod. He let go first and walked around me. When I heard the closing click of my front door behind me, I realized I was once again left alone with Skyla. I turned my attention back to her, the awkwardness hanging between us.

"I apologize about my brother. He can be quite lewd." There was no other way to put it. Tennyson never had time to mince words, and he loved toying with people and their emotions.

"He doesn't look like you," Skyla commented instead. She fiddled with the hem of her dress, avoiding eye contact.

"He is not my blood-related brother. We fought in arms together during the Fae Wars," I replied before realizing what I was admitting to her.

She nodded, refusing to look up as she continued to fiddle. I did not owe her anything. I had only met her yesterday, and the Fae wars had ended three hundred years ago.

"I see," she finally replied. I watched as she mulled that tidbit over in her mind. "That's a relief; you're a lot friendlier than he is." I could hear the warmth in her voice and saw the small smile gracing her lips. Her comment surprised me, considering we had barely spoken to one another.

"Tennyson can be intense." Was the only response I could give her.

"So, I can stay?" She asked, switching topics. I played out every scenario of how her staying here could go wrong. I had lived in solitude for the last two hundred years. When that sea bitch's initial rumors had started, I had plenty of females arriving at my doorstep for wishes, but then it stopped until yesterday. However, Skyla stated she had heard the story as a little girl. If I had to guess, she was probably in her twenties, and no one had shown up in the last twenty years. I could only hope she would be the last one to come to bother me from preposterous rumors.

"Temporarily, and don't get in my way."

Chapter Twelve

SKYLA

Temporarily. I had a place to call home temporarily. Giddiness bubbled up within me. I cleaned up the card mess that had been abandoned. Kierian said not to get in his way, but the least I could do was to keep my areas tidy. I looked over at him; he was pulling dried herbs from the ceiling and placing them on the lower countertop by the pestle and mortar.

Setting the deck of cards off to the side of the table, I came to stand on the opposite side of the countertop from him. Bracing my forearms on it, I used it to lean on. I took in every detail of motion. His eyes flicked to mine with irritation before focusing back on his task at hand.

"Does your friend visit often?" I asked, trying to make small talk while he worked.

"He comes and goes as he pleases." Kierian started crushing ingredients into the mortar. "I assume we will be seeing more of him with you here."

I grimaced, not certain how to take that. I kicked my right foot behind me, tapping my bare toes on the wood. I was curious what these temporary new days would bring me.

"Just be careful around him," he warned.

"Why?" I could guess why, but I wanted to know what light Kierian could shed on his brother. Why make assumptions when he could give me all the answers? Kierian stopped what he was doing to give me a level gaze.

"Tennyson generally only likes humans one of two ways -" Kierian paused "-he likes them dead at his fingertips or after he has fucked them thoroughly." I swallowed. My assumption had been correct, but the way Kierian had said it gave me chills.

"So, he doesn't like my kind?" I hedged, choosing to negate the second part of his statement.

"No, I am more surprised I didn't come home to the walls being painted with your blood . . . did he say anything peculiar when it was just the two of you?" It was apparent that Kierian was trying to figure out why his brother had not acted in accordance per his usual fashion.

I shook my head, unable to give Kierian what he was seeking. Aside from Tennyson's initial prodding of who I was, he really hadn't asked much about me. The deck of cards had appeared in Tennyson's hand, to which he lulled me into a game. As we played, he talked me through multiple strategies after each round. I knew he had been trying to distract me to lose, but that was the extent of our exchange.

Kierian sighed and pinched the bridge of his nose. Even though his eyes were closed, I gave him an apologetic smile. I should thank The Maker that I had made it out alive if that is how Tennyson truly was. I shook off the thoughts when Kierian went back to work.

"What are you making?" I inquired. His brows furrowed slightly. He probably had not anticipated me talking, and I wondered if I should be quiet. I didn't need to be kicked out immediately after I had just been granted a temporary stay.

"It's a healing salve for burns," he replied patiently.

"Why are you making it?" Instead of heeding my own advice, I chose to continue to pepper him with questions.

"Because I sell them."

"Do you make other things than burn salves?"

"Yes?"

"Like?"

Kierian set down his pestle from grinding and closed his eyes. I could hear his even breaths, and by the third, he opened his eyes to look at me. I pulled back a bit as I stopped kicking my foot behind me.

"If you need to keep busy, can you please go get me three pieces of aloe vera from the plant out front," he stated firmly.

"Aloe Vera?" I said it slowly, giving him a confused look. He sighed and held up a long green plant stem with small spikes along the edges.

"This is an Aloe Vera. I need three pieces, wide and long like this one. Can you do that?" Irritation filled his voice with a hint of exhaustion. I swallowed and nodded my head quickly. Pushing my hands off the countertop, I turned to head out the front door of his cottage.

As I passed the threshold, I looked to the right and instantly saw the plant with an identical leaf. I narrowed my gaze, trying to figure out which three leaves matched the one he had shown me. With an estimated guess, I broke the first one I selected from the stem. Surprise filled me when I noticed the green gooey gel coming from the bottom of the stem. Quickly, I broke off two more stems, similar to the first. I held them upside down to prevent the liquid from leaking out as I brought them back inside.

"Three Aloe Veras coming right up," I announced as I crossed the distance back to the kitchen. Kierian didn't look up from his work.

"Excellent. Please place them on the countertop there." He pointed to where the other one lay. I followed his instructions, rounding the bar top into his section of the kitchen. Placing them next to the other one, I took the opportunity to have a closer look at what he was doing. I accidentally brushed against his arm, which caused us to both still. He was the first to move, slowing going back to work.

"Please grab me a cup from the cupboard behind you," he requested. I turned around and looked at the cupboards set higher than I was accustomed to in a human house. They were set for his height. I opened them up and saw the cups on the top shelf. Looking down at the height of the countertop, I didn't think I would be able to climb on top of it to reach the cups. I looked back at Kierian for help, but his back was to me. I looked back up at the cups.

"Um, I don't think I can reach them?" I responded. My arm was outstretched towards the cups, my fingertips only reaching the first shelf of plates and bowls. He grumbled behind me. I startled when I felt his warm hand rest on my left hip as his chest pressed against my back. He reached above me and grabbed a cup from the top shelf. He froze when he realized what he had done, and just as quickly, I felt coolness from the absence of his body on mine.

"Thanks," I mumbled. My pulse raced with exhilaration. I couldn't contain my smile, which was silly. I turned back around, feeling elated to watch him work. Every time I thought, I caught him glancing at me; warmth, giddiness, and a feeling I couldn't put my finger on would run through me.

Chapter Thirteen

KIERIAN

It was difficult not to be aware of how near Skyla was to me. She didn't leave my area in the kitchen as I worked, watching intently everything I did. I continuously caught her glancing at me, and every time I made eye contact, she would quickly look away. Sometimes, she would ask about certain ingredients, and other times, her body would graze against mine. I had run out of ingredients to make her fetch.

Temporarily. What did that even mean? To a human and a Fae, that word had a very different meaning. *Temporarily, and don't get in my way,* is what I told her. Yet, hours later, here she was grazing against my body. I sighed to myself, and she froze, looking up at me. I shook my head and continued to grind together the ingredients. Maybe the years had made me lonely, and it caused me to agree to her question hastily.

"What's your favorite ingredient to use?" She asked, breaking my concentration.

"Cinnamon," I replied without thought.

"Why?"

"I like the smell of it."

"What does it smell like?" She asked curiously. I blinked, not quite certain I had actually heard what she had said. I took my attention away from my task to find her big green eyes peering up at me innocently. I looked at my shelves and started moving jars out of the way until I found the one with cinnamon sticks in it. Grabbing the jar, I offered it to her.

Skyla cautiously took it and fought to unscrew the lid. I withheld my chuckle from some of her facial expressions. Wordlessly, I took the jar back from her and opened the lid with ease. She made a face to which I dismissed. I hand tightened all my jars; human strength was no match against a Fae's. I handed the jar back to her.

She eagerly took a big sniff of the cinnamon sticks within. Even from here, I could smell the delightful scent. Her eyes brightened as her face lit up. She looked up at me, giving me the biggest smile, and I felt something flash through me. Desire. I dismissed the thought before it entered my mind. It was silly to even think that I could make this girl happy.

"It smells so spicy and sweet all at the same time. It's such a comforting smell," she gushed, holding the jar tightly to her bosom. "I have never smelled something as rich and warm as this." She swayed back and forth as she took additional sniffs from the jar.

"Have you smelled vanilla extract before?" I asked, hoping that she hadn't.

"No," Skyla rushed out excitedly. I quickly grabbed one of the bottles I had recently made from my last batch. Unscrewing the cap, I passed it to her. She took it while still holding the jar full of cinnamon sticks. Closing her eyes, I watched as she breathed in the smell. She opened her eyes as her giddy smile returned.

"Ohh, this is so sweet and rich but yet somehow smells creamy like. Is that even a thing?" she laughed.

"Now, smell the two of them back and forth," I suggested. A warmth spread in my chest as I smiled, watching her mix the two scents together. She hummed in satisfaction, repeating the process a few more times.

"I think this just became my favorite scent in the world!" She exclaimed.

"They are a lovely combination." I chuckled.

Chapter Fourteen

SKYLA

The next morning, I awoke to the smell of warm cinnamon. I smiled to myself, thinking about yesterday. I had never smelled such wonderful scents before. I was curious about what other luxuries I had been neglected of in my life. What else would Kierian introduce me to during my time with him?

The rest of yesterday had been simple; Kierian made simple sandwiches for supper last night. We barely talked after our moment. I noticed how he had put a mask back up after he chuckled. It had become awkward when it was time for bed. He had casually stripped down naked in front of me, and I quickly faced the wall to avoid seeing anything.

I rolled onto my back, feeling the throbbing pain in my right arm from lying on it against the cool flooring. I looked over to where Kierian stood in the kitchen. He didn't pay me any mind and I decided to take the opportunity to admire him.

He was tall, taller than the majority of the males in my village. I noticed how the cottage accommodated his height. It made me wonder how many places he needed to duck his head when walking from room to room in the human village. Various scars riddled Kierian's muscular body. He didn't need to flex; they were always on display. My eyes trailed down his abs until the countertop blocked the rest of my view.

I dragged my eyes back up to his face. I hadn't seen his antlers since the first day I arrived here, which made me curious: Where did they go? Moving past the thought of his antlers, he kept his hair half-tied back in a messy knot. I bet small braids or trinkets in his hair would be pretty.

My eyes fell upon his pointed Fae ears. I reached up to feel my round ones, curious what it would feel like to touch his. My eyes trailed to his prominent dark brown eyebrows, which were furrowed in concentration. His honey-brown eyes focused on cooking breakfast as I admired his high cheekbones and the straightness of his nose. I followed his chiseled jawline, sighing to myself. He was every bit the Fae male prince I had daydreamed about, without actually fitting any of my fantasy males.

"Breakfast is ready," his low voice made me jump. Had he known I was checking him out this whole time? I scrambled to get up and crossed the small space to collect my breakfast plate. I looked down at the interesting, swirled bread with white icing on top of it. I had never seen bread like this before. I looked back up to him for answers.

"It's cinnamon rolls," he replied calmly.

"Like the spice you had me smell yesterday?" I replied enthusiastically. I looked back down at the bread, my mouth watering. If cinnamon tasted nearly as delicious as it smelled, I knew I was in for a treat.

"Yes." Without another word, he led us to the table. He didn't say anything as he took a bite of his cinnamon roll. Kierian glanced up, noticing I was watching him. He swallowed his food.

"Eat," he commanded, and I eagerly dug in. I didn't mean to delay trying my breakfast, but he mystified me. I was beyond curious about him, and each new day meant I could learn something.

Picking up a cinnamon roll, I marveled at the soft, gooey feeling between my fingers. I inhaled the warm spice again and took a bite. Sugary sweetness burst onto my tastebuds. Closing my eyes, I moaned at how extraordinary it tasted. I would be asking for more of these if possible. Partially opening my eyes when I went to take the next bite, I noticed how Kierian watched me hungrily. His hand was frozen midway to his mouth with his cinnamon roll. I licked my lip nervously as I tasted the sugary icing on my tongue. Kierian tracked the movement, and I felt desire stirring within me.

My nose twitched, and I tried to ignore the sensation. My focus was on Kierian and the way he was looking at me. I wanted to reach across the table and take his hand in mine. How would he respond if I stood up and closed the distance between us? My nose twitched again, and I blinked a few times, trying to dampen the sensation. Focusing back on Kierian, I moved my hand toward his when I let out a sneeze that I directed into my elbow.

I opened my eyes from the sneeze and found Kierian had resumed eating his cinnamon roll. The moment between us broke. He was no longer looking at me. My heart dropped from the idea of what could have been. Maybe it was silly; we had only known each other for three days. We were complete strangers to each other, but a small part of me hoped for more.

When Kierian finished his breakfast, he didn't even pick up his plate from the table. It disappeared, and I squeaked. He looked at me curiously. No longer did desire radiate from his eyes as he cocked his head to the side with a furrowed brow at my behavior.

"Where did the plate go?" I asked in shock.

"Away?" He rose from his chair, his demeanor changing to amused.

"But where is away?" I pushed. I needed to know.

"In there, why?" He pointed to one of the cupboards in the kitchen.

"Did it clean it again today, too?" My eyes widened with wonder at this type of luxury.

"Yeah?" He tilted his head to the other side and shrugged before turning to walk around the bar into the kitchen. From where I sat, I could see him pulling ingredients out of his stashes and dropping them into a bowl. He had already moved on from this conversation.

I stood up, finished with my breakfast, and I wanted to watch him work. I took only two steps, and my plate disappeared. I whipped my head to look at the cupboard. Kierian didn't even glance my way as I walked over to the cabinet, standing with my back to him. I opened the door to find a stack of plates, bowls, and glasses stored away. I was amazed by this kind of magic; chores would be a breeze to have a house do everything for me.

"If you are done snooping in my cupboard, you can go out back and wash yourself," Kierian commented, and I could hear the irritation in his voice. I didn't understand why his mood changed within a matter of a minute. Did he not enjoy someone snooping through his things? I suppose no one really did, but I was temporarily living here, and that was the cabinet filled with plates and bowls. I wouldn't consider that snooping.

"Um, okay," I replied, uncertain.

"There will be soaps, oils, and towels ready for you."

"Thank you." I skirted around him to follow his directions. Maybe after yesterday, I had been in his way a little bit too much, or what if I smelled? I had just trekked through the woods for weeks; I was long overdue for a bath. To a Fae's nose, I was probably a very unpleasant thing to smell. My whole body felt a rush of warmth as embarrassment coursed through me. How badly did I offend his olfactory senses? I tried to calm my mind down, convincing myself that maybe he was only trying to be a nice host. Either way, I was not going to miss the opportunity to bathe.

Leaving the cottage, I smiled at all the herbs planted around it and in the planters under the windows. Butterflies were flitting about as were some bees. I gave the bees a wide distance, eyeing them nervously.

Looking out over the grassy knolls, I enjoyed the view as the wind blew grass waves across them. There was something about the crisp warmth of a summer morning that brought joy to me. My happiness subsided temporarily as a shiver ran through my spine while I surveyed the Fae Woods. At some point, I would need to venture back through them to a human village. Maybe I could convince Kierian to guide me to a more desirable place to live than the one I had come from.

I dismissed the notion from my mind, hoping he would let me stay here for quite some time. Due to a Fae's long lifespan, I was hoping that days could turn into weeks, months, and years before he realized how long I had spent in his company. I knew eventually I would need to find a home of my own, but for now, this would give me a moment to figure out my next steps.

I turned the corner to the back of the house and found the bathing area. There was not even a privacy screen to go around the tub, and I felt my face flush as I looked out over the grassy knolls and at the house. There was the kitchen window I could see from here, but I did not think it could have a great view of the bathing area.

"Some privacy would be nice," I grumbled. I didn't even blink, and a wooden panel screen surrounded the tub. My eyes widened as I blinked twice. "Thank you." I was not certain who I was thanking, but I preferred to stay on its good side for conveniences like this.

Cautiously, I walked to the now enclosed tub and moved a wood panel a bit to the side to let me in. It wasn't light by any means, which eased my fear of it blowing away or moving when I was naked. The tub was porcelain and laced with elaborate silver metalwork on the exterior. It was filled to the brim with steaming water. I glanced down at my dirty, barely held-together clothing. My face scrunched up with disgust, mentally preparing myself to undress.

As I pulled the dress over my head, I felt some of the dirt and grit fall from it onto my skin. A shiver ran through me from how gross it felt, and my eyes looked lovingly at the steaming, clean bath water. I was not going to enjoy bathing and putting this back on. I wondered if I could wash and have my clothes dried in time to head back in. I could wash my clothes with me in the tub, but they would brown the water quicker than I had time to bathe myself. I pulled down the leggings and kicked them off to the side. I would wash everything when I was done with my bath, hoping the breeze would dry them while I waited with a towel wrapped around me.

I braced my hands on the rim of the tub and hauled my left leg over, moaning at the warm, comforting feeling of the water on my skin. I did not waste time as I slid down into the tub. When was the last time I had a warm bath? The real question was when, had it been actual bath and not a washcloth with hard soap to clean everything?

I looked at the small ledge attached to the tub filled with pretty little vials of liquid. I reached and pulled out a pinkish-purple glass vial to smell its contents. It reminded me of lilies, and I found it peculiar that a Fae Male would have something smelling this feminine in his assortment of soaps and oils. Setting the glass back down, I looked around, momentarily forgetting I was hidden behind a wooden blind.

I took a deep breath and submerged my head under the water to wet my hair. Holding my breath, I vigorously rubbed my fingers through my hair and scalp. Surfacing again, I took a deep lungful of air back in and reached for the vial smelling of lilies. I poured the soup onto my head and massaged it in, making certain all of my hair was filled with soap.

Bubbles rose up from the water in front of me, and I watched them in amazement, one popping on my nose, causing me to giggle. The Fae magic had me in complete awe, and it made me wonder what other discoveries I would stumble upon. As I felt satisfied with my red locks being as good as they could get with the soap, I took another deep breath, squeezed my eyes shut, and submerged myself under the water again.

Working my fingers through my hair, I started to wash the soap out. My arms were beginning to feel the strain from the effort it took to clean my hair. I didn't dare open my eyes under the water to witness how much grime was being removed from my head. My lungs burned as I kept scrubbing and teasing soap from my hair. Coming up, I gasped in breaths for air as the water streamed down my face. My arms felt the tender relief as my hands gripped the sides of the tub. I shook my head back and forth, letting the excess water fly about.

Laughing, I started pouring more of the soap onto my hands and ran it all over my body, relinquishing the silkiness of it. This was nothing compared to the hard soap I had grown up with. I would need to ask Kierian if he could keep more of it on hand for me.

When I felt I was clean, I stood up from the tub, crinkling my nose from how dirty the water was mingled in with leaves and sticks that had been tangled within my hair. Hauling myself out of the grimy water, I shook my head again, letting the immediate area be covered in water droplets. Grabbing maybe the softest piece of fabric

I had ever dared touch, I wrapped the towel around myself. Turning back to my pathetic excuse for clothing, I sighed, knowing the task I needed to do before me.

Lamely, I walked to collect the discarded, rumpled clothes and noticed they weren't as dingy as before. I inspected the dress fabric, running it between my fingers. It was thin, and I feared one tear would unravel it all at the seams. I brought the material up to my face to sniff it gingerly. It smelled clean. I looked at my leggings, doing a quick sniff test, and they, too, smelled clean.

"Thank you," I whispered out loud. A wind picked up abruptly, and the wooden panel screen shook from the force. The gratefulness I had been feeling dropped when I watched with horror as the screen started to fall, and my eyes fell upon Kierian.

Chapter Fifteen

KIERIAN

I had come up short in quantity of dandelion and needed to collect more. I had a patch growing in the back of the house that should suffice to fulfill the rest of the recipe. I rounded the corner as the gust of wind picked up, whipping my hair around my face. It wasn't uncommon being on the knoll to receive vicious winds like this.

A wooden panel screen around the tub caught my eye, and I looked at it inquisitively, wondering where it had come from. The wind rattled the wooden screen until it fell away, and Skyla stood there, naked.

I inhaled sharply as I took her in. She stood there wide-eyed, staring at me. I trailed the way water droplets fell from her hair onto her breasts and ran down her stomach. A towel was pooled at her feet as she clutched her clothes tightly against her body. My eyes lingered on her breasts and the taunt pink nipples, hardening from the wind blowing on them.

I forced myself to look at her face, and when our eyes connected, she jumped into action. Skyla squealed, yelling at me not to look at her. I simply blinked and watched a multitude of emotions cross her face. She clutched her clothes to her chest, trying to cover herself, a poor attempt in reality.

I blinked again, trying to ignore the arousal I felt as I turned to head in the direction of my dandelion patch. She was still making squawking noises as I passed her. I glanced down at Skyla to find her face beet-red and her eyes wide open. I blinked and didn't say anything. I needed to keep myself under control, and the only way I knew how was to slip into a mask of indifference. I needed to feel nothing like I had once felt three hundred years ago. This girl would mean nothing but trouble for me.

At the dandelion patch, I forced myself to crouch and collect the flower heads in full bloom. I refused to pay attention to the sounds she made behind me. It would be ever so easy to turn my head and see what she was doing, but I stayed in place with my task. However, I couldn't stay doing this forever; it didn't even take me a minute to gather what I needed. I breathed heavily to build my concentration as I rose. I turned, and longing ripped through me when I found her standing there still naked and barely covering herself. We stared at each other as the wind whipped between us.

She clutched her clothes tighter to herself as a shiver ran through her body. I made the first move as I took a step to head back into my cottage. I needed to continue mixing my latest recipe, and maybe I could grind my frustration out on the dandelions. As I passed by her, I paused.

"I suggest putting those clothes back on before you catch a cold," I stated through gritted teeth. I didn't wait for her response as I left her to gawk at my backside.

I was in the middle of aggressively grinding the dandelion heads into a paste. The Fae magic straining to keep my mortar and pestle from crumbling into dust. My senses were on overdrive, and when Skyla trounced through the door, I didn't even look up. Her bare feet stomped angrily against my wood floor towards me. She smacked a hand on the bar top, and by the sharp sound it had made, I assumed it hurt, but she didn't withdraw her hand. She kept it firmly in place on my countertop.

"Apologize!" she demanded. I chose to ignore her and not acknowledge her statement. She huffed.

"I said apologize, Fae!" She growled this time.

I closed my eyes, collected my thoughts, and shook my head slightly. I did not need to deal with this. "I have nothing to apologize for," I replied, irritably. I kept my eyes shut; I needed to maintain composure.

"You saw me naked!" She screeched.

"And?" I chose to humor her. I opened my eyes and didn't even look at her as I continued to irritably grind my ingredients together. I could sense the Fae magic buckling now to keep the mortar and pestle intact.

"I was naked! It's indecent! Apologize!" She curled her hand into a fist and slammed it down on the bar top, trying to get her point across.

"I found nothing indecent about it," I replied, but not admitting the other feelings I had on the matter. Humans were far too modest in their ways when it came to their bodies. It bored me. Then again, if Skyla pranced around here naked . . . my jaw ached from how tightly I clenched it from the thought.

"Well, I did! Can't you respect that, Fae?"

It did not go amiss at how she used my kind as an insult. I stopped my grinding to look at her. Her hair was still damp, and water droplets were making a mess on my bar top and floor. She had a towel wrapped around her, and from here, I could see her clothes were clutched in her other hand. I found it peculiar that she was demanding an apology for her own modesty's sake but was indecent enough to stand here in a towel. Using my Fae abilities, I changed the energy in the room to drive my point for her to understand.

"*You* came to the Fae Lands," I stated firmly. "You sought *me* out, a Fae. Do not use *my kind* as an insult when I am the one allowing you to stay here in my own home. I could kick you out to fend for yourself right now." She jerked back from the realization, but I wasn't done as I growled angrily, letting out my pent-up frustration. "When your bones are being gnawed on by some Fae creature in the woods, just know I will be here, not giving you another thought. So, you ought to respect *my lands* and *me*. You are a *human*. If you think I have not had my fair share of naked female flesh, you are greatly mistaken. Now, if you are done throwing your little temper tantrum, leave me to make my salves and tonics." The last words came out as a threat. She stood there in shock. I watched as her mouth opened and closed, trying to grasp at words but coming up with nothing. I glared at her, raising my right eyebrow as I pursed my lips slightly, challenging her to argue against me.

She must have decided against it as she glared back at me. She, instead, stuck her tongue out at me and whirled away, stomping back out the front door, slamming it shut behind her.

I blinked a few times before letting out a bark of laughter. The energy in the room completely dissipated. I could not recall the last time someone had stuck out their tongue at me like an impudent child. Realization struck me that I had found the act quite cute. All the anger I had been feeling seconds prior had completely left me as I stood there laughing to myself.

Chapter Sixteen

KIERIAN

It was hours later when I had finished with the last of my salves. I heard the creak of my front door opening. I braced my hands on the bar top as Skyla's head popped in. Her eyes met mine, and they widened a bit. I raised an eyebrow at her as I thought about her earlier departure. I suppressed the smile, clenching my jaw instead. From here, it was apparent she was testing the waters to see if she was still welcomed. She must have moved on from knocking as she glanced nervously between me and the various items in my kitchen. She probably was afraid that, if she had knocked, I wouldn't have come to answer the door. I applauded her for this more direct approach to getting her way, even if nothing about her demeanor was bold at the moment.

"Um," Skyla started. My eyes tracked as she licked the bottom of her lip. Her fingers curled tighter around the door that hid the rest of her body. "Can I come back?"

I pushed my hands off the bar top and crossed them over my chest. It did not go unnoticed how she flinched ever so slightly. She was preparing for me to dismiss her and tell her to start walking to the nearest human village. I tilted my head to the side and lifted my chin up a bit, waiting for her to say more. Skyla nervously looked around the room and took a deep breath before opening the door and stepping through the threshold. She didn't close the door behind her, instead keeping it partially open. She tucked her hands behind her back and slightly rocked on her feet. Her fiery locks shadowed her face as she bowed her head.

"I am sorry for how I acted earlier. If you can forgive me, I promise I will not cause you to be angry again." She rocked faster, causing her hair to sway, but did not look up from the ground. A tender sorrow for this human girl spread throughout me. Sighing, I uncrossed my arms and walked around the bar to her. She braced herself as I stopped in front of her; Skyla's body was completely rigid. Crossing my arms again, I chose my words carefully.

"You shouldn't make promises you cannot keep." Her shoulders raised as her head buried deeper into her chest. I couldn't see her face, and I fought every instinct to reach out and lift her chin up.

"Look at me," I ordered, harsher than I had meant for it to be. She peaked one green eye at me and then the other, slowly shifting her stance to stand normal and not as withdrawn. She bit her lip and rocked again on her feet.

"What I mean is," I began gently. "You cannot promise you will not anger me again. That is an impossible thing to promise." Skyla looked at me warily, and I sighed. Relaxing my stance and uncrossing my arms again, realizing she did not understand my meaning. I wanted to reach out and rest my hands on her upper arms, but instead, I forced them to fall at my sides.

"We are strangers to one another; you do not know what will irritate me. Promising you'll never anger me is setting yourself up for failure." I tried to give her a reassuring smile.

She stopped swaying. Her eyes moved back and forth on mine, trying to determine if this was a trick. She bit the bottom of her lip again, and I desperately wished she would stop doing that. I ignored the twitch of my stirring cock.

"I can stay then?" Skyla asked slowly.

"Temporarily, and don't get in my way," I repeated the same words I had told her before.

I had to stop my natural instinct to defend myself from ripping her apart with my claws as she threw her arms around my waist, hugging me close to her. I reminded myself I was in no danger and slowly forced myself to relax. Awkwardly, I brought my hand down to pat her back. I had not anticipated the physical affection. Despite my thoughts on wanting to touch her, I was not prepared for her to initiate it. I questioned when the last time someone had touched me like this.

"Thank you, Kierian!" She squeezed me tighter, and I grunted in acknowledgment. The feelings began to stir within me again, and I quickly shoved them away. The smell of lilies on her hair tickled my nose, and I wanted to breathe in her scent. No, I needed to ignore those feelings. Skyla pulled back quickly, dropping her arms to her sides.

"Sorry, my emotions just overcame me," she squeaked.

"It's okay." I chuckled. She was adorable. *Adorably mine.* I slightly froze; why did that thought come into my mind? I thought about adding on more to my response, but I didn't know how to formulate into words what I was thinking. I felt the coolness from where her body warmth had been, realizing how much I had enjoyed it. If I hadn't stopped myself, this could have ended differently. My instincts reacted, and I was ready to attack her for the sake of defense. I knew humans weren't harmless, but Skyla was a threat to me in a different way.

Temporarily. I wondered how short of time it would be until Skyla moved on from my nomad lifestyle. She would want to settle down at some point and have a family, all things I would not be able to give her. She would become lonely living here, longing for female friendships and daily conversations. I preferred my solitude and went days without speaking. Eventually, one day, she would wake up and announce her departure, and I would go back to living the way I always have for the last three hundred years. Alone.

Chapter Seventeen

SKYLA

A week had passed since Kierian had told me I could live with him temporarily. It was a week of learning how to live together, but we fell into a semi-easy routine. We had breakfast every morning together. Sometimes I would watch him work on his salves, and other times, he would tell me to go pick certain herbs or flowers from his garden. In the evenings, it became an awkward dance of his nudity and polite conversations before bedtime.

Today, he told me he didn't need me to do anything and that I should enjoy the outdoors. However, I must be a glutton for punishment. I became more frustrated by the second. I weaved, knotted, untangled, and threw my attempts to the side, grabbing new materials to start again. Thankfully, being surrounded by wildflowers gave me plenty of new stems to braid together when I bent the previous ones beyond use. I never understood how all the pretty girls were able to do it, and they would never teach me when I

71

had asked. I tried to spy at a distance but could never gain a good enough view to understand the steps.

Five more attempts and I threw the poor flowers away from me, growling at them in frustration. I flopped onto my back, staring up at the sky.

"Why can't I figure this out!" I shouted, not that it helped my annoyance.

"Figure what out?" Kierian's low voice startled me. I jumped, sitting up abruptly. I looked around and found him standing behind me, wearing a curious expression. Internally, I argued with myself, debating if I should tell him this trivial matter.

"Do I need to come back?" Kierian asked, and I could hear the humor in his voice. I gave him a questioning look and then realized I had been moving my head back and forth as I contemplated how much I wanted to reveal to him.

"No, no!" I rushed out, embarrassed. He did not hide his soft chuckle this time. I warmed. I liked hearing him laugh. Some moments, he was cold, and the next, I would hear the richest laugh coming from him. I yearned for it.

"Then what is the trouble?" he pushed. I glanced down at all the destroyed flowers around me, and my shoulders sagged.

"I can't make a flower crown," I grumbled to myself, feeling defeated.

"What was that?" He sat down next to me in the grass, and it made me nervous at how casually close he was to me. I was certain his Fae ears had heard me, but I let out a heavy sigh.

"I don't know how to make a flower crown," I repeated, not wanting to look at him. I started pulling grass from the ground.

"Ah, is that all?" From my peripheral vision, I saw him picking a random assortment of flowers nearby that I hadn't destroyed, yet. I didn't hide my curiosity when he started weaving them elegantly together. I tried to follow his pattern but was more enthralled by the vibrant colors and the varying sizes of the flowers placed together.

When he finished, he gently placed it on my head, and I was surprised to find him smiling as he admired me wearing it. I looked upwards as if I, too, could see it upon my head and was only able to catch a glimpse of a fuchsia flower mingled with a yellow one.

"How did you do that?" I asked him enthusiastically, leaning into him.

"Here, let me show you. Grab some flowers," he instructed, and I quickly did as he bided. He picked more flowers and then slowly, with careful instruction, taught me how to weave my own flower crown. It was not as beautiful as the one he had created; it was quite clumsy and maybe on the verge of falling apart, but I had done it. I placed it on top of his head so we could match. His antlers weren't out today, which made the task far easier. Randomly, in the last few days, I would see his antlers, but not all the time. At some point, I would ask him about them.

"How do you know how to make flower crowns?" I asked as we sat there enjoying the summer breeze.

"Before I was decent at making my salves and tonics, I needed a way to make money. I realized that flower crowns and other flower varieties were an easy endeavor."

"Couldn't you have done mercenary work as a former Fae warrior from the Fae wars?" I thought it odd that he chose something completely opposite to what he had been trained to do. He didn't say anything for a bit, and when I looked over at him, he appeared to be somewhere else than in this moment.

"It would have been the sensible choice and maybe the easiest, but . . ." he trailed off as if trying to find the right words. ". . . I had witnessed enough bloodshed and death. I wanted a more peaceful life."

"And flower crowns gave you that?" I could hear the uncertainty in my own voice. He chuckled and shook his head.

"It taught me how to live again." His voice was light, but it sounded like there was more to it than what he was willing to tell me.

"What do you mean?" I asked, treading lightly. I didn't want to anger him again, but I was curious if he would tell me more. He looked up at the sky as if it could give him the answers he searched for with my question.

"I did some terrible things as a warrior. Unspeakable things."

"Did you enjoy it?"

"In the beginning, yes, but in the last five years of the war, I wanted it all to end. I was tired of the bloodshed and the deaths I caused from my own hands." He looked down and held up his hands to his face, looking at them. I followed his gaze and then back to his face, studying him.

"You killed a lot of humans, didn't you?" I quietly asked.

"Yes, and any Fae human sympathizers at the time." He dropped his hands back into his lap and stared out to the Fae woods.

"Was it difficult?"

"No."

I inhaled a sharp breath at his confession. Twenty years, the Fae wars had raged, and for the majority of it, he had no trouble killing my kind. I didn't even have to wonder; I knew if the war was still going on, he would have no issue killing me if I had crossed his path. I cocked my head to the side, looking at Kierian. Aside from a few of our conflicts, he was a quiet, peaceful male. He barely said anything unless I started the conversation. He had shown concern for me when it came to Tennyson visiting. Yet, there was a past to him that was dark and deadly.

"Does having a human temporarily live with you bring back memories of your past?" Fear slid into me as I became afraid to know the answer. He didn't respond right away, taking his time to mull my question over. My breathing became shallow, and I absent-mindedly broke pieces of individual grass blades from their stems. The silence stretched between us.

"Sometimes," he finally replied quietly. "But sometimes I don't mind it."

My eyes widened as I stilled at his confession. He didn't look at me as he said it, and I wasn't certain if I had heard him correctly. He looked at me, his golden-brown eyes holding warmth within them.

"You remind me of what I don't ever want to become again."

Chapter Eighteen

KIERIAN

I awoke, drenched in sweat and breathing heavily. Glancing frantically at my surroundings, I calmed down as realization settled in. I started the chant in my head: *I am in my cottage. I am leagues and centuries away from the Fae Wars. I am in no danger.* I started to repeat it again. After the fifth repeat, I sighed, noticing the drying flower crowns hanging carefully from the ceiling. I turned my attention to the human girl curled up in a ball in the opposite corner of the room. Skyla. I didn't understand why she didn't return to where she had come from; I had nothing to offer her. She had been misled here by lies from a woman weaving stories for children.

The only companion I have had in the last two hundred years was the cat, and we only occupied the same space together. Mytilda did her own thing, and I did mine. I had visitors over the years, but none stayed for more than a passing moment. I watched her body move with each breath; her back turned to me. I knew my nudity had been a bold statement, but I did not feel the need to change my living habits for someone who would eventually leave me.

She lay on the hardwood floors wearing the same clothes she had arrived in—the only clothes she owned, I found out rather quickly. It was summer and warm enough not to need a blanket, but she used her arm as a pillow. Her ratty knapsack had been holding the contents of barely passable definitions of food. I made her dispose of the knapsack with all of its contents. I had plenty of food to feed her.

I continued to watch her body rise and fall with each breath while I lay in my bed. I had spent many nights sleeping on the hard ground under the stars, not having much choice in the matter as a warrior, but she was not a warrior.

I commended her bravery of living in the Fae Woods for the time it took her to arrive here. She had survived some perilous nights and dangerous creatures. I did not think many humans, especially untrained, could do what she had endured. A human soldier may have had a chance, but maybe not the smarts for it. I had witnessed how humans trained their soldiers to be mindless fighting machines that took orders. Fae trained their warriors to take orders but to also think in a crisis.

I had been trained to be a lethal weapon against humans. I had been a higher rank than the majority of my Fae brothers and sisters when fighting. I had the power back then to order others what to do —something I used to relinquish.

Skyla moaned in her sleep, bringing my attention back to her. She rolled onto her back, and her face was scrunched up. From here, I could tell she was having a nightmare like I had awoken from. I halted myself when I realized I was moving to leave my bed. What could I, a Fae male, do to comfort her? If she awoke to find me looming over her, it would probably frighten her more than whatever night terror she currently faced in her mind.

I shook my head with a sigh, grabbing the blanket; I pulled it over my body as I turned onto my left side, putting my back to the girl and trying to find sleep again.

Chapter Nineteen

SKYLA

A few mornings later, Kierian gave me a basket to fetch ingredients. My wariness of him had lessened since the day we made flower crowns, and he had taught me how to preserve them. His silence still made me nervous at times, but after his confession, I was not as fearful of him.

I was more worried about having to travel back through the Fae Woods when my stay was no longer welcomed. It had been a bit disheartening to hear my childhood dreams had been a lie from the storyteller. It was a fool's mission, to begin with, but it was my one last hope before I figured out what I needed to do with my life next in order to survive. I had no intention of returning to Piggs Burough and wondered how close the next human village was. I knew each day was a day closer to my leaving here; the question was, would I be prepared to live on my own when that day came? I think it was an accomplishment that I had made it to his doorstep unscathed. Then, not only once but twice, due to my outburst, he told me I could stay temporarily. I did not believe I could be lucky twice to say the same later.

Kierian had sent me out to pick lavender, indicating where it would be growing. Upon finding the small lavender field, I made light work as I started picking it. I decided last week that I would prove myself to him as a valuable assistant; he would have to keep me longer. It made me sound a bit desperate and maybe a bit like a working barn animal. I didn't even have a bed to sleep in, just the corner of the room like a dog. Groaning to myself, I looked up at the sky. Maybe that's just how he viewed me like a lowly dog that gave him a mild form of entertainment.

Well, it was far better than trying to survive in the Fae woods on my own again. Kierian never stated how much lavender he needed, and I ended up gathering pieces until the basket he had sent me with was filled. I didn't particularly care for the smell of the lavender plant and realized if this was too much that, the cottage would probably reek of it. I scrunched my nose up at the thought of having to smell this full strength until it was used up.

Kierian had confirmed the rumors that a Fae's senses were stronger than a human's. If the lavender was this strong to me, how overly intoxicating would it be to a Fae's delicate nose? I shook my head, not even wanting to imagine how much it would give me a headache if the smell was even more prominent.

Walking back to the cottage, I casually swung the basket of lavender at my side. My gaze lingering at the woods lining the clearing, and wondering how many Fae creatures were currently watching me. A shiver ran up my spine. I hoped they would not dare leave their protected woods to feast on me. The woods to my right created a ruckus as a flock of birds came flying out of them, making a chatter. The wind whipped around me in a sudden gust.

I didn't even think as I started running towards the cottage. It could all be a coincidence, but I was not taking any chances. I ran until my lungs seared white-hot from the exertion. I felt a stabbing pain in my side, but I did not stop running. The birds were still chattering as they flew above me, and the wind had not died down. I skidded to a halt in front of Kierian's door and looked back wild-eyed at the empty clearing while I gasped for air.

I placed a steady hand on the door and fell forward into the cottage onto the floor. Kierian dropped what he was doing and was at my side instantly; lavender had been tossed about the floor as it had fallen from the basket.

"What is it?" His low voice rumbled in concern. I still was gasping for air as I turned to look up at him. I must not have fully shut the door that my weight had pushed it inwards. I glanced back out at the door and then back to him. It was then I noticed he had a dagger angled, ready to fight, and he followed my gaze to the door. He stood up and walked to stand in the door frame, surveying the clearing of any potential threats. When he looked back at me, he gave me a questioning look.

I gulped and, through panted breaths, replied, "Something was out there. I don't know what it was, but the wind picked up, and the birds started acting strange. I felt eyes on me." He looked back out to the clearing and stepped back into the cottage, shutting the door to block the outside world from us.

"Whatever it was, it is gone now," he replied calmly as he flipped the dagger in his hand and slid it with ease back into the sheath at his hip. I did not miss how comfortably he handled the dagger, as if by second nature. "Probably some creature wanting to scare you and nothing more." He added. He glanced at all the lavender on the floor surrounding and covering me. My nose twitched as I pulled some of it from my hair.

"I think you picked enough that I won't need to harvest anymore for quite some time," he commented, his voice filled with warmth and humor. I blushed. I had not known how much to gather, and I would rather not have to return to pick more anytime soon.

"Sorry, you never specified, so I didn't want to disappoint," I replied as I sat up and looked down at my lap, watching as bits and pieces of lavender fell upon it. I was nervous to meet his eyes, bracing myself as I awaited my punishment for incompetence. He had never disciplined me, but the worry of the potential still lingered within me. Hesitantly, I glanced up at him and found him staring down at me with a hardened expression. My heart dropped; I had upset him again. Gritting my teeth, I involuntarily flinched back and looked back at the floor.

He shifted and bent down in front of me as he started picking up pieces of the lavender, not saying a word. Slowly, I relaxed, not anticipating that. I figured he would have made me clean up my mess and then some. I watched him pick up pieces for a moment before I jumped into action and gathered all the pieces near me. We worked in silence, filling the basket full again.

He remained silent as he picked up the basket and carried it to the kitchen. Curiously, I followed him and grabbed my barstool to sit on as I watched him work. The barstool had been a silent gift from him; one day, he had procured it for me. It became my permanent spot to sit and watch him work. I had yet to tell him my appreciation for the seat but was too nervous to break the current silence.

Kierian started tying bundles of lavender together and then looping the string around their stems. He hung the plants upside down on the ceiling via an empty hook, adding to the collection of herbs he already had drying alongside all the additional flower crowns I had been making. My newest ones were an improvement compared to the first successful one I had made. It sat on a shelf overlapping with the one Kierian had made me.

"You've gathered enough that I may make additional batches of my wares, thank you," he complimented. I blushed under the praise, and a small warmth of happiness spread throughout me. He glanced at me and raised an eyebrow. I looked around the kitchen, searching for an answer. I wasn't certain what he wanted me to respond with, and I mumbled out a "welcome," when I came up with nothing else.

He continued to stare at me silently, and I tried not to squirm in my seat under his gaze. What more did he want from me? I had done a good job, and there was no additional context to the conversation for me to contribute to. Maybe I had made a careless mistake, and he was waiting to see if I realized what it was. I sifted through my memories of any place where I had made an error. I collected the lavender; he had hung it to dry, there were no additional ingredients he had asked for, and I don't think I had damaged anything when I fell.

"While you were collecting lavender," his voice broke my thoughts, and I brought my gaze back up to him. "I pulled an additional mattress to your corner of the room. It is not much, but it is better than the hardwood floors." My eyes widened, and I whipped my head to my area of the room to find on the floor was a mattress with blankets and pillows set on top of it. My eyes began to burn, and I gritted my teeth harder as I fought back the swell of emotions that were surging forward through me.

"It's mine?" I whispered, disbelieving.

"It is, if you want to stay here," the low timber of his voice confirmed. I nodded, bringing my hands up to my cheeks and ducking my head into my chest. I squeezed my eyes shut, trying to prevent the tears from falling. I didn't want Kierian to know how much giving me a comfortable bed meant to me. I had never had a bed to myself. In the orphanage, we were forced to share, and usually, what was classified as a bed was really just straw over a scratchy drop cloth.

"Skyla?" He asked, prompting.

I made a squeaking, muffled noise in my throat.

"Is everything alright with the bedding?"

I nodded my head quickly, still not wanting to face him.

"Then why are you crying?" He asked.

I jolted, thinking he wouldn't notice. I shook my head, not wanting to answer.

"Skyla," he said, my name evenly. I heard his footsteps as he left his area of the kitchen to come around the countertop to me. I stared at the floor, feeling him stop on my left. I dared not look at him.

"Skyla," he repeated my name. His hand came up under my chin and directed me to look at him through blurry eyes. I tried to remove my chin from his finger, but he held firm. I squeezed my eyes shut, trying to will away the tears.

"Look at me, Skyla," Kierian's voice softened, and I obeyed. Opening my eyes, they trailed from his wrist, up his arm to his jaw, and then met his eyes—a smoldering concern burned in them. My mouth went dry, and I willed myself to have the courage to speak, but it came out as a cracked whisper.

"I just . . . I Just had not anticipated that you wanted me to stay living with you, is all." My voice felt strained as I tried to get the words out as I felt the tears threaten to spill. I repositioned my body on the barstool to face him. He went from only a finger under my chin, to his hand cupping my cheek. I leaned into his hand, resting my face against it, relinquishing in the warmth.

"Do you not want to live with me?" He asked. Hurt flashed through his eyes.

"I do! But . . ." I trailed off and swallowed. I pushed past my fear to admit, "I did not think you would want me to stay here."

"Hmm." He assessed me, and then, dropping his hand from my face, trailed it down my arm. Bringing his other hand up, he placed both of them on my hips. My heart began to race from the contact, and then he knelt on both knees before me. At this height, he came up to my breasts, and I had to look down at him.

"Do you enjoy living with me?" He asked. My heart lurched as I leaned in closer to him.

"I do," I rushed out, stumbling over my words. "I don't want to live anywhere else," I replied earnestly, shaking my head. His face was barely a foot away from mine, and I felt the weight of his forearms on my thighs. His hands moved slightly from my hips to behind me, his fingertips pressing slightly into the lower part of my back. He searched my eyes, and I leaned in closer to him, closing the distance.

"My cottage is at your disposal." He breathed. "For however long you want to live here."

I brought my hands up and tentatively rested them on his chest. When he didn't react, I slid them over his shoulders. I allowed myself to put more of my weight on him as I tediously balanced on the barstool. I could feel the warmth radiating off him as we breathed in each other's air.

"It's not much," he said, his lips brushing against mine as he spoke. "But I enjoy having you around and helping me out."

"Kierian?" My heart was hammering in my chest, enjoying the sensation building between us.

"Yeah?" He whispered.

I kissed him, loving the feeling of his soft, warm lips against mine. All my nerves melted away as I felt him kiss me back. His arms circled around my waist, pulling me tightly to him. Spreading my knees apart, I cradled his waist between them. He deepened the kiss, and my heart soared as I wrapped my arms around his neck, wanting to close any space between us. In doing so, I lost my balance on the barstool and crashed into him.

Our kiss broke as we fell onto the floor, the barstool tangled in my legs. He kept his arms wrapped tightly around me, and I looked down at him, ignoring the stinging pain in my legs. He was breathing heavily as he looked me over. His lips captured mine again, and I kicked the barstool away from us. He kissed me as if I was the air he needed to breathe.

Then, just as quickly, he held me up at arm's length away over his body. I looked down at him, confused. Why did he stop? His eyes flashed between desire and coldness. Gently, he placed me to the side and sat up, breathing heavily as he stared at the floor in front of him. Confused, I reached my hand up to touch him.

"Don't," he barked, and I noticed how his fangs were elongated. I flinched back, withdrawing my hand to cradle against my chest.

"Kierian –" I began, but he cut me off.

"We shouldn't have done that." His shoulders rose and fell in quick processions. He closed his eyes and then got up from the floor. Standing there, he didn't even look at me as he said, "You can still stay, but we cannot do that again." He walked back behind the kitchen to resume making his salves. He didn't even glance my way, acting as if nothing had happened between us.

My shoulders slumped. What had happened between us felt like lightning. I wanted to feel it again. The press of his body against mine, the sensation of his lips tasting mine. I wanted him, and yet he denied me. I let myself wallow a bit more and then looked about the cottage. I wouldn't call it home yet, but I could only hope maybe one day I would. I realized the implication that would mean, despite what he had just stated. I don't think either of us believed him. I wanted to kiss him again, and by how he responded, I knew he wanted to kiss me, too. The idea of staying by his side made me happy, and there would be more opportunities. Maybe I was getting ahead of myself, but for now, I had a place to live. I had a place where I was wanted.

Chapter Twenty

KIERIAN

I broke temptation. The moment her lips touched mine, my willpower shattered. I knew I had been flirting with a dangerous game. When I spoke, and my lips brushed against hers, I felt the spark go through me. She was euphoria. I wanted to breathe her in as I made love to her. I wanted to be the only one she ever looked at and loved.

My fist slammed against the countertop. Skyla squeaked from the sudden noise, and I closed my eyes, forcing myself to focus. All I could think about was the way her body felt pressed against mine when she lay on top of me. I wanted more, but I knew why I was torturing myself like this. I didn't want to fall in love with her because I knew what it would mean for me. She was human, and I didn't believe I was strong enough to lose someone I loved again.

I felt her arms wrap around my waist as she hugged me from behind, and I sighed. All the pent-up irritation with myself dissipated as my head dropped to my chest. She hugged me tighter, and I felt her face pressed into my back. Bringing my hand up, I rested it on her arms, to keep her holding onto me.

"We can't do this, Skyla," I murmured to her. I needed to set this boundary in place for my own heart.

"Let me hold you, Kierian," she replied. "There's no harm in holding you."

A chuckle rumbled through me. She was trying to find a loophole, and I enjoyed the feeling of her body against mine. I sighed again and shook my head. I gently squeezed her arm before letting her let me go. She stood behind me, and I needed to decide what my next move would be. I turned around to face her and found concern and worry in her eyes.

"Skyla, I just can't." It was the only answer I could give her. The memory of my lost love heartbreak tried to push its way forward. I shoved it back; I didn't need the reminder.

"Is it because I'm human?" She asked quietly as she bit her lip nervously. I felt the crack form in my heart, and I didn't stop myself as I reached my hand up to cup her cheek again. This is what got me in trouble mere seconds ago, but I couldn't stop myself from wanting to touch her more.

"That is a small part of it, but I . . ." The words failed me. There was too much of my background to tell that a simple answer wouldn't be able to cover it all. How could I tell Skyla she was everything I had been searching for, but someone I didn't deserve? My past was riddled with murdering her kind. What right did I have to be with a human? She knew this already, but she still chose to stay here.

"But what?" She asked, waiting for my answer. My hand moved from her cheek to the back of her head as I pulled her into my chest. I held her there as her arms came up to wrap around my waist again.

"I'm just not ready to give you a piece of my heart," I lied. She had already been taking pieces of it since the day she walked through my front door, but I wasn't ready to admit the truth out loud.

We stayed like that for a few minutes until I dropped my hand, letting it skim down her body. She didn't let go as she looked up at my face. Worry still riddled her eyes, and I gave her a sad smile.

"I'll be fine; go along and keep yourself busy," I replied to her silent question. She searched my eyes for more truths than I was giving her. I shook my head, indicating to let it go. She let out a tiny sigh through her nose and then dropped her arms from my waist. She tilted her head to the side, and I shook mine again. This time, she let out a loud sigh, turned, and walked to the other side of the bar. Skyla picked up the barstool we had knocked over, placing it back in its location. She positioned herself to sit upon it, and I realized we were in the same predicament moments earlier before everything unfolded. I would need to do something to change that.

Chapter Twenty-One

SKYLA

'*I'm just not ready to give you a piece of my heart.*' He had said it so tenderly and afraid, but he never realized that he already was claiming my heart. It made me nervous and a smidge scared, but everything I felt during our kiss melted those fears away. There was a nagging sensation that I needed to be patient and gentle with him. I had found sorrow in his eyes when he let a little bit of me in.

I continued to watch him work, my heart pitter-pattering every time our eyes connected. He was always the first to look away, while I remained hopeful. I glanced over my shoulder at my new bed along the wall where I had been sleeping. A fuzzy sky-blue blanket was on top of the mattress, along with a lighter green throw blanket. Two of the biggest, fluffiest pillows rested against the tiny headboard. He may not be ready, but everything he was doing for me told me otherwise. I was not an expert on love, but even these small actions were enough to convince me. I rested my head on my arms on the bar top—slouching forward as I continued to watch him work.

Calmness fell on me, and I tried to keep my eyes open, but it was difficult. I thought about the feel of his lips against mine, and I smiled.

I felt the warmth of Kierian's body as he cradled me to him. I felt the sway of his steps as he carried me, and I snuggled into him. My right hand clutched a handful of his shirt to hold onto. I didn't open my eyes as I pressed my face against his chest, breathing him in. He leaned over and gently laid me on top of a soft mattress. Was this his bed? He started to pull back, but I held fast onto his shirt with my grip.

"Don't leave me," I whispered as I felt the absence of his warmth leave my body. He stilled, and we lingered like that for a moment. He leaned back down to me, and I once again felt his warmth encumber me. I pulled his shirt closer to me and felt his warm breath on my face. I cracked my eyes open, knowing his nearness. We were almost nose to nose as we watched each other. My heart began to beat harder in my chest.

Lifting my head up from my pillow, I closed the small space between us, our lips barely brushing against each other. I tried to maintain my breathing as my heart hammered in my ears. I searched his eyes, trying to confirm the answer to my question.

His eyes, once again, held desire and fear in them. I went to kiss him, and he pulled away, untangling my hand from his shirt as he did so. Hurt and disappointment flashed through me. My heart still beating rapidly from what could have been.

"I can't," Kierian rasped out, defeated. He turned and walked away from me to his side of the room. I watched him pull his shirt over his head and irritably toss it to the floor. His thumbs hooked into his pants, and he paused. I watched with fascination and hunger, but the moment he started yanking them down, I closed my eyes and flipped around in my bed. I blushed from almost seeing him fully naked after what transpired earlier between us.

I heard his bed creek, and the Fae lights chimed out. We were both cloaked in darkness, but neither of us was falling asleep. I listened to every little move that came from his side of the cottage. He was just as still as me; I could barely even hear him breathing. We stayed like that for a long time until sleep finally captured me again.

Chapter Twenty-Two

SKYLA

Two weeks had passed since the day we kissed. He kept me busy every day after breakfast by sending me off with a list of ingredients to pick. When those were collected, he would have me either grind the herbs or tend to the boiling pot over the fire. The only task he would not allow me to do was pour any hot salves into their tins. I was okay with this. The cast iron pot was too heavy for me, and I preferred not to have any burn marks. I'm sure his burn salve would prevent that, but I wasn't looking to take a chance.

If there was nothing else for me to do, he would simply send me off to attend to his gardens. Every few days, I would need to check for new weed growth and remove them. The one thing I refused to do was collect honey. I avoided those Fae bees as if my life depended upon it. Kierian would sigh and mutter something before he went out to collect the combs himself.

When there was nothing else for him to have me do, I would ask him about the various properties of plants. Patiently, he would explain them to me. We maintained that I stayed on the opposite side of the bar than him, while he worked in the kitchen. It did not go unnoticed how he kept a distance between us.

Sometimes, if I accidentally became too close to him, I could feel the zing spark between us. For a moment, it would feel like we were entering back to that space two weeks ago. Everything around us would melt away as the energy shifted in the air. One of us would move to reach for the other, but he would always withdraw. Never allowing it to go further. It left me feeling agitated with longing for him. I tried not to push too much; I didn't want to ruin what we had going. Just, I wanted him to kiss me passionately again.

I sat on my barstool, watching him work. He had already run out of things for me to do today. I had become more brazen in admiring him. My heart was fond of him, and whenever our eyes connected, it would skip a beat.

"I wish that –" I began.

"Do. *Not*. Finish that sentence." Kierian growled, baring his fangs at me. My eyes widened as I moved back into the barstool. The room's atmosphere changed from calm to threatening, the Fae lights flickering above us. "Words have consequences, and I see you have not been taught the importance of them."

"I have not the faintest idea as to what you are referring to," I snipped, glaring back at him. The small fraction of fear I had was replaced with irritation from his insult.

"That there is a Fae cat." He nodded over at Mytilda. I tore my gaze from him to where he indicated her to be; she watched us intently with her vivid cerulean-blue eyes. Her tail swished excitedly while her eyes stayed pinned on me. I had tried to coax her to communicate with me, but she had been silent since that initial day.

"Okay, and you're a Fae male. What does that have to do with anything?" I dragged my gaze back to Kierian and rested my hands on my hips, tilting my head to the side, trying to get a sense of what he was implying. He rolled his eyes and snarled again.

"Fae cats are different than other Fae creatures. If you befriend them, they are prone to grant your heart's desires."

"You mean wishes?"

"Yes," he responded hastily, "but don't say that word."

From the corner of my eye, I saw Mytilda swishing her tail back and forth even more quickly, her front paws kneading the floor where she sat. Her eyes had become the size of saucers, solely intent on us.

"But you told me Djinn's grant wishes and not the good kind."

"Fae cats are rarer than a Djinn. Now, I need you to stop saying that word before you accidentally use it." He continued to bare his fangs at me, so I bared mine back. His nose scrunched up further, and then he elongated his canines.

"No fair, you cheat!" I shrieked, throwing my hands up in the air. He chuckled darkly.

"Perks to not being a human, I suppose." He shrugged. He slightly froze as he said the word, and I knew we were both thinking the same thing. My being human was a hindrance to the lust that swirled between us. Some moments, I loathed it, because what could have happened if I were Fae like him? Would he have already dragged me off to his bed?

"So, what happens if they grant a," I cut myself off to remedy with, "one." I wanted to break the new awkward tension that was forming.

"They lose a life," he replied bluntly, relaxing a bit.

"How many do they have?" I leaned in, becoming more curious.

Mytilda crossed the short distance to us and nuzzled her face against my legs.

"Depends on the Fae cat. Some only have one; some have hundreds. There is no telling."

"Have you ever used one?" I hopped off the barstool to pick Mytilda up and began petting her. She purred loudly in response. Kierian didn't respond right away, and I took my attention from Mytilda to look at him. He wore his faraway expression, and I knew he was living in his memories again. This had become a regular thing. Sometimes, he would stay lost in them for minutes if I didn't speak up.

"Kierian?" I prodded, trying to regain his attention. He shook his head, returning to the present.

"Not me, but I witnessed one." His voice became quiet.

"What was it for?" I leaned in slightly with the cat clutched tightly in my arms. Her little body radiating more heat than I was expecting. It didn't help with how fluffy her coat was.

"We're not discussing it." I felt the wall rush up between us.

"I hit another nerve, I see," I replied, curious as to what he was hiding. He didn't respond, turning away from me as he grabbed a book off the top of his shelf. He handed it to me without even glancing my way. I looked down at the title through Mytilda's fur, 'Fae Creatures.' I carried her and the book over to the bench with pillows, plopping down on it. Mytilda nestled herself in my lap as I opened the book.

Kierian had been kind enough to add another seating area to the cottage for me to use as needed. While he didn't mind his minimal rigid furniture, he had made a comment that I would probably enjoy something more cozy. I glanced around the room, noting my bed in the corner with blankets and pillows, the barstool for me to sit on to watch him work in the kitchen, and now this comfortable bench seat.

He never balked at the privacy screen that stayed surrounding the bathtub outside. I smiled to myself when my gaze fell on our dried flower crowns as I petted Mytilda. I've been here for over a month, and he has already done so much to make this feel like a home for me.

Mytilda must have become agitated with her arrangement; she moved off my lap to land onto the floor. She looked back at me over her shoulder, and then with a flick of her tail, walked to the other side of the room. We both watched as she jumped onto Kierian's bed and curled up to take a nap. Kierian chuckled in response, and I shot him a look of annoyance.

"Can Fae read minds?" I asked.

"Not usually," he drawled out slowly. "But some can. Why?" He was working on a new batch of salve and was pouring the hot liquid into the metal tins he had lined up on the bar top. The day prior, he had informed me that he would soon need to head to a village town to sell his stock and pick up a few items.

"Can you project your thoughts into my mind?" I ignored his question and continued with my curiosity.

Yes, I can. Why? His voice filled my mind. I jumped, realizing his mouth had not moved. He quietly chuckled in amusement.

"Because the Fae Cat, on my first day here, told me her name was Mytilda, I was curious," I answered.

"She communicated to you?" He said out loud, his eyes snapping up to mine. All amusement vanishing from his face as wariness replaced it.

"Yeah, why?" I asked nervously.

"Just be careful. I don't know how many lives she has left, and you will be mournful to know she passed away because of a careless desire you spoke out loud," he warned. He maintained eye contact, his task at hand on pause.

"I see." I wasn't certain what else I could say in response. I was the first to break eye contact as I turned my attention back to the book in my lap. I opened it up and found the chapter on Fae cats, settling in for the long read ahead as I began to hear liquid hitting and filling metal tins from the kitchen again.

Chapter Twenty-Three
KIERIAN

I took one of the few rare moments to watch Skyla as she read the Fae Creatures book. Her red curly hair had become more manageable since her arrival, gaining a nice shine to it. I didn't mind mixing up additional bottles of the lily shampoo for her. She had tried the other aromatic types, but the lily one was her favorite. She didn't know it, but it was my favorite smell on her. She also was unaware that I had mixed up the various scents the day after her arrival.

She no longer looked as ragged and starved since living with me, and I smiled at the glow her skin was beginning to take on. My gaze fell upon her lips, and I thought of our kisses. I quickly dashed them away. I had been trying to keep her as busy as possible to prevent it from happening again. Every so often, the feeling would linger between us, and I had to use all of my strength to pull away. Due to my continuous efforts to keep her occupied, I was ahead of schedule. I would need to make my annual trip to one of the local villages sooner than I had anticipated.

Skyla's nose scrunched up as she read, making me smile. While she hadn't admitted it to me, I had gathered that her reading comprehension was low. She would hedge around certain topics that I would patiently explain to her. When I would hear her let out an angry sigh, I would ask if there was certain Fae terminology I could help her with. I didn't want to wound the poor girl's pride. I admired her determination to work through her struggles instead of throwing in the towel. I already had decided that I would need to pick up more books to keep her entertained and help with her reading abilities. When she had nothing to keep her occupied, she became a distraction to me with her relentless curiosity.

I glanced at her pathetic clothing, which was being barely held together. My clothing would swallow her whole, and unfortunately, the cottage's magic did not extend to the point of creating new wardrobes for anyone who dwelled within. I would need to buy her new clothing. I tried to tell myself I could pick out clothes for her, but the argument raged in my mind as I realized I would need to bring her with me. I couldn't keep her locked away in my cottage forever.

I poured the last of the salve into the final tin and placed the now empty pot off to the side. I started capping all the tins while they cooled and mentally took inventory of the rows of marked jars. There were healing salves, pregnancy preventatives, scar removers, illness cures, and burn relief, amongst many others. I had been perfecting these recipes for two hundred years and was quite proud of how far I had brought them in effectiveness.

"Do you want to go to the human village with me?" I asked, breaking the silence. She looked up at me, completely surprised. She probably had not anticipated me welcoming her on a trip like this. Then again, I wasn't certain at what she expected of me. I sometimes barely knew what I expected of her each day. She helped fill a void in my life, and I enjoyed her company even though I knew our time together was limited.

"Which village?" She asked hesitantly. She chewed on the bottom of her lip, and my cock twitched, changing my appreciation of her to self-irritation. *Fucking hell*, a few weeks with this human, and she did one little thing like that, and it drove me up the wall. Often, I scented Skyla's curiosity and lust upon her. I tried my damndest to withhold myself from ever acting upon it. She had been the one who initiated the first kiss. Currently, I was glad the bar was placed in between us. She couldn't see my twitching cock. The only relief to my sexual frustrations was masturbating each morning. It was a blessing in disguise that she never caught me.

"Up north, a village called Fairfield," I replied, not thinking much of it. My cock was fully erect now. I watched as she relaxed a bit; she probably was unaware of how stiff her posture had become until I said the village name.

"Sure, I'll come along," she replied excitedly, Skyla's smile beaming on her face. "When are we going?" I surveyed all the jars and tins on my countertop, twisting my lips to the side. I really could not make another batch of anything. Any more items and carrying it all would become too cumbersome.

"I suppose tomorrow if the weather is nice?" It was too late in the day now to make the trek. I was running low on supplies such as jars and tins, and I did not feel like having a lazy day tomorrow to relax. I needed to be diligent about taking advantage of traveling when the weather was nice out.

She bolted up from her reading position.

"Tomorrow?!" She yelled. I flinched from the loudness of her voice. My Fae ears were not used to her random outbursts of excitement. "I hope it's the perfect day to go!"

"I'm surprised you are this excited to head to a human village?" I smiled at her enthusiasm. Seeing her smile delighted me. She scrunched up her nose.

"Fairfield is a huge city! I have never been, but I heard it has so many wonderful things, and I always wanted to go," she rushed out.

"Which village did you hail from?" Despite her incessant chatter, she had never told me, and I had not expressed enough interest to ask.

"Piggs Burough," she replied dully, her shoulders slumping with embarrassment. I refrained from revealing to her how I wanted to react to the information of her home village. I assumed the place had not improved in the decades since I had last visited. The people there were ill-mannered and generally illiterate, hence why the town's name was misspelled. Knowing this, it made sense why she struggled with reading. It made me intrigued that she was able to read; I commended her for it. I questioned where her kindness had derived from, considering the interactions I have had with the people that dwelled there were less than pleasant.

Maybe the village had improved in the last few decades, but they had not been a kind-hearted community either. It did explain why Skyla was as scrawny as she was, along with why her clothing did not suit her. The dress had been oversized and looked second-hand worn. I did not have much faith that it would last a year still intact.

"Well, you don't need to go back there if you choose not to," I replied, the words leaving my mouth before I could stop them. I realized I had been potentially promising her a permanent place to stay with me. I opened my mouth to retract my statement but closed it when I watched how much she perked up. I noticed rather quickly that Skyla wore all her emotions on her face, and I did not want to take away her current happiness.

"Really?" She asked, hopeful. I turned back to begin packing away the wares I planned to sell.

"Maybe I'll leave you in Fairfield," I teased, and I heard her choke on a shriek.

"You wouldn't dare!" She accused.

I glanced over at her and, with a devilish smile, replied, "Better stick close to my side tomorrow."

"Deal!" She rushed out, and I chuckled to myself.

By the following morning, I had everything organized and packed away in my bag to carry to Fairfield. Slinging the bag over my shoulder, I glanced down at Skyla, who was eager to begin the journey, and by eager she was literally bouncing on the balls of her feet. I hoped today would be the last day I ever had to see her in those rags.

"How long of a walk is it from here?" Skyla asked.

"Walk?" I raised an eyebrow at her.

"How else do you plan to get there?" She asked inquisitively. I mulled over her words, realizing I could not Fae sprint while traveling with her. I blinked at this conundrum; if I carried her, she might become sick from the speed at which I traveled. I was not inclined to wear her breakfast on my attire while selling my medicinal wares. An idea sparked in my mind; it would be humiliating on my part, but I did not see any other way around it to get to Fairfield in one day.

"Are you against riding on the back of a stag?" I asked, masking my true thoughts on the matter.

"No?" She replied slowly.

"Good, take this and wear it," I said, shrugging off my backpack and handing it to her. She umphed from the weight and struggled to put it on. I suppose I had overfilled it. I did not wait as I shifted into my deer form. Looking at her, I kneeled on the grass before her.

Get on, I commanded into her mind. She looked at me warily.

Don't dawdle; we don't have all day. I barked, which caused her to scramble into action. She swung her leg over my back, and I felt the weight of her and the heavy bag. She repositioned herself, moving her ass back and forth to become comfortable. I stood up immediately, and her hands landed on my shoulders as she caught her balance. I felt the warmth of her thighs as they tightened around me, my thoughts traveling upwards to what lay between them. Fuck, this trip was going to be my fucking undoing.

Hold onto my neck. I communicated one last time, feeling her do as I instructed; I took off at a full sprint. She shrieked as I dashed over the grassy knolls, heading toward my walking path to Fairfield.

I had to force my focus on where I was going and not how her thighs squeezed around me. The thin barrier of fabric between my back and her sex was riling me up by the second. With every leap I made over a log, I felt temporary coolness as her body rose up and came back down again.

I tapped into my Fae speed to get us there sooner. I needed her to stop touching me as soon as possible. I was positive that if I tried to make bargaining deals with my buyers and had a hard on, they would be less inclined to talk to me. I was almost just as positive if I continued this torture, I would stop mid-journey to take her right here in these very woods. I needed to think of something else to keep my mind off the female riding my back. I started recounting the ingredients in my pack and how I had strengthened them in quality over the years. Which batches had failed me versus the ones that came out on top. I was desperate for my distractions.

Chapter Twenty-Four

SKYLA

Off. Kierian's ragged voice filled my mind. I quickly obliged, sliding off him. I lost my balance from the weight of his bag on my back. Falling backward, I landed on top of the bag and felt the pain from all the items digging into my back. I was still coming down from the adrenaline rush I received from how fast we traveled together as he sprinted through the woods.

Kierian shifted back into his Fae form and shook his body as if he was still a stag. He glared down at me, annoyed. I realized why as my eyes fell upon his cock that strained against his pants. Flushing, I looked away quickly. My heart still raced from the adrenaline, but now it was laced with desire and curiosity.

"Give me the bag," he growled. I tried to sit up but couldn't and decided to shrug out of it and let him retrieve it off the ground. I moved out of his way, and he grunted as he picked it up and swung it onto his back. I glanced at the bulge in his pants again, unaware of him watching me.

"You either can take care of that or keep quiet," he growled gruffly. I gulped, my eyes becoming wide, and shook my head frantically. He growled again and started walking in the direction of the village. He had stopped us on the side of the road before the entrance when he had shifted. I chased after him, afraid if I lost him, he would make good on his threat from yesterday and leave me here to survive on my own.

Despite my better judgment, I grabbed onto the bottom part of his shirt to avoid losing him. He slowed his pace and glanced over his shoulder at me. I shrugged with a shy smile, hoping he didn't mind. He shrugged back in response and kept walking. As we walked through the village gate entrance, it became rather crowded quickly, and I clutched tightly to his shirt.

There were more people in Fairfield than I had ever witnessed in Piggs Burough. Many paid attention to Kierian and parted out of his way; very few looked past him to me. The ones who did would give me a curious look and then turn their attention away. Everything was brick here: brick fences, brick houses, brick roads, and even the vendor stalls were made of brick.

Stay close. Do not let go. Kierian's voice entered my mind. I pulled myself up to his side and looped my arm through his, clutching him tightly to me. With all the activity going on around us, I barely reacted to the touch of his warm skin against mine. I was too worried that if enough people passed by or didn't see me, they would make me lose my hold on him.

I suppose that will do. He said it with approval, no longer coming off as irritated. *When I am dealing with vendors, please stay quiet.* I had no desire to talk to a bunch of strangers, especially with how I looked compared to the rest of the people here.

They were dressed in deep, jewel-tone fabrics. Some had stripes, some lace, and many of their clothing was multi-layers of fabric. I noted that most of the females wore some pendant around their neck and bobbles on their ears, while the men either wore bowties or top hats. My attire had been on the sad side in Piggs Burough, but here I was in beggar rags. Which, I did not see any poor people about, and it made me curious if there was homelessness in Fairfield.

Kierian led us to the first of many storefronts. I witnessed him exchange his jars and tins for more coins than I had ever seen in my life. It made me wonder what he planned to do with all his money.

Chapter Twenty-Five

KIERIAN

A few hours later, I glanced down at Skyla; she still clung to me as if her life depended upon it. I had warned her to stay close to prevent us from being separated. I knew if that did happen, I should be able to track her scent even in a crowd this large. If it didn't work, I would tear this town apart until I found her.

Even through the noise of Fairfield, I still heard her stomach begin growling. Her grip tightened on my arm as she withdrew into herself a bit. We were nearing lunchtime, and I glanced around for any nearby places to grab a bite to eat.

"What are you hungry for?" I asked her as I started leading the way to cross the street to the side with some of the more favorable restaurants I had eaten at in the past. Her grip tightened further.

"Umm, I'm okay," she replied, quieter than her normal self. Interesting. I found it quite . . . intriguing that she was being shy now when it came to something as nourishment.

"I can hear your stomach growling. Come along; there are a

bunch of restaurants to pick from. We won't be home until later tonight when you will be well beyond starving."

"What about you?" She ignored my question.

"What about me, what?" I asked, confused, maneuvering us amongst the crowds.

"Won't you be hungry too?" She pushed, and I chuckled.

"I trained and lived the life of a warrior." I paused, noticing her shoulders falling a bit. "But I suppose I could go for a bite myself."

She smiled at me, and I smiled back. We had slowed in pace until we stopped walking. People milled about us, and I ignored them. Turning, I faced Skyla and reached my hand up to tuck a stray strand of hair behind her ear, causing her to blush. Warmth spread throughout me. It would be easy to lean down and kiss her here, let everyone know she was mine. A wave of sorrow and shock crashed through me; I couldn't claim her like that. No matter what the Maker had intended when she showed up at my door, I couldn't do that to her or myself.

Our eye contact broke when a male roughly ran into Skyla, jarring her off balance. I caught her in time, preventing her from falling and being trampled or swept into the crowd away from me. Holding her protectively close to my chest, I looked up, spotting the offending male disappearing into the crowd, and snarled at him. Even if he couldn't see it, it was enough to make everyone else nearby give us a wide berth.

"Are you okay?" I growled, still baring my fangs at everyone who looked our way. Her arms were wrapped tightly around my waist. She loosened her grip as she pulled back to look up at me, still keeping her arms in place.

"Yeah, I'm okay. . ." Skyla's eyes darted to look at everyone around us. "Um, you can stop threatening everyone," her voice raised nervously. I snarled once more and whipped my head to the side, closing my eyes. I breathed deeply, tuning the world out. I needed to focus. I needed to stay in control. I could not lose my grip. If I did, I probably would not be allowed back amongst humans. Skyla would be separated from me. I inhaled deeply again and let it slowly out my mouth.

"Okay." I opened my eyes to find everyone still giving us wary looks from a distance. "Let's eat, Skyla." I led us to a place I knew she would enjoy. The humans continued to keep their distance while other Fae watched me warily until we ducked out of sight into the cafe.

As we entered, I noted the fresh white paint on the walls. They must have recently been remodeled, as the once bright colors were now subdued to pastel pinks, blues, and olive green with sprinkles of yellow stars throughout. There were three other customers in the ten booths, which were now a light wood color with pastel blue seats. Instead of cramped-in tables in the center, there were five white high tops with bar stools spread throughout.

I led Skyla to one of the booths along the windows. I took the far side, which would make it easy for me to see the door and anything happening on the street. She eagerly grabbed one of the menus that was placed behind the napkin holder. I glanced at the bar, where there were more bar stools for seating, and to find a Fae male filling drinks. Behind him, another Fae male and a human male could be seen through the small kitchen window. Ivy vines covered various parts of the interior, and if I had to guess, it had been strategically placed.

This cafe had once been donned in dark woods and a more relaxing setting. Now, it was bright and welcoming. Judging by Skyla's expression, this had been a good choice. I watched how her eyes eagerly scanned the menu, flipping the pages back and forth as if she might miss something. I found it amusing; she probably had become tired of our mundane meals. She glanced up at me, catching me watching her. Skyla's face changed to startlement.

"Is something wrong?" She asked as she tilted her head to the side.

"No?" I furrowed my brow, wondering why she would believe something to be wrong.

"You were smiling at me." She stated and it was then that I realized I was still smiling. I dropped it immediately, distracting myself as I reached for a menu. She gave me a quizzical look, which I chose to ignore. As I opened my menu, she watched me a moment longer before eagerly turning her attention back to her own menu.

"Hello, I'm Rhoda. I'll be your waitress today. What can I get you both for drinks?" A husky female voice asked. I glanced up at the Fae female whose eyes were trailing down my body appreciatively before her eyes connected with mine, and she smiled. Rhoda had short mint green hair in a long bob, and her delicately pointed Fae ears were adorned with multiple hoop piercings. She had aquamarine blue eyes and pert pink lips. She wore a loose, off-white tunic dress that did not hide her ample bosom, with multiple belts and chords wrapped around her waist. The tunic dress only fell midway to her thighs to show off her long Fae legs.

I'm surprised I hadn't noticed her coming with all the bangles and bells on both of her wrists and ankles. She wore strappy sandals on her feet and had sky-blue painted toenails that were adorned with multiple toe rings. I noticed then the various rings she had on her fingers and the long, matching sky-blue nails. They were long and sharp enough that I knew they would leave some marks.

"May I have a strawberry lemonade?" Skyla's voice took my attention away from Rhoda, who had arched her eyebrow silently, asking if I wanted to play. Rhoda didn't even look at Skyla as she nodded, keeping her focus on me.

"And you?" Rhoda's voice warmed. I knew she was asking for more than just my drink order.

"Water," I replied dryly.

"Just water?" She looked amused.

"Yes." I was a bit curt as I turned my attention back to the menu, pretending to browse it. Rhoda stood there a moment longer before turning to grab our drinks. They were placed down in front of us a minute later. Rhoda didn't linger this time as she headed back to the bar where the Fae bartender stood watching, bored.

"You can order whatever you want," I offered Skyla, not looking at her. I grabbed a glass of water and took a drink.

"I think our waitress wants to order you," Skyla replied, and I choked on my water, causing me to cough. She gave me a challenging look. I didn't respond.

"Well, she does," Skyla added, returning her attention to the menu. I detected annoyance in her voice.

It didn't take much longer for Rhoda to return to our table to collect our orders. I wanted a simple sandwich. Meanwhile, Skyla ordered a sandwich and three different types of desserts.

"You're going to make yourself sick," I commented as Rhoda walked away to put our orders in.

"It'll be worth it," Skyla countered.

"I'll remind you of that later when you're complaining about your upset stomach," I replied as I leaned back in the booth, crossing my arms. She rolled her eyes.

"How many more places do we need to go to?" she asked, changing the subject. I glanced at the bag of wares at my feet, calculating the number of vendors and shops I still needed to visit.

"It'll be a few yet. We've only sold half of my wares, and I still have plenty of merchants from whom I need to buy supplies from. We most likely won't be home until dusk." She nodded and then turned her attention to take in the café, not hiding her awe.

I noticed a new hole growing larger on the shoulder of her dress. It was one of many I had come to find on her apparel. When Skyla tied up her wild red mane, I noticed the most how her clothes didn't suit her. They reminded me of some middle-aged women's clothing who worked in a grimy sweatshop and were probably miserable with their life. Skyla was anything but that; she needed vibrant clothing that matched her ray of sunlight. I glanced around the cafe at the colors again; clothing that matched this atmosphere would look darling on her.

Rhoda brought a tray with our food over soon after. She lingered again, but I did not give her attention. Aside from the thank you for the food, she was dismissed until we needed her.

I ate my sandwich and watched with amusement as Skyla inhaled hers before she sampled back and forth between her three desserts. She reminded me of a bird flitting about on the ground when they were scavenging for seeds.

"You need to try this!" she exclaimed, cutting a healthy serving of the strawberry dessert onto her fork and holding it out for me.

"I don't particularly care for sweets," I replied gingerly, eyeing the contents on her fork to what I assumed would be sugar overload.

"Come on, just this one bite for me," her voice turned into a plea, and I gave a small sigh. Giving into her wiles, I took the offered fork and ate the contents. Sugary sweetness exploded on my tastebuds. Quickly, I handed her the fork back.

"See! Good, isn't it?" she pressed. I swallowed, assaulted by the sugar buzz I could feel.

"It's something," I replied, taking a drink of water to cleanse some of my palette.

"How can you not like it? It's strawberries!"

"How do you know I don't like it?" I challenged.

"Your face is practically screaming in disgust." she pointed out. I immediately masked my facial expressions from her. I was not particularly fond of how often my façade slipped around her. I did not like her being able to read my thoughts on my face.

"It is far sweeter than I would care for. Now eat up." I tried to ignore how she lingered on watching me. She swirled her fork around on her plate, and I braced myself for the question she was mulling in her head.

"Why did your eyes turn black earlier?"

I stilled. I had not been aware that had happened on the street. I tried to keep that side of me locked up tightly, but it had momentarily slipped out. I needed to have a better hold on myself. If that side of me had been unleashed, I would have been put down like a rabid dog. I shivered from the thought of what it could have meant for Skyla.

"Kierian?" Her voice had changed to tender concern, and I met her eye.

"It's just another part of me, nothing more," I answered, trying to shake her off. She cocked her head to the side, the wariness still lingering in her eyes. I dared not look away until she finally shrugged and continued to eat her desserts. I would need to be more conscious of my reactions around her.

For the rest of the meal, we ate in silence. When it came time for the check, Rhoda gave me another offering look, which I ignored. I guided Skyla and myself back outside to continue selling the rest of the contents in my bag. Once I started restocking my supplies, it didn't take long for me to notice the way Skyla lagged behind me. She still held onto my arm or had a grip on my shirt, but she no longer excitedly looked around at the businesses of Fairfield. I gave her clothing another glance and spotted the shop we would head to next. She followed in tow; if I didn't know any better, I would think she was sleepwalking with how zoned out from the world she currently was.

Chapter Twenty-Six

SKYLA

I was exhausted. The crowds, the noise, and the constant business dealings had worn me out. Even though I had kept quiet all day, it had been a lot to take in. I still mulled over why Kierian's eyes had gone black on the street, but I knew better than to push on the topic. I tucked away the new detail about him for later. He said it was a part of him, and I planned to ask more about it when we were home, and the timing was right.

We entered yet another shop, and I tuned everything out to let Kierian buy more supplies that he needed. I did not even pay attention to the shopkeeper or the shop we were in; I wanted to go to sleep. I tightened my arm around him as I nuzzled my head against his arm, not caring if the merchant took notice of me or not. I just wanted to go home.

"Dearie?" An elderly woman's voice withdrew me from the thoughts of my bed. I glanced at the older lady standing there, looking at me expectantly. She had gray hair streaked with white that was piled into a bun on top of her head. Her brown eyes were warm, friendly, and patient as she waited for my answer. She wore a simple lilac dress with a blue half-apron tied around her waist. I looked up at Kierian questioningly. He had told me not to talk to anyone.

"She asked what color fabric you preferred for your dress," Kierian supplied.

"My dress?" I asked, confused, looking down at the one I was wearing.

"The kind sir." the lady began, and I looked back up at her as she nodded to Kierian. "Is buying you new dresses. I am curious what kind of fabrics you prefer." The old lady smiled kindly at me. My eyes widened, completely shocked. I tried to take a step back, but Kierian's arm locked in on mine, preventing me from escaping. I looked up at him.

"You're buying me dresses? I have no money to pay you back with," I confessed.

"I never asked for you to pay me back. Accept the gift and go pick out some fabric swatches." He nodded his head at the bolts of fabric on the shelves to our right and loosened his grip on my arm to release me. I stood there in awe, looking at all my options, and looked back at him. He nodded again, encouraging me.

I slid my arm from his and hesitantly walked toward the bolts of patterns, looking over my shoulder at him. He nodded, and I turned back to look at the swatches in front of me. Lightly, I trailed my fingers over the soft fabrics. I was afraid, even with my regular baths, that I would soil them. I was surprised that none of the fabrics were coarse or itchy. Carefully, I picked a pretty jade bolt from the pile and turned, offering it to the elderly lady.

"I like this one," I stated.

"Matches your eyes," she complimented.

"Any others you would prefer?" Kierian asked. "You can have multiple dresses made." Happiness bubbled within me, and I picked out five more bolts of fabric: an emerald green, a sky blue, a dark blue, a lavender, and a simple slate gray.

The elderly lady started taking my measurements, not commenting once on my figure, which calmed me. She hummed along the way and then had me sit down to wait while she and a few of her workers whipped up the dresses. Kierian did not say a word as he sat there with his arms crossed over his chest.

An hour later, the elderly lady returned with my six brand-new dresses, along with leggings that would complement beneath the dresses. When she procured the panties, I blushed. I hadn't wanted Kierian to see them. I was in awe at her thorough thoughtfulness. She told Kierian the amount, and I made a strangled sound in surprise. He paid it without blinking an eye. She told us of two more shops we ought to visit for my wardrobe, one for accessories and another for shoes.

He took me to the shoe shop first, and the cobbler was horrified at the state of my current pair. He set me up with three different types: a hiking pair for the woods, a sporty type for around the yard, and lastly, a pair of strappy sandals.

Next was the accessory store. The lady offered me new belts, ribbons to tie my hair up in, and a unique pouch bag that I could use when gathering my ingredients for Kierian. He paid for everything without complaint.

As we left the shop, it became a habit for me to loop my arm within his. All of my items were safely tucked away in his backpack, which was now filled with empty jars, tins, and things for the cottage. Something glimmered in a shop window, catching my eye. I slowed, pulling slightly away from Kierian to look at it. It was a metal pendant, handcrafted in the likes of deer antlers with a gemstone in the middle.

"Do you want it?" Kierian asked me. I looked up at him and

shook my head. I could not ask this of him; he had given me so much already. He sighed. "Come on." He did not wait for me to respond as he pulled me into the shop. The bell chimed, and the shopkeeper came out from the back.

"How may I help," he stopped mid-sentence, noticing the Fae male standing in his shop. Straightening himself, he started again. "How may I help you, sir?"

"The antler necklace in your shop window, the lady would like to see it." He nodded in my direction, and I tightened my grip on him. I blushed with warmth from him calling me a lady. The shopkeeper turned his attention and seemed to notice me for the first time. I clutched Kierian's arm tighter.

"Ah yes, excellent taste," he replied instead of whatever else he had been thinking. He moved past the counter to the store window to retrieve the necklace. "This piece had just come in this week, new designer to the store, but their work is exquisite."

"Human or Fae made?" Kierian questioned. I found it peculiar that Kierian would care about who had made it.

"Human," the shopkeeper replied, unphased by the question. He handed the necklace to me, and I looked at Kierian, not certain of what I was supposed to do.

Look it over and make sure you still love it in your hands as you did in the window. I slightly nodded and did as he told me. I turned it around in my fingers before bringing it up close to my face to admire the exquisite details. The little lines that had been hand-carved into it made the antlers appear realistic in the metal setting. *If it meets your approval, tell him we will take it.* I glanced up at him, making certain he meant it. He nodded, and I looked back at the shopkeeper with a smile.

"We'll take it."

Outside Fairfield, Kierian handed me the bag filled with all my new items, along with other supplies he had stocked up on. The antler necklace felt warm on my skin, and making me smile as I reached my right hand up to touch it. I had never had something this lovely before in my life, and it reminded me of him. I looked over at him, and he had already shifted into his stag form, kneeling on the ground before me.

I barely swung my leg over and was seated comfortably on him before he shot off at a full sprint. I shrieked as I threw my arms around his neck for support. A low, dark chuckle rumbled in my head. It felt as if he was sprinting faster heading home than he had been coming to Fairfield. The dim lighting made it difficult to track everything, and I wondered if he wanted to be back at the cottage before any of the Fae creatures awoke for the evening.

We came to a jolting stop, and I peeked over his shoulder to see the full moon rising above the cottage in the clearing. I had lost track of time as I recounted all the Fae creatures I had read about in his book, worried we might cross a few. I felt the weight of the books on my back that Kierian had picked up for me to read. I didn't complain because I found the Fae creature book fascinating. My reading speed had started out slow, but I felt I was improving with the more I practiced. I still stumbled over many of the words, but I felt an accomplishment at what I had achieved thus far in my readings.

He kneeled in the grass, and I crawled off his back. This time, the weight of the backpack did not cause me to fall backward. He shifted back into his Fae form, panting heavily. The moonlight did not conceal the stiff bulge in his pants again, and I looked away, not wanting to make eye contact.

I felt his hand on my shoulder and I jolted before realizing he was removing the bag to carry for himself. I stood there nervously. Earlier, he told me to either take care of it or keep quiet. I chose to stay silent again. I took a few steps to the cottage but was halted when his hand firmly grasped my wrist. I looked back at him as I chewed on my bottom lip.

The moonlight caught his golden-brown eyes, and I felt my heart slow. I glanced between the cottage and him. Making my decision, I took a step back and faced him. It had been two weeks with no intimacy. I had felt the spark between us earlier when that man had bumped into me. I was certain that before that happened, Kierian was going to kiss me in the middle of the street with everyone passing by.

He closed the small distance between us, the moonlight illuminating him. I waited with bated breath as I looked up at his face, and he looked down at mine. Kierian raised his hand to cup my right cheek and leaned down until our faces were mere inches apart. I searched his eyes, my heart hammering in my chest.

Reaching up, I lightly touched his cheek. His pupils contracted from my warmth as he leaned into my hand. I rose up on my tiptoes to close the distance between us. Both of our eyes searched each other's, and I pressed my lips against his. His eyes widened before his other arm snaked around my waist, yanking me close to him as he kissed me deeply. Heat rushed through me as I felt his hard cock pressed against me. I wrapped my arms around his neck for support. He kissed me hungrily with desperate need as he moaned into my mouth.

Kierian broke the kiss and closed his eyes, resting his head against mine. He breathed heavily, and I was unsure what it meant as we stood there silently. His breathing picked up; his brows furrowed as his face scrunched up in anguish. He bared his fangs and pushed back away from me.

"Get in the cottage now," Kierian ordered with a low growl.

"What?" I asked, confused by the sudden change.

"We have unwarranted company," he answered, and I looked past his shoulder to see hideous creatures emerging from the shadows of the Fae woods. My heart leaped into my throat from fear. He turned to face them and snarled.

"Run to the cottage and shut the door behind you, Skyla," he ordered again. Fear coursed through me from the sheer number of creatures making their way towards us.

"Go!" He shouted, breaking through my frozen stupor. I jumped, moving into action as I ran to the cottage. It was so far away, and there were too many Fae creatures; could Kierian take them all on? I was too afraid to look back at him and the sight I would see.

Running down the grassy knoll had been easy but tedious. I had to make certain I didn't stumble or lose my footing and send myself tumbling. However, running up the next hill to the cottage caused me to breathe heavily. The first shriek behind me sent me falling forward. Pain shot up my hands and arms as I tried to catch myself. My face slammed against the cool grass. I breathed in the smell of damp dirt before I pushed myself back up. The adrenaline in my body caused me to ignore the ground burn I received from the slide. I would deal with it later. I continued to race towards the cottage as more shrieks and roars sounded behind me.

Worry coursed through me for Kierian. What if they tore him from limb to limb? He was all I had now. I suppose I had Mytilda too, but if something happened to Kierian, my only hope would be for Tennyson to visit soon. Otherwise, I would be on my own again.

My hands closed on the cottage door. Feeling safe enough, I turned back to look at the grassy knoll over from me to where Kierian was. The sight unfolded, surprising me. Kierian was painting the grass with the Fae creature's blood as he tore through them. He moved and twisted around them, slicing their bodies with his bare claws as he went. I couldn't help but to view him as a beautiful vision to behold.

Get inside, Skyla. His voice growled against my mind. I snapped out of my daze and did not need to be told again. I pulled open the door and slammed it shut behind me. I didn't even think as I raced to Kierian's side of the room. It was completely cloaked in darkness, and I didn't want to be seen. I wrapped his blanket around me as I crawled into his bed. Instantly, his scent enveloping, giving me a small sense of security. The screams and roars grew louder outside. I clapped my hands over my ears, trying to muffle the noise. What if they made it inside? I had no way to protect myself. Without warning, it became deathly silent.

Hesitantly, I pulled my hands away from my ears and stared frightened at the door. My body shook involuntarily as I flicked my gaze to the windows, wondering if they would give me any indication if the monsters were coming for me. Unless they had night vision, any creature looking in through the windows would not see me tucked away here. I hoped.

Minutes ticked by, and my anxiousness grew. Everything was quiet, and I dared not leave my spot. I clutched his blankets tighter around me. I wouldn't move from here until morning light streamed through the windows, but what if Kierian needed me? A human had no chance against Fae creatures. I was fooling myself; I needed to listen and stay in here like he had told me to.

The cottage door opened, and I froze. A tall figure entered, and the Fae lights chimed on. I scrambled out of his bed, running across the room to throw my arms around his waist tightly. I cried into his chest as I felt relief that he was okay. He stilled momentarily and then gently rested his hand on my back.

"I am okay," he comforted, and I sagged against him. He pulled away from me, and I flushed from embarrassment. I looked up at him and realized he was covered in a mixture of red and black blood. I looked horrified down at myself, now covered in it as well from touching him.

"Come along, we'll wash up outback," he sighed. I was scared to go back out there, but he pulled me along regardless. He did not let go of my hand as he rounded the back of his house, where the washing tub sat hidden behind the privacy screen. He stopped us before it, and I looked up at him questioningly. He must have realized what I had been thinking.

"You wash first. Tonight, the privacy screen will be removed as a precaution." I tried to argue against the idea as the screen disappeared, but Kierian held up his hand to silence me. I obeyed as I noticed how his hand slightly shook and that he once again had pure black eyes.

"I will keep my back to you and stand guard. We also are burning those clothes you are wearing," he commented dryly. He turned his back to me, and I looked at him and then the tub. In the moonlight, I stripped down naked, tossing my ratty clothes to the side, and stepped into the warm water. I truly enjoyed Fae magic. No matter when I entered this tub, the water was clean, and the temperature was perfect.

I watched Kierian as I scrubbed the blood off my body, making certain he did not turn around to sneak a peek, and true to his word, he stood guard. I was a smidge disappointed he did not try. When I felt clean again, I left the tub to grab one of the fluffy towels from the bin and dried myself off. It dawned on me that the bag with my new dresses had been left in the cottage.

"I'm done," I said quietly, breaking the silence. Kierian turned around and sucked in a breath as I stood there with only a towel wrapped around me. I gave a meek smile and tried to escape past him. He grabbed my wrist, halting me, and I looked up at him, waiting for what would happen next. Half his face was covered in black and red blood, and he looked down at me silently. His eyes still hadn't changed back. Then, just as quickly, he let go of me and started to undress for his own bath. I quickly ran to the cottage door and did not pause as I grabbed the bag, pulling out the light sky-blue dress, panties, and gray leggings to go with it.

I curled up in my bed, putting my back to the door. I was too shy to face Kierian if we made eye contact after his bath. I knew he would walk through that door completely naked, and I did not think my poor heart could handle it after tonight.

Chapter Twenty-Seven

KIERIAN

Sinking into the bathtub, I needed to get Skyla out of my system. The fear I had felt from the thought of those Fae creatures getting ahold of her still had my heart racing. I killed them all, not wanting a single one to ever be a threat to Skyla in the future. I paused, realizing I had lived in peace with the Fae creatures of the woods until tonight. They had never bothered me, and I had never sought out to bother them in the last two hundred years. Why tonight?

I glanced at my home, where I knew Skyla was safe. Did they crave human flesh? By this point, Skyla's scent would be all over the clearing as I had been having her collect various ingredients. I looked up at the full moon, wondering why they chose tonight. Maybe it was because she had never been out in the evening since arriving here. My scent would have been mixed with hers, but that hadn't stopped them from coming for her.

I would need to be more aware of her safety when she was alone outside. I stilled, realizing I could not hoover around her every time she was out of my sight. I needed a workaround to ensure her safety when I could not be present.

The necklace. I jumped, which caused water to slosh in the tub from having a forgotten voice enter my head. Mytilda jumped onto the edge of the tub and sat there staring at me as the moonlight reflected off her cerulean-blue eyes.

You stopped communicating with me three hundred years ago. I accused angrily.

No, you blamed me for granting a wish and shut me out. Her tail swished irritably. I leaned my head back slightly, narrowing my eyes as I looked down my nose at her.

You shouldn't have granted it. I argued, gripping the edge of the tub tightly.

I choose what I should and should not grant. Her eyes slitted slightly as her ears flattened back.

The wrong life was taken that night, and you lost lives too.

My choice, not yours.

I bared my fangs at her, and she hissed back at me. I had never forgiven her for that night. Then a hundred years had passed by before I saw her again when she had shown up at my cottage. I had not wanted her here she was a constant reminder of what she had done that night a hundred years prior. No matter how much I tried to get rid of her, she continued to come back. Eventually, I had given up on trying to remove her from my life, and now she flitted in and out of my cottage as she pleased.

What are your intentions with Skyla?

Simmer down, Fae. I like her. Mytilda's tail swished again as her ears pricked forward. She stared at me.

You have been more present with her here.

I am here to watch the future I had predicted unfold. I only want to know if I will be correct. She blinked.

The future you predicted? My brows furrowed at her, but instead of responding, she hopped off the tub's edge and walked away. There was not a lot known about Wishing Cats. The books were filled with speculations, theories, and handed-down stories, but none that I had ever read contained about future sight. Had Mytilda witnessed three hundred years ago, what would have happened if she hadn't granted the wish I cursed her for?

Chapter Twenty-Eight

SKYLA

My back remained facing the door when Kierian entered. Mytilda nestled closer to me, and I took comfort in her presence. I heard Kierian stop walking and wondered what he was doing, but I dared not turn back around as I clutched the pillow tightly against my chest.

"Skyla," his low voice broke the silence of the cottage.

"Yeah?" I asked as I studied the wall in front of me.

"May I borrow your necklace?" he asked. Letting go of the pillow, I brought my hand up to touch the antler tines around my neck.

"Yeah, but why?" I worried he would take it and not give it back.

"Please, Skyla." I could hear the impatience and exhaustion in his voice. I moved to sit up, still not looking at him. I reached back and undid the necklace clasp from behind my neck. Grasping it in my left hand, I held it out at arm's reach. I heard his footsteps approaching, and I kept staring at the wall. He gently took the necklace from me.

"I'm not naked, by the way. You don't need to feel uncomfortable."

Slowly, I looked over, nervous it would be a joke to find him naked as I thought back to earlier, either take care of it or be quiet. Instead, I found him wearing a kilt bottom of some sort made of sage green fabric. It was not like his usual loose brown pants. The kilt was the only bit of fabric he was wearing; the rest of his muscular body was on display.

"In the beginning, I was okay with making you feel uncomfortable by my nakedness if it meant you would leave quicker. But now . . . I want you to feel safe here with me." He held the necklace up, looking at it. "I'm going to take this to a spellcaster I know to have it enchanted."

"Enchanted?" I interrupted, perking up at this tidbit. I had never owned anything enchanted, the cost being too steep. I eyed his kilt again and wondered if he would wear it every night.

"I am going to have a protection enchantment placed on it." He took his attention away from my necklace to meet my eyes. "That way, you can walk outside without fear."

"But it's safe during the daylight?"

"It should have been safe tonight, too, with me there, but that didn't stop them. I do not want to worry about something bad happening to you while collecting ingredients." My heart skipped a beat.

"What will the protection enchantment do?" I asked, leaning forward on my bed. My throat felt tight. He looked back at my necklace that he held.

"I will let you know when I come back in the morning about the logistics of the enchantment when I understand it from her. You may need to make your own breakfast."

"Wait! You're leaving me here alone tonight after what

happened?" My blood ran ice cold through my body. I had not slept alone since the last night I spent in the Fae Woods, which that had been over a month ago. Kierian may have killed all the Fae we had seen, but what if there were more lingering in the woods? They could be waiting for him to leave for an opportunity to get ahold of me.

"The enchantment on the cottage does not allow anything in without permission. You will be safe." He paused before finishing with, "And you have Mytilda." He nodded at the lavender cat. I nodded slowly, easing myself into a more comfortable sitting position. My muscles relaxed, and I felt the burning sting from keeping them clenched. I watched him turn and walk to the door. He stopped to turn back and look at me.

"Sleep well, Skyla."

He didn't give me a chance to respond as he opened the door and left into the night. Sleep did not find me easy. Despite him telling me the cottage would protect me, I worried and listened to every sound I heard from outside. Mytilda nudged my face and purred loudly to comfort me.

After a bit of tossing and turning, I gave up. I scooped Mytilda into my arms and carried her and my blanket over to Kierian's bed. Crawling underneath his blue covers, I breathed in his scent. I felt safer here than I had across the room, in my bed. Mytilda had not fought me and remained nestled close to my chest.

I must have dozed off at some point because when I cracked open my eyes, sunlight greeted me by streaming through the windows. My eyes felt gritty, and my skin felt dirty. I needed another bath to wipe away the sweat and cleanse the tiredness from my body. I glanced at the door, wondering if it would be safe for me to go outside. Based off of Kierian's comment, I would wait; he said he would be back in the morning.

If he had gone through the trouble of having my necklace

enchanted only to come home and find me dead because of a Fae creature, everything he had done last night would have been for naught. I rose from his rumpled bed. Mytilda was still sleeping partially on my pillow. Padding over to the kitchen, I looked around at what was at hand.

The door opened, and I turned to find the half-naked Kierian standing there. He was still wearing only the green kilt from last night. His hair was rumpled, and dark bags were under his eyes. It was evident that he may not have received any more sleep than I had last night. I bristled slightly at the thought of him being at a female spellcaster's house, barely clothed.

"Morning, have you had breakfast?" Kierian asked, sniffing the air.

"No, I was just figuring out what to make," I replied, coolly. I told myself it did not matter what conspired between him and the spellcaster. That was his business. After all, we had only shared a couple of kisses —kisses that I desperately wished would go further if he hadn't put a halt on them each time. I gritted my teeth, anger and jealousy flooding through me.

"Excellent." He appeared to be in a good mood as he crossed the room and pulled my necklace from his kilt pocket. I held out my hand, but he shook his head. He twirled his finger in a motion to indicate that I needed to turn around. I did as I was told and jumped when I felt his hand moving my hair off the back of my neck.

Gathering my fiery locks, I raised them off my shoulder to help him. He placed the necklace on me, and I felt it as he clasped it together, but he didn't move away from me. We stood there, and his hands trailed from the back of my neck down to my sides, resting on my hips. My breathing slowed, and I wanted to look back at him to see what he was doing.

I felt his warm breath on my neck as my heart picked up in pace. I angled my head to give him better access. I wanted him to kiss me there. I knew he desired me. I felt his fangs graze my neck, and I inhaled sharply. I leaned back into him, trying to tip him over the edge.

Instead, I stumbled backward trying to catch my balance as coolness settled behind me. I glanced back, and he was pressed against the bar top, panting as he stared at me. I turned and crossed the small distance in the kitchen. He eyed me warily as I placed my hands on his chest, leaning into him. I rose up on tiptoes as my body glided against his. He clenched his jaw as he breathed in short, rapid sessions through his nose. I could tell he was trying everything in his power to maintain control.

"We can't do this, Skyla," he breathed. Ignoring his comment; I wrapped my arms around his neck. He made me nervous; he made my heart race and after everything that had happened yesterday; I didn't want to hold back any longer. His hands skimmed up my sides and elation ran through me only to become disappointed and confused.

He stepped around me and grabbed a skillet off its hook along the wall. He didn't look at me as he grabbed ingredients, and I speculated we would be having pancakes. He cleared his throat, but it did nothing to hide the huskiness and lust in his voice.

"The enchantment will protect you as long as you're wearing the necklace. Other creatures will either not notice you or will think you are a danger to them as it is imbued with my Fae properties and scent. Meaning, as you wear it, you will not be recognized as a human." He focused solely on breakfast. I wanted to demand his attention, I wanted to tip him over the edge and shatter the last bit of self-preservation he had left when it came to me. Yesterday, he was telling me to either take care of it or be quiet, and now, today, he was restraining himself. I wanted to know that nothing happened last night with another female.

"I could walk out in the evening, then?" I touched my fingertips gently on the antlers, attempting a new approach.

"You could, but let's not test the waters until we are certain during daylight hours." He mixed the ingredients in a large bowl.

"How did you pay for it?" I asked him suspiciously, once again eyeing the green kilt. I highly doubted he had taken any money with him, and he continued to stay half naked as he made breakfast. He stilled slightly before responding casually.

"That is none of your concern; just be grateful you will be protected." He didn't look at me, and I breathed heavily out of my nose in irritation at what I speculated may have been the truth. Despite how close we had almost come seconds ago, we were not together. I had to remind myself once again to quit those thoughts; we were only living together. I didn't belong to him, and he didn't belong to me. However, it couldn't stop me from becoming jealous at the notion of him being with a female spellcaster whose name I didn't even know. I wanted to be with him, but he kept preventing it.

Chapter Twenty-Nine

KIERIAN

Skyla was a bit guarded, and I dismissed it. I had come too close to letting her in again; despite knowing what she was to me, I needed to keep that wall up between us. I was certain that she probably was still recovering from last night's events. People became highly emotional in life-threatening situations. She probably had rationalized with herself that coming that close to death from the terror she felt meant she should show gratitude towards me. A sense of self-bravery had washed over her, and I knew how that would end. She would feel regret after chasing her adrenaline high. I did not want her living with that on her shoulders. That did not negate the other times we kissed. I shook my head and decided not to dwell on the thoughts anymore; it wouldn't do me any good.

I glanced at the antler necklace hanging off her neck feeling calmer to the addition of protection she now wore. I could have her collect honey from my hives without having to heal any bee stings. The necklace would make all attack bees fly away as she collected from their hives, and they would only return when she left. It was one less task I would need to do.

This was an additional perk on top of driving away any monsters wanting to eat her. The Spellcaster promised me that Skyla could walk in the dead of night through a den of bloodthirsty Fae creatures protecting their newborn young and walk out unscathed. I was not ready to put the necklace that far to the test, but it was a comfort nonetheless.

After breakfast, I sent Skyla out with a list of ingredients to collect so I could start on my next batch of wares. When Skyla started pushing on how I had paid for the enchantment I needed to deflect. Despite what The Spellcaster had revealed, I couldn't allow more to happen between us. She was a human with a short time to live compared to me, and I couldn't give her an answer for what kind of payment The Spellcaster would ask for in the future. I thought back to the events that had unfolded last night.

"It's been some time since your last visit, Kierian," her silk voice purred when I walked through the door. Her cottage was opposite of mine. She had items stashed in every direction. Herbs, feathers, pelts, and more all hung from the ceiling, and if I was not careful, I would either bump into something from above or below. There were goat paths to move in any direction of her home. She had become worse since the last time I had visited in collecting magical items. A magical hoarder is what she was.

"I suppose it has been," I replied casually. She emerged from the back of her cottage. The familiar long silk-spun black hair now sparkled with silver strands running through it. She wore a sheen gold dress that depending on how the light hit, I could see her full naked body underneath it. My mouth going dry as I swallowed, my cock beginning to stir from the familiarness.

"You used to visit me regularly." Her smoke-gray eyes trailed appreciatively over my almost naked form. I still wore the green kilt. A part of my heart tugged at the reason for me wearing the kilt and knowing what I would need to do for payment. "I'm glad to see you have not let yourself go in the last how many decades."

"I could say the same." I nodded in appreciation to her. She graced me with her sweetheart smile. It was a game between us as we figured out our next step and move. Nothing was ever easy with her.

"How can I be at your disposal tonight?" Her eyes trailed back down to my already hard cock, hidden by the little bit of fabric covering it. My body knew exactly where I was and what would happen next, but I needed to tell her my request first. I pulled the antler necklace from my pocket and held it out in front of me, letting it dangle between us for her to see.

"I need you to do a protection enchantment on this."

The Spellcaster reached up and lightly touched the necklace; her eyes widened ever so slightly before she smiled even deeper.

"Thee Kierian has a lady friend, I see," she said approvingly.

I chose not to reply, waiting to see if she would agree to do what I had asked.

"She must be exceptionally special if you are wanting to protect her. . . Do I sense she is a human as well?" The Spellcaster gave me a knowing look.

"Aye, she is." A gleam entered her eyes as she glanced back downwards.

"But no sexual relations with her." The Spellcaster may have enjoyed playing the game, but she preferred going for the jugular at the right moment.

"No," I gritted out.

She brushed aside the necklace, coming to stand with her breasts pressed against my chest. Only the soft fabric prevailing as a barrier between us. She blinked up at me with her sultry eyes.

"Then humor an old spellcaster with your wicked ways," she purred. I was never certain of her age, and I didn't even know her name — a spellcaster's name being sacred to them. For hundreds of years, she had appeared to be in her late twenties and very adept with the pleasures of the body.

"I would hardly call you old," I chuckled gruffly. "Do we have a deal?" Unspoken words passed between us, and she nodded, knowing exactly what she would be receiving in our deal.

My hands came to rest on her hips, and I looked down at her clothes, questioning. She laughed and undid the fabric, letting them pool at her feet. I stilled and took a step back as she looked up at me speculatively.

"I'm sorry," I said, taking another step back and taking my hands off her hips. She laughed whimsically.

"Ah, should I be cursing a mere mortal human for preventing me from a good time?" The Spellcaster's eyes twinkled mischievously, and I froze from her implications. "Kidding, kidding. Give me the necklace." She held out her hand impatiently, still laughing to herself.

I dropped the necklace into her hand. She did not even ask as she took a quick step toward me; reaching up, she plucked one of my white strands of hair. I did not miss a beat at the way her naked breast brushed against my chest. I took another step back to keep the distance between us. She laughed in response.

I watched her turn and walk over to the work desk. Laying the pendant upon the worn wood, she grabbed various vials. The Spellcaster wrapped my strand of hair around the antler pendant and started muttering in a language I couldn't understand while she dropped various liquids onto the pendants.

Silently, I stood there.

"There," she announced, bringing my attention back to her. She held the pendant up, inspecting her work.

"Thank you, and the payment?" I asked, curious what she would demand now that sex was off the table. She smiled, letting her gaze roam my body.

"I'll come to collect it when I am ready. For now, enjoy the mortal." Her voice was but a promise as to what she may have in store for me in the future. I nodded, not saying another word. I tried to take one step toward her, but the necklace floated to me from where she stood. When I reached up to grab it, it pulled back slightly out of reach, and I looked at The Spellcaster.

"If you deny my request of payment in the future, the mortal will die a terrible death in front of you," she warned, and I nodded again. I wouldn't let on the unease I felt at what this request could potentially be. The Spellcaster continued with, "I only hope your fated mate, Skyla, will understand."

My eyes widened as she cackled out loud, tossing me out of the cottage. I landed on my back roughly, with the necklace falling delicately onto my chest. I rubbed the back of my head, trying to soothe the pain I felt from it smacking against the ground. Sitting up, I grabbed the necklace and glared at the cottage, where I could still hear The Spellcasters laugh. Her voice echoed around me, telling me of all the things the enchanted pendant now would do for my human.

I came back to the present and eyed the cottage door, knowing Skyla was out there somewhere. My mate was protected and safe as long as she never took it off.

Chapter Thirty

SKYLA

Three days later, we were sitting in the field of wildflowers. We still had not talked about what had happened and how he had colored part of the land in the blood of Fae creatures. I purposely avoided venturing to said area, but as I peeked at it now, from a distance, I could still see the black stain their deaths had left behind. Shaking my head to clear my thoughts, I resumed braiding the wildflowers in my hand together. Kierian sat next to me peacefully, not saying a word. I felt as if I had been tiptoeing around him, even though nothing had changed between us.

I noticed a bug crawling on my arm and raised my hand to rid the world of the offending creature. Kierian caught my hand mid-death slap on the insect. I looked up at him with confusion, not understanding why he would prevent me from killing this annoying pest. I was positive I was doing the world a service by eliminating one less of its kind from being able to repopulate on this planet. What consequence of this insect's life did it bear merit to him?

Kierian wore a frown on his face, and his brows were slightly furrowed. I felt I was in trouble but had no inkling as to why.

"It's just a bug," I stated blatantly. I did not see the big deal.

"And you are *just* a human," he replied back in the same tone as mine, which caused me to bristle. How dare he insult me like this? Maybe I was not some all-powerful, immortal Fae, but that did not mean he should treat me this inconsequential.

"What is *that* supposed to mean?" I challenged. Kierian held my gaze for a moment and then sighed, looking down at the bug. He held out his pointer finger for the bug to crawl onto him. I shivered, wrinkling up my nose from the idea of the bug even remotely touching me, let alone him.

"Do you feel your life is more important than this creature?" He asked, not looking at me. I gave him a bored expression, even if he didn't notice.

"Seriously, Kierian, it's a bug." I rolled my eyes, not wanting to hear a lecture or receive any form of a lesson from him today.

"And you are a human. You don't care about this creature's life, but expect everyone should care about your life because of what you are. Do you not believe this insect wouldn't feel the same way?" Kierian began. I just glared at him, bored.

"I don't think bugs have big enough brains to have the capacity to think past eating, fucking, and sleeping," I argued.

"Such language," he tsked, and I groaned.

"You are hundreds of years old. I am sure you have heard far worse," I countered.

"You are feisty today, Skyla. Taking a stab at my age," he sighed, resting his hand with the bug still on it in his lap. He braced his other hand behind him and looked up at the sky. I looked at him and then glanced up at the sky, trying to figure out what he was looking at. Kierian continued, "When you have lived as long as I have and seen what I have, you begin to value life a little more."

"Even a tiny bug?" I pressed, regretting that I had ever made the motion to murder the insect. Even more so now that it had become one of Kierian's calm teaching lesson moments.

"Yes, even a tiny bug." He looked back at me, and it felt like he was a hundred years away from me in this mere moment. He lifted his hand with the bug crawling on it to above his head as he studied the insect. "The way you could have easily killed this bug, I could do to you with these very hands. I could do it without even thinking about it; your blood would be the most inconvenience of it all."

Ice ran through me; sometimes I forgot how comfortable I had become with him. His gentle and calmness had lulled me into a sense of security, but I felt like I was now betraying my own thoughts. Kierian, for the most part, has always been kind and patient with me. I never worried about my safety around him, but in a simple sentence, he had me questioning everything.

He sighed and leaned forward, resting his head on his knees. He shook his head. I reached my hand out instinctively to touch him, but hesitated, letting it linger on the air above his back before pulling my hand back to my chest. I was uncertain if I should comfort him or not at this moment.

"My past is not who I am anymore," he said roughly. "I am no longer that warrior." This time, when I reached my hand out, I let it rest on his back and felt him stiffen under my hand before relaxing again.

"Promise you'll always protect me?" I quietly asked. I didn't realize how much I had wanted to know the answer to that particular question until it had slipped past my lips. I sat there waiting with bated breath, but he sat there quietly, and my heart started to feel the pain of being hurt once again in life.

"Only if you'll protect me in return," he replied finally, and I let my breath out with a small giggle.

"What could I possibly do to protect you?" The notion seemed silly. I was a human. Anything that came to hurt Kierian would kill me in the blink of an eye. I had not a fighting chance in protecting him.

He turned his face to look at me while continuing to rest his head on his hands. The soft breeze blew through his hair, moving it that it flowed around and in front of his face. I became conscious of the energy between us as I took in every detail about him. I wanted to lean in and kiss him. Unconsciously, I didn't realize I had begun to move towards him. I found tenderness in his eyes as he smiled at me.

"You are more powerful than you leave yourself to believe, Skyla. If ever a moment came down to it, I only hope you would save yourself if there was no other choice." His words were betraying his face. His soft, sweet expression had me confused to the words he had just uttered.

"What are you saying, Kierian?" I breathed, my heart slowing.

"If there is a choice in saving my life or yours, always choose yourself."

I shook my head slightly.

"Kierian," I trailed off.

"Always choose yourself, Skyla," he repeated. I didn't know what it meant or why my skin felt like pins and needles.

"Why?" I asked. He studied me, and his smile turned to one of sadness.

"Because I have lived my life, it is your chance to learn to live yours."

"You're talking as if you are dying," I joked, but the fear was lacing through me that maybe he actually was, and he didn't want me to know. What if that had been the payment for the protection spell on my necklace? I froze, reaching my hand up to touch the warm metal. He chuckled softly.

"No, I am not, but I have done a great many things in my past. Horrible things and the past always has a way of catching up to one. If mine ever does, and you're here to witness it, I need you to save yourself. You shouldn't be punished for what I have done," he replied quietly as if reflecting upon his memories and the horrible things he had done.

I nodded slowly, not knowing how else to respond.

He leaned back, allowing himself to lay back in the grass and look up at the sky. I looked down at him as he raised his hand to the air once again, studying the bug still crawling on his arm. Somehow, I had forgotten the insect was the whole reason this conversation had started. He didn't invite me to, but I laid back in the grass next to him. I watched the bug with him until it became bored and flew off. We lay there staring after it until the bug disappeared from sight. Neither of us said a word to one another. The growing question I had was gnawing at me.

"Did you have sex with her?" I blurted out a little more loudly than I had intended. Heat radiated through my body, but there was no going back now. I felt at odds with him, even though he appeared more cheerful than normal after his return. Then the sting of rejection from the other night hit me, and that laced with the curiosity of needing to know the truth. It bubbled up within me until I couldn't take it anymore.

"Excuse me?" he asked, his voice sounding incredulous that I even had the gull to be this bold. He stayed lying there, not even turning his head to look at me.

"Did you sleep with The Spellcaster for the enchantment?" I pushed. I felt myself flushing, but I chose not to back down. I needed to know what the payment was for the thing I wore around my neck.

"What I do is none of your concern." He replied briskly. I could feel his guard locking into place, but I would not let it deter me this time.

"I think it is when I am wearing a sex-paid object," I spat back. Kierian ran his hands down the front of his face and looked up at the sky as if seeking an answer from it. This was becoming a habit of his, always looking upwards for the answer.

"I did not pay for it with sex." He stated, sitting upright suddenly.

"Then how?" I hounded, pushing myself to sit as well.

"The Spellcaster said she would come to collect in the future and only hoped you would understand. I do not know what those implications would mean, so let it lie," Kierian warned. I glared at him, and he glared right back.

"So, no sexual favors occurred?" I pushed.

"No." Everything about his demeanor snarled to back off.

"Why not?"

"Because I couldn't go through with it because of you!" He roared. He stood up abruptly and changed into his stag form, bolting away. I sat there watching his white tail become smaller, completely confused. He had admitted that sex had been on the table, but what did he mean because of me? What had I done to prevent him from having sex with her? Was it because he had feelings for me? A rush of giddiness overcame me at the thought. Sex had been on the table between, but he couldn't go through with it because of me. I wanted more answers, but there was not a chance I would be able to chase after him. I would need to wait until he came home to find out more.

Chapter Thirty-One

KIERIAN

As I sprinted away, I shouldn't have admitted that out loud to her. Skyla knew how to get under my skin. I did not enjoy how comfortable she made me feel. She angered and annoyed me, and what I wouldn't do to bend her over and make her take my cock. She was like an addiction in my veins, one I had barely even tasted, yet I needed —her constant curiosity about what had happened between The Spellcaster and myself was damning me. Skyla being my fated mate was damning me.

I shouldn't have held myself back. I should have followed through with the payment. Maybe then my balls wouldn't ache as much as they did. My hand could only do so much work, but eventually, I would need some female attention. Unfortunately for me, the female I wanted was still a virgin and would not be ready for what I wanted to do to her. The Spellcaster could have handled everything, but I knew I would have frightened Skyla if I tried the same things. She had tempted me multiple times, and each time, I had come too close. No, the truth wasn't that I shouldn't have held myself back with The Spellcaster; it was that I should never have held myself back with Skyla.

I was beginning to develop a pattern. I had to remove myself from her premises, and this wasn't like me. Was it my pride or the now growing fear of allowing a mating bond to snap into place that caused me now to run away from my home? I didn't have time to ponder more on the subject because a scent on the wind caught my attention.

No. I changed my course of direction, sprinting back from the way I had come.

Chapter Thirty-Two

SKYLA

I was crouched, pulling weeds angrily from Kierian's herb garden. I figured I would keep myself busy and take out some frustration until he returned. A shadow covered me, and my heartbeat picked up at the thought of Kierian standing behind me. I turned with a smile on my face but instead was greeted by a scowling Tennyson. My smile faltered when realization hit me of who truly stood there.

"Can I help you?" I asked, dusting my hands off. I refused to wipe them on my brand-new blue dress. If I had been wearing my old ratty one, I wouldn't have given it much thought, although Kierian made certain that one was burned like he had promised. I completely treasured the new dresses and leggings. I wanted them to last as long as possible because I didn't know when I would receive another new dress.

"I see my brother chose to keep you, Petal." His eyes trailed over me, taking in every detail. I sat there frozen like a statue, trying not to give away how I truly felt to him scrutinizing and taking an interest in me. Despite how Tennyson had lulled me into a sense of relaxation the last time he had been here, Kierian made it evident I needed to be wary of him.

"I also see my brother has decided to decorate you in pretty attire," Tennyson added, eyeing the antler necklace. I controlled my breathing and swallowed, forcing myself not to reach up and touch it. I tried to think of a response as I sat there staring up at the predator before me. Tennyson's energy crowded me in, and I had a sinking feeling that if Kierian wasn't nearby, I wouldn't live to see the evening. Maybe the protection enchantment didn't work against Tennyson.

"Why so quiet, Petal?" He pushed.

"What do you want?" Kierian's low voice asked. My head whipped to find my savior leaning with his shoulder against the corner of the cottage. Tennyson's eyes traveled over me once more and then turned, spreading his arms wide with a relaxed swagger towards Kierian.

"Since when am I not allowed to pop in to see how my brother is doing?" He glanced over his shoulder at me. "I see you choose to keep her as a pet." I scrunched up my face from the insult, but he had already returned his attention to Kierian, who stood there with a grim look on his face. He was half-shifted with his antlers on display.

"When you are bothering my help," Kierian replied flatly, ignoring the second part of Tennyson's statement.

"Testy, testy," tsked Tennyson. I watched the two; there was a casual ease about them, but it felt as if, within a moment, everything could change. I tried to keep myself still, not wanting to draw attention back to me and preventing whatever may happen from unfolding.

They stared each other down, and I could feel the crackle in the air between them. Tennyson's shoulders eased as he gave a light chuckle, the heavy energy disappearing immediately. Kierian shifted, and I noticed his hand was no longer angled to grab the knife at his side. I felt the hairs raise on the back of my neck. Something was wrong.

"What do you want?" Kierian repeated his original question. Tennyson shifted his weight on his right leg and held out his arms again to show he was not a threat.

"I simply came for a visit, nothing more," he replied with casual ease. Kierian's eyes narrowed slightly; his gaze flicked to me for a mere second, and I almost thought I imagined it until Tennyson looked back at me. He smirked over his shoulder, his smiling widening as he looked back at Kierian.

"Are you worried I am going to hurt your precious flower?" Tennyson asked him. Fear slid through me as I leaned away from Tennyson. My heartbeat hammered in my ears as Kierian's frown deepened. He tracked every single one of Tennyson's movements.

"You touch her . . ." Kierian trailed off, baring his fangs at Tennyson. I gripped the edge of my dress tightly between my fists, hanging on to his next words. Tennyson let out a dark chuckle and put his hands up in defeat, interrupting what Kierian would say next.

"I can take a message when I am not welcomed." And with a snicker, he looked over his shoulder at me, giving me a wicked grin. "Take care of him, Petal." I couldn't even respond as he shifted into a black raven. His wings flapped him upward until he was a speck soaring in the sky away from us. My gaze left the disappearing speck of Tennyson and found Kierian watching me. I swallowed, letting the silence linger between us.

"Never let your guard down around that one," he warned me once again, and I nodded.

"He may look friendly and may have been nice to you the first time, but to him, you are only a means of entertainment. There is no telling how far he would go."

I nodded. Kierian had already told me once Tennyson's favorite pastime to do with humans, I didn't need a reminder of that. His gaze flicked to the herb garden.

"You missed a few weeds," he commented and turned to leave. I looked at the weeds I still needed to pull and back to him disappearing around the side of the cottage.

"I wasn't done!" I yelled. I heard his amuse chuckle in response. The thoughts of our earlier departing conversation came to the forefront of my mind, and I stood up to chase after him.

"What did you mean it was because of me?" I huffed as I grasped his wrist. He stopped walking but didn't turn around. I stared at his back as he remained quiet.

"Kierian," I stated more firmly. I wanted answers.

"It's best you go a little while longer in the dark," he replied, still not facing me.

"But why? Do you like me?" I pushed. His shoulders tensed from my question, and hope spread throughout my body.

"Don't ask questions you're not prepared to hear the answer to." His back heaved as he took a breath in. He shook his arm, and I released my grip on his wrist.

"I'm sorry," I replied.

"I just don't want to hurt you."

"You won't." The tears pricked my eyes. I was trying to understand what he wasn't telling me. I wanted to know what was going on in his mind. Did he have feelings for me? Why wouldn't he tell me? My heart raced in my chest. If I told him how I felt, would he reject me? I opened my mouth, ready to speak.

"Don't." he warned. "Don't say it, Skyla." His voice broke on my name, and I tried to push myself to utter the words I wanted to confess but closed my mouth, listening to him.

Hesitantly, I reached out and touched his back; he stilled. I heard him sigh, the only sign that it was okay for me to touch him. He shook his head and started walking. My hand dropped, and I felt the lonely coldness from the absence of his warmth.

"Come along, I'll prepare dinner, and you can read one of your new books," he offered. I trailed dully behind him. I wanted to tell him my feelings, but could my heart handle the rejection? The way his voice had broken on my name made me scared he couldn't handle rejecting me if he had to. It was silly when I thought about it. Kierian had made it abundantly clear multiple times that we were different. He would still be alive when my soul drifted on in the afterlife.

I stared after him and puzzled over why he would reject me. He could use me, lead me on, and then desecrate me for his own pleasure. He could play out my fantasies and not have to worry about strings attached in a hundred years. As a Fae warrior, had he ever become close to anyone romantically in his life? Maybe he pushed everyone out, like he was doing with me.

Chapter Thirty-Three

KIERIAN

A week later, things had returned to normal for us, or at least as normal as they could be. Skyla stopped pestering me with feelings of affection or about information on The Spellcaster. We fell back into our former routine, and I started to feel like I could breathe again in my home.

I mixed up a new batch of cold medicine as I sent her out to collect honey and honeycombs from the hives. She had been skeptical the first time I requested it with her protection pendant in place, but now she did it without grumbling . . . too much. I suspected I would be making additional trips to Fairfield and maybe a few other side villages to sell my wares with how far ahead of schedule she put me.

Mytilda sat perched on my bar top, staring at me, and I narrowed my eyes at her. She licked her paw as if to say she didn't even notice I was there. The wishing cat stayed extra clingy to Skyla, not that the girl seemed to mind. She completely adored Mytilda but remembered my earlier warning to be careful about what she said out loud with the cat around.

The front door opened, and I had anticipated for Skyla to be tromping through it with a bowl full of honey and combs. Instead, I was let down. My brother waltz in and looked as if he was in on a secret. I gave him a bored look, turning back to my measurements. He had never visited this regularly in the past, and now I was becoming curious as to what he wanted.

"Tsk, tsk. Sour as always," Tennyson commented dryly. I chose to ignore him. It usually worked when I did not want him about. He eyed the barstools and pulled one out to sit where Skyla sat when she watched me work. Usually, her incessant chatter slowed down my progress, but it was not unwelcomed.

"I think your flower is eating more of the honey than she is collecting it," he said flippantly.

I stayed quiet, continuing to measure and mix.

"If she keeps eating it, your honeybees will surely starve. You worked so hard cultivating those hives, did you not?" Tennyson continued.

"If that is true, she will not be feeling well later on. Some lessons need to be taught the hard way," I answered unphased. Tennyson had a way of exaggerating things to gain a rise out of someone. Since Skyla was not here, I assumed he had not talked to her yet.

"Hmm, and I suppose you would have the cure if she fell ill." He eyed my work.

"Aye," I answered.

"Pity." he sniffed. I remained silent again. The door opened a second time and Skyla paused mid-step when she noticed Tennyson sitting in her spot at the bar.

"What is *he* doing here?" She asked me, and I shrugged in response.

"Is that any way to greet me, Petal?" Tennyson pouted, and I tensed from the nickname he called her. I needed to calm down before he figured out it bothered me.

"It is when you are a cheat at cards," Skyla snipped back. Tennyson turned back to me, giving me a droll look, and I shrugged my tensed shoulders. He swiveled back around on the barstool to face her, propping his elbows behind him on my bar top. I eyed every weapon I had at my disposal in reach if Tennyson tried anything.

"Petal, how about I make it up to you?" He offered. I paused in my measuring. Tennyson was not a kind Fae. The most kindness I had witnessed from him in all my years of knowing him was in the first hundred years of me living in this cottage. He would check in to make certain I was okay, and that was the extent of how far his kindness would go.

"I think I would rather take my chances in the Fae Woods," Skyla argued. I looked at her and gave my head a quick shake. I did not need her planting ideas in his mind, and with his back to me, I could freely communicate with her in these subtle movements. She noticed but did not give away anything to my brother.

"That . . ." Tennyson paused; viciousness laced his voice. "Could be arranged." Skyla stood her ground, her eyes narrowing at him. The deathly calm I was familiar with from our time in the war fell upon the room. I had warned her multiple times about Tennyson. I didn't understand where this defiance was coming from with her.

"I suggest you leave her alone," I warned him.

"I can show her a good time," Tennyson promised, but I heard the threat. Skyla shifted ever so slightly, and Tennyson leaned forward, propping his elbows on his knees. He breathed in deeply.

"Still haven't fucked." It was a statement, not a question. Skyla glared at him outright, and I put down the bowl I had just dumped my last ingredient in. I extended my claws, preparing for Tennyson's next move. He was in between Skyla and me, and I could not tell her to outright run. She wouldn't be fast enough compared to his speed, and I needed to maneuver around my bar to intervene between them. By then, I could be watching her choke on her own blood from Tennyson's claws or fangs. Fear ran through me from the mental image. The faint mate bond screamed to protect what is mine.

"What we do in here is none of your concern, crow," spat Skyla. The part of me that wanted to be proud of her bravery was squashed by the fear of how Tennyson would react.

"Crow?" He leaned forward. I couldn't see his face, but I could hear the coldness in his voice. I had to stay still. If he had the faintest inkling I was moving into motion to protect her, he would be across the room in a heartbeat.

"Ravens have more pride than you. A crow is far more fitting. A scavenger," Skyla answered with steel in her voice. Tennyson slid off his barstool, and I slowly followed him step for step behind him. I didn't dare look at Skyla as she stood there holding the bowl of honey on one hip, and her free hand rested on the other. She didn't take a step back as she glared at him.

"Call me a crow again, little human," Tennyson threatened. He stopped when he was looming over her as she glared up at him. I stood behind him, ready to move into action, hoping I could track his movement before harm came to her. Every alarm in my body went going off as the lethal calm came over the room.

Skyla don't. I sent to her mind, but I wasn't fast enough, because simultaneously she repeated her slur.

"Crow."

Everything blurred as it slowed down and sped up again. I caught Tennyson's wrist before he could slash Skyla's throat and stomach apart. She stood there, her human eyes not able to track what unfolded until I had Tennyson pinned beneath me, snarling at his face. He snarled back at me, struggling to break free.

I heard Skyla gasping from behind me. She had been flung across the room. I wasn't certain if I had been the one to push her out of the way or if it was from the force of me knocking Tennyson to the ground. She continued gasping for air and coughing as I heard her feet running past us until she stood behind the bar. It was better protection than I could give her currently. At least there, she would have knives for weapons.

"Release me!" Bellowed Tennyson.

"You are not in charge here." I snarled back. "When I release you, you will leave. I am letting you off this *one* time."

"I am your brother!"

I growled louder in warning.

"She is a human!"

It took everything in my willpower not to scream at him that she is my mate. I glared at him as I allowed three beats to pass before I responded, "And yet, you let her bother you. Leave, and if I catch you attempting to harm her in the future, brother or not, I will not hold myself back," I threatened thickly.

He snarled at me, and I snapped my fangs in front of his face.

The next moment flashed again as I released him while throwing him towards my front door. He didn't even hit the ground as he transformed into a raven and flew away. The cottage door slammed shut behind him. I whirled toward Skyla, who was still standing behind the bar for protection. Both her hands were holding steak knives.

Chapter Thirty-Four

SKYLA

"Do you have *any* idea what he could have done to *you*?! You're just a *weak human girl*!" Kierian roared at me. "You have not the faintest idea as to what Tennyson is capable of."

I stood my ground. My hands gripped the steak knives tighter as I gritted my teeth, seething at him. How dare he be this insulting toward me.

"Yeah, well, if being Fae is so great, then why do you live alone?" My insult did not even cause a reaction; he only blinked with his haughty expression. I had not been expecting a reaction, but a small part of my pride had been hopeful.

"I live alone, so nuisances cannot find me, but apparently, you managed to still get through, just like a weed." He shot back, and while I tried to prevent the sting, it did not stop the pain that laced through my heart. I felt the tears threatening to expose my feelings, and I needed to leave.

"Fine! If I am such a nuisance, I'll get out of your antlers!" I spat.

Throwing the steak knives down on the countertop, I stormed past him toward the door.

"Good riddance," Kierian growled behind me. I yanked open his front door and slammed it as hard as I could shut. It worked because I heard his annoyance rumble through the house, which gave me a small sense of satisfaction. I needed to collect my thoughts; I would worry later if I was still welcome. I was angry; Tennyson had threatened my life, and instead of any comforting words, Kierian was being rude to me.

If my tears hadn't already started blurring my vision, I would have stomped off, but instead, I found myself running in the direction of the woods. It was as if I believed if I ran fast and far enough, I could outrun the tears trailing down my cheeks. I ran until I tripped over a tree root, which caused me to crash onto the wooded grounds.

"Oof!" The wind was knocked out of me for the second time today. I looked back, glaring at the offending tree root. It lowered back into the ground, and my anger surged again, burning like the tears in my eyes.

"Kierian quit playing games and leave me alone," I shouted as I pushed myself to rest on my knees. I hadn't witnessed all of Kierian's powers, but being able to control nature, like moving a tree root, wouldn't surprise me. I glanced down at my dress, which was now covered in dirt and leaves. Roughly, with the back of my arm, I rubbed my eyes and sniffed loudly. This was the first of my new dresses to become dirty and I noticed a small rip in my leggings. Kierian didn't emerge from the trees like I had been anticipating.

"Kierian, I am being serious. Leave me alone!" I yelled, becoming angrier. He insulted me, calling me a dumb human and then a nuisance. Okay, he had said 'weak', not dumb, but I felt he had been thinking it. So, what if he had hundreds of years on me? I'm sure I would be just as smart or more intelligent than him if I had been on this planet just as long.

I pushed myself up from a kneeling position to stand as I wrapped my arms around my waist, hugging myself as I sulked. I glared at the shadows in the woods, trying to figure out where he would emerge from. It occurred to me that the woods were deathly quiet, the birds no longer chirping, and the wind rustling the leaves made a chill run through my body as the hairs stood up on the back of my neck. Something or someone was watching me, and deep down, I already knew it wasn't Kierian. Whatever they were, it wasn't friendly.

Thankfully, I had my enchanted pendant to keep me safe. I reached up to touch it, but it wasn't there. I frantically searched for it on the ground and double-checking with my hands that it wasn't on my neck. Where had it gone? Had I dropped it? I looked back the way I came, but I traveled such a distance that I didn't think I would find it that quickly.

I sucked in a breath, I knew I couldn't outrun a Fae creature, but I wouldn't just stand here to make it easy on them. It was daylight still; it didn't mean creatures weren't out, but the deadly ones were less likely. I glanced to my left and right, wishing I knew which way they were. The clearing and Kierian's cottage were straight ahead. Maybe I wouldn't make it, but then again, maybe if I did, Kierian would notice and prevent my death. He had enough herbs and remedies to sew me back together again.

A twig snapped to my left, and that was all the encouragement I needed as I tore off into a sprint back the way I had come. I ignored the pain in my body from the fall as I heard a high-pitched laugh from branches crunching close behind me. A scream of terror tore through my lungs as I picked up more speed. I dared not look back in fear of what I would find.

I was closing in on a low branch ahead of me, one that I had thought nothing of while coming this way when I had ducked under it. It could hinder my escape, and I glanced at the surrounding paths, but it was all dense underbrush. Quickly, I bent to go under and heard it crack as the branch came down, scraping off my back. I stumbled, my hands hitting the ground as I pushed back up and propelled myself to keep running forward. The high-pitched laughter sounded closer, and I shrieked again, trying to escape this Fae creature.

I screamed when the bush in front of me shook. I did not have anywhere else to go, and the high-pitched laughter sounded closer. I had not the faintest idea of what was going to emerge from the bush I was closing in on. Could it be another laughing Fae creature? I only hoped luck stayed on my side and I could escape it as well.

I couldn't stop the new tears falling from my eyes as I watched Kierian emerge from the brush, and hope soared in my chest. I ignored the mask of death on his face. He bared his fangs with his focus on the creature chasing me. The relief that surged through me made me lax, and I tripped, causing myself to skid and tumble through the rough ground. I could feel the rocks and sticks slicing into my exposed arms and cheek. I knew my clothing would be completely ruined.

The Fae creature landed on my back, its weight pressing down on me as I felt its claws tearing into my flesh. I screamed as that high-pitched laugh sounded next to my right ear.

With tears streaming down my face, I forced myself to look up at Kierian. If I was going to die, I wanted the last thing I remembered to be this beautiful Fae male. But he was not where I had last seen him. Instead, I was staring at his brown slacks and felt the Fae monster being lifted from my back. I whimpered as the claws ripped through my skin again. My body involuntarily shook, and as frightened as I was, I forced myself to roll slightly onto my side and look up to find Kierian growling into the Fae monster's face.

The laughing beast looked like a disfigured dog. It had a black coat with brown horseshoe spots and a long, sleek tail that ended with a tuft of hair. It had long claws on all four of its paws, and I feared for my back and the state it was in. The dog-like creature had a long nose; its mouth was open, exposing fangs longer than Kierian's. Its tongue lolled lazily out of its mouth that was still laughing. Its tail swished back and forth, clearly unphased by the danger it was in.

Kierian bared his fangs. "You do *not* touch what is not *yours*!" It started as a hiss and ended in a roar. Then Kierian tossed the dog Fae beast with ease into the woods out of sight of us. A growl rumbled in the back of his throat, glaring in the direction of the woods, and then he glanced down at me. I cringed away from his glare; maybe death would have been a far better option.

I felt the burning pain in my back and winced, a whimper escaping from my mouth. Kierian's pupils contracted. He leaned down and scooped me up into his arms. I yelped from the pain. His grip tightened on me. I felt the vibration of the rumbled growl that he emitted from his chest, but he did not speak a word as he turned and walked us back to his cottage.

I was too frightened to speak up. I wanted to know what kind of Fae creature that was and why it did not fear Kierian. I worried about how deep the cuts in my back were. It was difficult as I tried to withhold the whimpers of pain when Kierian's arms pressed into them with each step.

He took me around the back of his cottage towards the bath. I protested against his body. The idea of stripping down naked with the pain searing through my back did not sound appealing. He ignored me and led us behind the privacy screen. Gently, he set me down to stand on my own two feet.

"Can you strip, or do I need to remove the rest of your clothing?" He asked, his voice hard.

"Get out." I wrapped my arms around myself; the movement caused me to cry in pain. The flesh on my back burned from the pull of skin and muscles. Kierian's hands came up to brace me on my upper arms, steadying me in place.

"I'm going to cut you out of this dress. We need to wash these wounds to prevent infection."

I started to cry, causing more pain to lace through me. He gently guided me until my hands were on the porcelain tub, helping me maintain my balance. He let go of me as I stood there, and then I heard the fabric of my dress ripping from his blade. It fell away when the last bit was sliced apart. My head hung there as I squeezed my eyes shut from the embarrassment and raw pain. My first pretty dress now lay in a heap at my feet, completely destroyed.

"Can you remove your leggings, or do I need to?" Kierian's voice changed to gruff tenderness.

I tried to reach my hands to do the task he had asked, but when I curved my back more, it screamed in pain. I shook my head, heat blazing my face. Gently, I felt his hands at the top of my waistband, and then he was pulling them down with my panties. He didn't make a sound behind me, and when the fabric was at my ankles, I stepped out of it.

"I'm going to pick you up and place you into the tub, okay?" Kierian asked.

I nodded my head, not wanting to look at him. I felt his warm hands fall on my waist, and then he picked me up with ease and slowly placed me down into the warm water. I hissed the moment the water touched my wounds, new tears falling from my eyes.

"Lean forward on the edge of the tub while I clean these," he instructed. I did as he ordered, folding my arms over the tub lip with my back to him. It was embarrassing and unnerving to be this close to him while naked. I was vulnerable, and if I tried to move too much, pain laced through me.

I cried out when I felt a warm washcloth going over my wounds. He made calming, shushing sounds as he continued cleaning my wounds. I whimpered over every claw mark. I was not made to endure pain.

"Do you want me to wash your hair?" He asked gently. I was pretty certain it was covered in dirt, leaves, and sticks, similar to the day I had arrived. Against my better judgment, I nodded my head.

"Tip your head back then." I listened, and he began pouring water over my hair via a pitcher. I sighed as he poured the lily vial of soap on my head, and I felt his hands begin to massage it in. I leaned back my head more, enjoying the pleasure I felt. A moan escaped my lips, and we both froze. Slowly, he resumed washing my hair. We didn't say another word until he was hauling me out of the tub and wrapping me up in a fluffy towel.

Once again, he picked me up and carried me. When he pulled open the cottage door, I started to protest as he headed toward his bed. He ignored me and placed me gently on my belly into his bedding. I was immediately encumbered by his scent; a sense of feeling safe washed over me as I relaxed slightly.

I jumped as I felt his fingers graze my clean, bare-back flesh, and he hissed at my reaction. Without a word, I heard his footsteps retreating. Cautiously, I snuck a peak to find him grabbing herbs, methodically adding them to his mortar bowl as he used the pestle to mix them together. A heaviness began to come over my eyes, and I fought to keep them open. I was uncertain as to why I had become this drowsy from simply being in Kierian's bed. Maybe it was better than sleeping in my bed on the other side of the room, out of the way, or maybe it was because I knew I would always be safe with Kierian.

I jerked awake, not realizing I had dozed off when I felt a white-hot coldness being pressed into my wounds. I tried to escape, but Kierian silently held me in place.

"That hurts!" I stated, hoping he would let up with the pressure.

"Maybe if you didn't go for a stroll in the woods, we wouldn't be in this mess currently," he chided.

"Maybe if you weren't such a cold-hearted asshole, I wouldn't have felt the need to leave," I countered, taking my pain out on him through anger.

"Well, if you had been more cautious and not provoked Tennyson." His voice rose.

"Your brother needs an attitude check." I shrieked as he pressed more of the salve into my injuries.

"And a mere human such as yourself is going to be the thing that whips him into shape?"

"Well, it sure won't be you!"

"Stop moving; you're bleeding all over everything," he warned.

"Oh, *so* sorry for bleeding on your things."

"Well, we know it isn't any of your things."

"Because I have nothing but the dresses you bought me. And now one of them is ruined!"

"Because the clothes you arrived in were horrendous. Did your family neglect you or something?"

"I didn't have a family growing up!" Tears pricked at my eyes.

"What did they not want you? Too much of a nuisance?"

"I'm an orphan!" I screeched back.

"That is not my problem!" He roared, his eyes flashing black. "You are not my problem!" The cottage shook. I wanted to escape him, but I was trapped here in his bed. I glared at him. All his emotions were hidden behind that glacier mask. He stood up abruptly, sneering down at me. How could he have been so tender moments prior when I was naked in a bathtub to now a complete stranger?

"Do not leave that bed." He ordered and stalked to his front door.

"And *where* do you think you're going?" The underlying tone of threat hung in the air from my voice indicating the potential consequences if he left me.

"I don't answer to you." He replied coldly.

Chapter Thirty-Five

KIERIAN

An orphan, it enraged me that no one had wanted her as she grew up. It wasn't that I was unfamiliar with the concept of orphans. I had witnessed my fair share as a result of the Fae wars. The maker knows I probably created more orphans than I cared to admit to. Why did Skyla, being an orphan, irritate me this much? Yes, she had her quirks, but she wasn't outright annoying like I claimed her to be. She was polite and kind. Why did a family not want her?

Then, it occurred to me that maybe her own family had not wanted her, and that enraged me more. Had they abandoned her as a babe in a basket outside of the orphanage, or had they waited until she was older and then dropped her off in a state of confusion? I fought the urge to raze her human village to the ground in her honor. I wanted to tear the limbs off of every human who had ever hurt her.

A tree was in my path, and with one calculated swift side kick, it cracked and fell to the ground. A growl erupted from my throat at the realization of what I had done. I had planted this oak sapling over a hundred years ago with the rest of the oak trees that lined the edge of the timber, and in a moment of rage, I destroyed it. I needed to reign in my emotions; I could feel my other self itching to break free.

I glanced back at the cottage to where Skyla still lay in my bed, injured. The half-Fae that had gotten ahold of her in the woods was harmless, for the most part. It had not done a significant amount of damage to her back. My main concern was keeping infection out of her wounds. Who knew what had laid in those beast's claws? The creature didn't have a name, but it had crossed my path a few times. Friendly on every occasion, until today. If I had to guess, it was probably because Skyla was not wearing her necklace and reeked of human. If she hadn't run from it, it probably wouldn't have chased her. It was more like a stray, friendly dog than anything. Her running probably made the creature view her as either prey or as something fun to play with. Maybe a bit more roughly than either of us would have cared for, to say the least.

I realized I had ended things poorly and needed to find out the truth. I needed to know if the sacrifice of my oak tree was worth it in honor of my anger to the possibilities I had felt for Skyla's past. What had led her to become an orphan?

My shoulders slumped as some of the air left me, and I headed back to my cottage to retrieve my answers.

Chapter Thirty-Six

SKYLA

There had been a loud crack outside, causing the cottage to shake. I watched in fear as Kierian's herb jars rattled on their shelves, threatening to fall and break to the floor. I dared not move from his bed. I had tensed my muscles, causing a flash of pain through my back. Everything had gone silent after the crack.

Mytilda jumped up on the bed beside me. She gave my back a disdainful look, before curling up next to my side. I wrapped my arm around her, ignoring the strain on my back muscles, and pulled her closer to me for comfort. I half expected her to protest, but to my surprise, she purred loudly.

The front door was yanked open hard enough that the hinges buckled to stay mounted into the wooden frame. I flinched, watching warily as Kierian stalked through the door. His piercing eyes settled on me, and every fiber of my being screamed to run as he stalked towards me. He had the same predatory energy that Tennyson cloaked himself in. Everything about him screamed murder, and I had not the faintest inkling as to why. Could my being injured have been his tipping point for how much I burdened him at times?

He stopped abruptly, and my heart pounded in my chest. Mytilda didn't even bat an eye to what was going on. Lying on my stomach, I didn't have a fighting chance of escape. Then again, what chance did I have against a Fae warrior like Kierian?

Chapter Thirty-Seven

KIERIAN

She looked up at me, frightened, and it pained me. I was angry at her past and had not controlled my emotions. She was injured and did not need me stressing her out more. I dropped the enchanted necklace in front of her on my bed.

"Never take that off again," I growled. She looked down at the necklace, her hand covering her neck where it should have been, and back at me questioningly.

"I found it hanging from some tree limbs."

"Then it must have snagged on them. I never took it off," her voice rising with panic.

I sighed, all the anger leaving me at once. I sat on the bed next to her and did not miss how she tried to put distance between us. She turned her face to not look at me, and I knew I deserved that.

"I'm sorry, Skyla." She remained quiet. I groaned internally, trying to find the words I needed to tell her. She didn't understand how vulnerable her life was or how she kept putting herself in risky situations. The salve I had concocted up would have her wounds cleaned from infection and healed with no scars within a day. I used witch magic and a bit of my Fae healing powers to speed up the recovery process. She aggravated and frustrated me, but most of all, she had brought an emotion back into my life that I had not felt in centuries. Even if I refused to admit it out loud, I knew why she was the one.

It was the reason I kept putting off making her pack her things and leave or discard her in some human village of her choice. I was being selfish, but I didn't want her to confess her feelings. Every day was a constant battle of how far we flirted with the line. Some moments, she would be extra cautious around me, and the next, she would brush her lips against mine. I could sense her wanting to confess everything, and I had to shut her down every time.

Today, had become too much. Why Tennyson kept poking around with her here, I had not the faintest idea. He kept me on edge with every visit; I feared one of these times, I would find Skyla mangled in his claws. I knew if he murdered her, he would stay away for a century or two, letting me calm down from her death. Then, he would be back to randomly visiting me as if nothing had ever happened. I knew how he operated. The only catch was that I would never come back emotionally from her death if I allowed the mating bond to snap into place.

"Skyla, please look at me," I begged. She shook her head, and I watched as her back heaved. She was crying again. I sighed and lightly rested my hand on her back where her flesh wasn't torn. Her muscles tensed from my touch, and she hissed from the pain.

"Skyla, I have never been this scared in my life, not even when I fought in the Fae wars," I began. "Twice today, I watched you come close to the hands of death, and it's not been the first time since your arrival that I have felt this fear." I took a deep breath through my nose, trying to organize more of my thoughts. "Before you came here, I lived a quiet, peaceful life. I didn't need anyone, and no one needed me; I was content with that. Then, one day, you arrive at my doorstep, and now I don't know which way is up, which way is left, but I know you by my side feels right. I don't want to lose what we have. I don't want to lose you because I couldn't have prevented your death in time."

She still didn't turn to face me, and I let out another sigh. She had every right to be upset with me. I had reacted poorly. I had allowed my emotions to go unchecked for the first time in a long time. I was uncertain how I could make it up to her. She lay injured in my bed, and the best I could do was apply a fast-healing salve to undo the physical damage. Nothing I could do would fix the mental damage that had been created.

"Do you mean it when you say you don't want to lose me?" Her quiet voice quivered, and my chest ached.

"Yes, I mean it." I didn't add on that it took a lot for me to even admit that out loud to her, let alone to myself.

"I'm sorry I made you worry."

"Please, be more mindful of your necklace in the future." I knew it must have snagged on a branch without her being aware. Accidents happen, but the fear that lingered within me was what would have happened if I hadn't chased after her. If another creature had found her? If I hadn't reached her in time?

"I will be." She turned her head to look at me. Tears glistened in her eyes, and I saw the drying, wet track lines that had streamed down her red cheeks. I reached my free hand up and wiped away the tears from her face before smoothing her damp hair back.

"How did you become an orphan?" I asked, and I regretted it immediately. Her tears started forming again as her face scrunched up.

"I'm sorry, I shouldn't have asked that," I rushed out.

"No, it's okay," she hiccupped through the tears. "My parents had been murdered when I was maybe four or five. When they found me, I was covered in their blood. For some reason, they believed it had been a Fae, but no idea on why it had left me alive to witness their deaths."

I stilled, listening to this confession. There were still Fae out there, like Tennyson, who believed humans shouldn't be alive, but to murder them without cause was prohibited. It made me question who her parents had been to warrant their deaths. Were they Fae hunters, which was also illegal, or were they innocent victims in some Fae cause, a hidden society, perhaps?

"I was taken to the orphanage in Piggs Burough, and as you probably know, that village is very poor. Very few kids were adopted out, and once we aged out, we were left on our own."

"How old are you?" I interrupted. I had never asked her in the past, not thinking that it consequently mattered.

"I'm twenty. Agatha, the lady who ran the orphanage, kept me for two additional years as an extra measure because no one knew how old I was. I knew my age, but I didn't reveal it." She paused, mulling something over in her mind. "It's not like I wanted to stay there those two additional years, but I also did not like the idea of living on the streets either. I figured dealing with her was the better option than being a beggar." I felt my other self beginning to stir again from anger, and I closed my eyes. I needed to calm myself down; this was not the time.

"Were you treated badly in her care?" I asked.

"I'd rather not talk about it." She looked away, not wanting to meet my eyes.

"If you ask me to, I will take care of her," I offered, and her eyes flicked to mine in shock. She shook her head rapidly.

"N-N-No! Don't do that! There are still children who depend upon her. Where would they go?"

"I could have them delivered to a nice orphanage in Fairfield and any other towns that deem acceptable," I answered. I was already calculating everything out when her hand rested on my arm.

"But what about you? Killing humans is treason for your kind?"

"Did they ever catch whoever murdered your parents?" I asked, choosing to not answer her question.

"No, they never did, to my knowledge," she replied dully.

"Do they know why it happened?" I pushed.

"It was speculated as a wrong time, wrong place kind of situation."

"Do you remember?" My voice came out soft, fearing the answer.

"Yes." My heart broke for Skyla and the trauma she had experienced at a young age.

"How do you not fear me?" I was incredulous that she had purposely sought me out even after that kind of beginning to her life.

"Because I knew not all Fae were bad. Agatha proved to me that humans could be just as bad, and when I was kicked out, I had nothing left to lose but my life in search of you. I know I should fear Fae. I should resent them if they are the cause of my parent's death, but growing up, none had shown me cruelty. Why should I take it out on the whole species?" She talked as if she had lived for hundreds of years and not as a mere twenty-year-old. I knew Fae with a few centuries under their belt that were not as mature as she was with that one answer.

We stayed like that in silence. I had no answer to give to her statement, and she did not add more to it. Despite all that had happened in Skyla's life, it had brought her here to me. I shouldn't have been, but I was grateful for it.

Chapter Thirty-Eight

SKYLA

Groggily, I opened my eyes and looked around the cottage. Evening had already fallen, judging by the hazy dusk light reflecting through the windows. I repositioned myself in Kierian's bed from my stomach to my side. My back no longer hurting due to his healing salves.

A thrill ran through me when I noticed Kierian sleeping with his head on his arms on the edge of the bed. He had been diligent on tending to my injuries. Prior to my falling asleep, he was regularly changing out the bandage cloths, while continually applying additional layers of the salve. It had been rather awkward when he refused to let me get up to eat supper. Instead, he chose to spoon feed me a chicken herb broth. It was mortifying and enduring, and I still couldn't tell if I cared about being fed by another person or not.

I trailed my eyes over Kierian as he slept. He looked peaceful; his eyebrows weren't even furrowed. I reached my hand out, threading my fingers in between his hair. It was so soft and silky that I smiled as I continued to play with it. He stirred a little bit in his sleep, and I paused with his hair still entangled in my fingers. After a few seconds, his breathing returned to long, heavy breaths.

Withdrawing my hand, I repositioned myself in the bed until I was able to fold my arms next to his. Laying my head down, I rested on my arms. I watched as he slept, our faces close together. I probably should wake him; he would be sore if he stayed in that position all night. The notion of us sharing his bed more intimately crossed my mind. It was big enough. He smiled in his sleep, distracting me from my thoughts. Tentatively, I reached my hand out again and twined his hair in my fingers. Feeling the lull of sleep pulling me back under.

Chapter Thirty-Nine

KIERIAN

Hard ground and an uncomfortable body with numbness. I must be sleeping outdoors; it was the only logical explanation. My muscles would feel the kinks in them for a few hours, to which I would ignore the pain. Tennyson must still be with some virgin lover otherwise he would be causing a racket already. Erilea typically stayed quiet in the mornings, but I didn't smell her anywhere on the premise either.

I kept my eyes shut, letting my breathing stay even as I tried to assess my situation. I was in a building, but my partners were not nearby. I didn't sense any bindings on my limbs, which deduced I hadn't been captured. The smell of lilies tickled my nose, and I felt a warm body shift against me. Lilies, why was the smell of lilies important to me?

Slowly, I cracked open my right eye and found myself on the ground in my cottage, next to my bed. It had been quite some time since I had forgotten where I was or how many years had passed by.

Due to sleeping on the hardwood floors, my mind probably had assumed it was three hundred years ago.

The warmth shifted against my left side again, and I turned my head. Skyla was on the ground with me, wrapped in blankets, nestled close to my body. Everything from the previous day came rushing back to me, and I worried about her injuries. I tried to move away from her, but her hand gripped my shirt tighter. I smiled to myself, the selfish part of me wishing she would never let go. She was small and fragile but so full of fiery life. She was everything I needed but everything I didn't deserve.

Again, I started to move away from her. Carefully, I untangled her hand from my shirt and gently placed it on the floor as I moved entirely out of her range. I sat there, watching her sleep peacefully. I would need to check her back and ensure everything was healing properly with no infection. I should put her back in the bed. She would be a lot more comfortable there. It did make me curious as to how we both ended up on the floor next to each other. The last thing I remember was sitting on the floor talking to her.

I got on my knees and looped my arms under her legs and upper shoulders, carefully picking her up. She didn't even stir as she nuzzled her face into my chest. I didn't want to let her go; if I could, I would stay there holding her. She needed more rest, and my pestering her sleep wouldn't do either of us any good. I lowered her back into my bed, positioning Skyla on her stomach. I did a quick check of her back and found the salves and my Fae magic had done their jobs. Her flesh was completely mended with barely any trace of scarring. Without knowing where to look, it was difficult to see where her flesh had been ripped open.

My fingers traced the faint lines. If Skyla stayed with me, I could take care of her like this forever. I would never have to worry about if she was okay in the world; she wouldn't forget me. I longed to keep her, but it wasn't my decision. It was hers. It would always be hers. The Maker must have had a great malicious joy when he chose who my mate would be. He had to delight in picking a human for me. Someone I wouldn't be able to spend the rest of my life with. It would be a fleeting moment of love and nothing more. Mates were too rare for my kind, and to be given a human . . . it was a cruel joke. I had suffered enough in this life; I didn't believe it fair to suffer more by having a mate with a short life.

The day she showed up at my doorstep I felt a pull to her. I tried to ignore it; I tried to reject her. When The Spellcaster revealed that Skyla was my mate, it elated me, but to know I would only have maybe forty years with her . . . I had suffered enough with losing one love of my life. I wasn't ready to watch my own mate die before me. We both would have been better off if she had gone to another human village and forgotten about me. I didn't want her to forget me because I knew I would never be able to forget about her. She was my sunshine that had cleared my stormy skies. I had been living a shell of who I once was. She gave me meaning, and all I wanted was to live the rest of my life with her.

Chapter Forty

SKYLA

"Why do you sometimes have antlers?" I asked him the following morning after breakfast. I sat on my bar stool, watching him mix ingredients. I fiddled with the antler pendant on the chain around my neck. Just as Kierian had promised, my back had already healed from the cuts. There was not even a mark to indicate where the cuts had been. The only haunting pain was the fresh memory of it happening yesterday. If it weren't for that, I would think I had been dreaming.

My heart warmed, and I smiled to myself. *You by my side feels right.* I played those words on a loop and fell asleep thinking about them. I wish I had been looking at his face when he had said them. If I hadn't been injured, would I have reached up and pulled him against me in a kiss? I blushed at the thought of kissing him again.

The Fae Prince, I had grown up fantasizing about, changed from silver or black hair to having brown with a white streak running through it. Golden-brown eyes and a body that had been sculpted by The Maker herself. Even with clothes on, I fantasized about what lay beneath.

Initially, I had been flustered by his nudity in the night, but now I missed it. As he had promised to make certain I didn't feel uncomfortable, he now wore that confounded kilt or other bottoms to bed.

He paused and looked at me; I flushed. Even though I knew he couldn't read my mind, I still felt as if I had been caught in the act.

"That is a personal question."

"Your antlers are a personal question?" I found that quite odd, considering all the things I had asked him already. I felt this was a little less invasive than the rest.

"Why do you have red hair?" He ignored my question and asked his own.

"Usually, that could be attributed to a parent. Your half-shifts intrigue me," I pushed again. He sighed, setting down his pommel to look at me.

"Many times, I do not notice when I half-shift; my antlers are just a part of me," he answered patiently.

"Do you shed them like a normal deer? I notice they look velvety to the touch." I had been wondering if they felt soft. He looked down his nose at me, giving me a bored expression.

"Yes, I shed them like a regular deer, and yes, they feel the same way they look."

"Can I touch them?" I couldn't contain myself as I sat on the edge of my seat.

He blinked. A startled look flashed over his face. He paused for a few seconds longer than normal, as he mulled my question over in his mind.

"I suppose so?" he replied slowly.

I hopped off my seat giddily and walked around the bar into the kitchen. He bent his head downward, and I reached up to trail my fingertips over the velvety softness of his antlers. He jerked back a bit, causing me to jump. Kierian relaxed, and I brought my other hand up to touch his other antler.

He watched me from under his brows as I ran both my hands over the softness, enjoying the feel of his antlers. I became aware of how close of proximity we currently were to each other. My fingertips trailed up to each of his antler tines and back down to move to the next tine. Kierian shivered.

"Can you feel my touch?" I asked quietly, and he cleared his throat.

"Yes," his voice was strained. I wondered why he was acting like this was torture for him. I grasped both of his antlers in the palm of my hands, enjoying the feel of the velvet. He groaned, and I glanced at his face. His eyes were scrunched closed, and then I noticed the hardening bulge growing in his brown slacks. *Oh.*

Both my hands clenched tighter on his antlers, and he groaned more. His head jerked upright with my hands still gripping them that I became flushed to his body, feeling his hardened cock against my lower abdomen. I stood on my tiptoes for balance. He looked down at me through lust-glazed eyes.

"Um, Kierian?" I asked nervously, licking my bottom lip. He tracked the movement, slowly blinked, and then his hands circled around me, jerking me to him as his lips crashed on mine. He kissed me deeply, stepping forward as I became pressed against the lower countertop attached to the bar top. His hands skimmed down my side. Breaking the kiss, he lifted me up, placing me on the lower countertop.

Kierian stepped between my legs and leaned me back. His lips were inches from mine as he searched my eyes with heavy lids. We breathed each other in, and then he closed the space, kissing me deeply. I wrapped my legs around his waist, feeling his cock pressed flush against my entrance with only our clothes as a barrier. My back rested on the bar top.

He grinded into me, and I felt him try to pull away from our kiss. I still held his antlers and slid my hands down to the base. Gripping them tightly, I guided him back to me. I didn't want this kiss to end. He moaned into my mouth, and I kissed him harder. His tongue started playing with mine. I jerked his antlers closer to me, not wanting this to end.

He shook his head, forcing the kiss to break, and I made a noise in frustration, trying to protest. We were both panting as we looked at each other. I moved to kiss him again, but he pulled back, my body following as I refused to let go of him.

"If we do not stop," he panted, "I will not have any remorse for taking you to my bed." His jaw clenched. He searched my eyes, trying to warn me.

"What if that's what I want?" I whispered. Kierian groaned, giving in. He captured my lips to him again. His hands came under my ass and pulled me up to him. I tightened my thighs around his waist, releasing my hands from his antlers. I wrapped my arms around his neck, and he walked us to his bed. With one knee, he kneeled on the bed as he lay me down on it.

He broke the kiss to remove his shirt. I clenched my thighs tighter around him, excited and nervous at what was coming. He threw his shirt off to the side and looked down at me as he began undoing the laces on his pants. My mouth became dry as I watched his cock come free of restraint from his pants. I had become used to seeing it, but now the thought of his size entering me scared me.

His hands reached down to the edge of my green dress, and he started pulling it upwards. He paused momentarily as he took in the scene.

"You're certain you are still okay with this, right?" His voice was low and husky. I searched his eyes quickly, made a decision, and nodded.

"You're sure?" He pushed.

"Yes, Kierian," I replied, and that was all the confirmation he needed. I helped him get me out of my dress, and then he was pulling my panties off. He tossed them on top of the pile of clothing on the floor. I licked my lips as I watched him stroke his cock, a bead of pre-cum forming at the tip.

"I promise to be gentle, but I have not been with a female in a very long time, so you need to forgive me." His eyes met mine, trying to make me understand what he was trying to convey. I nodded, but my mind was too focused on the size of his cock.

He leaned forward, resting his hand on the right side of my head as he guided himself closer to me. I gasped, my heart racing when I felt him press into my entrance. He slid up in between my folds and back down.

Leaning down, Kierian kissed me softly on my lips. I hissed against his mouth as I felt the stinging pressure of his head push into me and pause. We stayed there for a moment, my heart hammering as I calmed myself down to relax. He pulled back and then pushed in further, and I whimpered into his mouth. He kissed me deeply, the hand braced by my head now tangled into my hair as his thumb stroked my temple gently. He pulled slightly out and then thrust all the way into me. I cried into his mouth. He broke the kiss, breathing heavily.

"Skyla, the restraint I am feeling is killing me," he groaned. "You feel like euphoria." His body spasmed as he held himself, hovering over me.

"Then why are you holding back?" I whispered.

"Because," he gasped. "Because if I don't, I'm afraid I will ruin your first time." He growled out the last part.

"How?" I asked, shifting my hips a bit, and he moaned.

"Because I want to fuck you hard and fast, and I don't want to hurt you," he gritted out, his whole body shaking now.

"Do it," I breathed, giving him permission. His eyes snapped to mine, ensuring he had heard me correctly.

"Do it," I repeated.

"Are you sure?" He asked, his voice breaking with desperation. I reached my right hand up and rested it endearingly on his cheek.

"Yes, I can take it," I promised. With his free hand, he grabbed my left hand and brought it up to rest on one of his antlers. Kierian moaned when I grasped it.

"The velvet on my antlers makes them sensitive. If it becomes too much, use them to break through to me." He was giving me a way out.

"How?" I asked, my heart hammering in my chest. I was afraid to know what was going to come next.

"Dig your nails into them or something, yank my head to the side. Anything to make me stop," he replied, and I nodded in response. His lips crashed against mine as he pulled his cock slightly out and then drove back in. Kissing me deeply, he moaned as he roughly thrust into me, picking up speed. The sharp pain melted into pleasure, and soon, I was falling into rhythm with him. I stroked my hand up and down his antler.

In response, he hiked my left leg up, fucking me deeper. A new sharp pain I felt from the depth made me whimper, but he didn't pause to stop. He kept rhythm as I whimpered and moaned into his mouth. I felt something build within me, and I chased it, accepting the pain and pleasure he was giving me.

I cried out as my orgasm crashed through me, wave after wave. I wrapped my free arm around his neck, pulling Kierian closer to me. He fucked me harder as the waves of pleasure continued to surge through me. Breaking our kiss, he let out a roar as I felt something snap through me before he crashed down onto my body, panting into my neck. I could feel his heart pounding against my chest, a mirror image of my own.

As our breathing slowed, he shifted to lay beside me, pulling me close to him. I laid my head on his shoulder and wrapped my arm around his torso, snuggling into him. We lay there naked in silence, enjoying the moment we shared. I felt like I was glowing from the new bond that formed between us.

Chapter Forty-One

KIERIAN

This human nestled beside me felt like the salvation I had been searching for in all these centuries. How many years had passed me by without knowing what I had been seeking? She was the answer to every question I didn't even know I had. Skyla wasn't some mere mortal girl; she was mine. She was my fated mate. She just didn't know it yet. If she hadn't touched my antlers, I wondered how much longer I would have lasted in suppressing my desires for her. I shivered involuntarily from the pleasure I found in my mate.

My cock was already hardening from the thought of taking her again, but her breathing turned heavy, and I knew she had fallen asleep. Instead, I pulled her tightly to me, nuzzling my nose in her hair to breathe her in. Someday, she would leave me, and I would have these memories to reminisce on, but for now, she was mine. The bond had snapped into place. I could no longer run from her; she needed to know the truth. Skyla needed to know how I felt about her. She needed to know we were officially fated mate.

Chapter Forty-Two

SKYLA

I woke and gingerly stretched, feeling Kierian's warm, naked body against mine. I glanced up sheepishly at him. Our legs were intertwined, and he smiled down at me with amusement. I ducked my head, flushing with how exposed I currently felt, and he chuckled.

"How are you feeling?" he asked with concern in his voice. I quickly checked over my body; aside from a soreness and a unique feeling with my thighs, I didn't feel much different.

"I feel good. You?" My voice came out higher pitched, and I realized how nervous I felt.

"Marvelous." I could hear the warmth and contentment in his voice, and I relaxed into him.

"Was- Was I okay?" I gritted my teeth, afraid of the answer. I pressed my head into his shoulder, bracing myself for the complaint due to my lack of experience. He rolled onto his side, and I tried to keep my head hidden in his chest, but he brought his hand under my chin and forced me to look up to meet his eyes.

"Skyla, if I had known it would have been like this, I would never have held myself back since your arrival." He kissed me softly on the lips. I felt the emotions surge through me as tears welled in my eyes. He pulled back quickly.

"What's the matter?" he asked, concern lacing his voice.

"It's nothing." I hiccupped. "I am just happy, is all." I wiped the tears from my eyes, giggling from the giddiness I felt for this Fae male. I had arrived looking for a wish, and instead I found Kierian.

The cottage door banged open, causing us to jump. In strolled Tennyson. I was in between him and Kierian. Fear coursed through me. Was I fully covered by the blanket? Tennyson's eyes fell upon us, widening slightly before he smirked. He let out a low whistle and then darkly chuckled.

One moment, I was lying in front of Kierian, and the next, he had rolled me behind him with the blanket firmly wrapped around me. He stood naked with his claws angled at Tennyson. I gripped the blankets tighter to me, my happiness completely evaporating.

"I came to apologize for my behavior from the other day, and imagine my surprise to find you both like this." Tennyson's eyes, not leaving me, danced with amusement. Kierian snarled at him. I couldn't see his face, but if I had to guess, he was baring his fangs right now.

"I bet she tastes heavenly; you could share her with me." An evil glint entered Tennyson's eyes, and I tried to shrink back, but the wall prevented me. Kierian snarled louder.

"Get out of here, Tennyson," Kierian threatened. Tennyson laughed and rolled his eyes. His gaze shifted from me to Kierian.

"Brother, you are aware that one day she will have grown old and have died. She'll be dust on the wind, just like every other human before her," Tennyson growled, irritation reflecting in his eyes.

"Shut up, Brother," Kierian roared, the cottage rattling.

Tennyson didn't even flinch from the outburst as I gripped the blanket tighter.

Tennyson released a sigh. "Come outside, Brother. I need to speak to you. Alone." His gaze flicked to me as he said it before returning his attention back to Kierian. Tennyson turned around and went out the door to wait for his brother to join him. I watched as he breathed heavily before roughly grabbing his pants from the floor.

"Stay here, do not leave the house as I go deal with him." He didn't even look at me as he said this. I knew the anger radiating off him wasn't because of me. Tennyson had ruined everything by barging in on us. I listened, staying in place as I watched him walk out the door.

Coldness settled in my stomach from Tennyson's words. *One day, I would be dust on the wind, leaving Kierian all alone again.* How did the happiest moment of my life turn into this? Why did Tennyson have to come and ruin this for us? Fear laced through me at the realization that Tennyson could be convincing Kierian to get rid of me.

My mind started running rampant. What if Tennyson murdered Kierian out there and came in here for me next? Would Tennyson go rogue against his own brother? Could he be like the Fae that had taken my parent's lives? I started to shake as I felt trapped within this cottage, only hoping the worst of my nightmares wouldn't come true.

Go to him. Mytilda jumped onto the bed and tilted her head to the side.

"What, I can't go out there," I replied, completely flabbergasted by the notion.

Put a dress on and go. Mytilda said more firmly in my mind.

Chapter Forty-Three

KIERIAN

I found Tennyson standing outside with his back to me. Either he was really cocky about this situation, or he was trying to prove he didn't pose a current threat to me. My blood felt like steel in my veins as I clenched my jaw, glaring at him. How dare he barge into my home and find my mate in that state of undress. I didn't want him to see her like that.

"Kierian," Tennyson's voice came out quietly. "You need to let her go." He didn't turn to face me, and I was grateful I had shut the cottage door to prevent Skyla from hearing what he was saying.

I chose not to respond; I didn't need to justify my decisions to him. I wasn't going to deny what he stated. I knew it to be true, but it was already too late. When the bond snapped into place, it secured that I would never let Skyla go. No matter the aftermath, I would never let her go.

Tennyson and me may have been brothers in arms once, fighting side by side, but now we were both free. We lived our own lives freely.

I didn't need him coming here to push his own personal agenda with thoughts on my matters.

"I watched you become lost one other time when you had lost Erilea." He turned to face me as he said it. A flash of vulnerability displayed on his face before he masked it again. I wasn't the only Fae to keep my feelings locked up tight. After all, he was the one I had learned it from.

"Don't." I sharply cut him off. I felt my eyes changing to black as I shut my mind to the images that were threatening me. They were surging forward and I tried to keep them held back at bay.

"Do *not* speak her name," I warned. Flashes of memories kept trying to force their way through. I squeezed my eyes shut, bracing myself against them. I could not relive them. I couldn't do it with Tennyson here.

"Brother," his voice came softly, and I felt his hand rest on my forearm. I jerked back, making him drop his hand from me. I could not handle the warmth of his touch. If he kept pushing, I knew I would need to get away from here. Skyla momentarily flashed in my mind and I worried that she wouldn't be safe with either Tennyson or myself right now.

"Don't." I gritted out. More scenes flashed in my mind as I kept shoving them back away, forcing myself not to remember. My body shook as a sheen of sweat coated my skin. My jaw ached from how badly I gritted my teeth, but I knew if I succumbed to the memories Tennyson would not understand how to respond to my condition.

After a few minutes, the memories started to subside, and I gulped in ragged breaths of air. Finally, when I trusted myself enough, I opened my eyes, glaring at Tennyson. I knew my eyes were still pitch black and would be for some time until I completely calmed down.

"I never realized it was this bad," he replied with concern. My gaze flicked out over the clearing. My thoughts began to tunnel as everything else started to disappear from sight.

"Kierian." Tennyson rested his hand on my forearm again, jerking my gaze back to him. I breathed in ragged breaths. Concern washed over his face, and I knew I needed to snap out of this. "I should have visited you more– if I had known . . ."

I took one final ragged breath and stood up straight, staring at him. He wouldn't have known if it were not for his arrival now; he still would be in the dark. I never had any intention of Tennyson finding out how badly the wars still affected my mind. How I feared when Skyla passed, I would revert back worse than the time directly after the wars. If I didn't die from her death, I would hole myself up even deeper away from the world to be left undisturbed.

"Brother, I think it's best that you leave," I growled out, trying to restrain myself.

"Will Skyla be safe with you like this?"

"I didn't think you would care what happened to her?" I snapped, even though I wanted to roar it at him. My body vibrated with the simmering rage that was beginning to bubble beneath the surface. It had been pent up for decades, maybe even centuries at this point. I wasn't certain; I never had kept track of the time that passed when I lived in an existent state.

"I don't really. I worry about you." He took a step back, retreating with his hands up to show he was not a threat to me.

"Leave."

Tennyson didn't respond. He simply nodded, and I watched him take a couple of steps backwards. He was mid-step when he shifted into his raven form and flew away. I tracked him until he disappeared from sight. Taking deeper ragged breaths, I knew I needed to calm myself down.

"Kierian, is everything alright?" Skyla's hesitant voice came from behind me. I closed my eyes, I couldn't be trusted around her in this state.

"Get back inside Skyla," I bit out.

"Kierian, I'm scared. Why does your voice sound different?" She didn't listen. She never listened. I heaved mouthfuls of air in, I couldn't trust myself to shift right now. The other side of me could take over mid deer shift and then I wouldn't be able to control what would happen to Skyla. A small voice whispered in the back of my mind that my mate would be safe regardless. I didn't trust it enough when it came to my other form.

"Just get inside!" I shouted at her.

Arms wrapped around my waist, pulling me tightly to her. My ragged breaths turned to even calm ones. I closed my eyes and gently rested my hand on her arm, careful of my extended claws.

"Why don't you ever listen?" I sighed, tilting my head back to look up at the sky. She pressed her head harder into my back, gripping me tighter. I could feel the blackness leaving my eyes as I gained better control of my other self. I waited another minute to be certain my other self was locked away deeply within me once more.

"Come on, let's go back inside. I'll make breakfast."

Skyla's grip on me released when I turned around. She was already walking toward the cottage door. I reached out and grabbed her arm, twirling her back to face me. She looked up at me, blinking rapidly. I captured her mouth against mine, pulling her close to me. Dammit to all hell, she would stay mine. I kissed her passionately, running my fingers through her hair until they were nestled within the curls.

"Bed, now." I panted, breaking the kiss. She nodded eagerly and turned to race toward my bed, dragging me with her. She fell onto the soft mattress, pulling me down on top of her. I shifted my body lower until my shoulders were between her legs. She looked down her body at me and lightly bit her index finger in her mouth. A fiery passion blazed in her eyes as she watched me lift the bottom of her dress up and I noticed she wasn't wearing any panties.

"Naughty girl," I commented, becoming more turned on. One strong enough breeze could have exposed her nakedness outside. She giggled again as a blush graced her body. Lowering my head to in between her legs, I inhaled the delicious smell of her sex. Unable to resist, I dragged my tongue right up her center, and she moaned. I swirled my tongue around her clit, playing with it, lavishing in how she moved her hips against my face. Teasingly, I licked her down one-fold and back up the other, sucking her clit into my mouth. I gently grazed the tip of my fang against it, letting the adrenaline spike within her as I pierced it slightly. I ran my tongue back and forth on her clit, not allowing her to escape from the pleasure I was giving her.

Gently, I slipped two fingers into her, feeling her muscles tense around them before she relaxed again. I created a rhythm with my fingers and teased her clit, feeling her orgasm build. Skyla fell into a rhythm with me and then she was crying out as I felt her orgasm crash through her. I wasn't done yet; I stayed in rhythm, chasing her orgasm harder. Her hips began to buck, trying to escape the pleasure I was giving her sensitive clit, but I followed her every move.

"Kierian!" She cried out in a begging moan, which I ignored. Her fingers raked through my hair, clutching my head as she rode my face. I licked and sucked her clit harder as her body started shaking. She gasped my name multiple times, and it was like music to my ears. I didn't stop until the waves of her orgasm ceased and she was a trembling mess. Her skin completely flushed red. I did one last long lick on her clit, her body shuddering. I smiled and repeated the action three more times, eliciting the same response. She begged me to stop, her words becoming incoherent. I chuckled, lowering my mouth to lick and suckle her clit as she whimpered and shook, her breaths coming in fast pants.

When I was thoroughly happy with how I satisfied her, I kissed her clit and removed my fingers from her. I hauled my body up to lay next to her. A layer of sweat covered her body, and she looked up at me through thoroughly satisfied, lust-filled eyes. I leaned down and kissed her on the lips, letting her taste herself. She tried to kiss me back with the same passion, but I knew she was still recovering. Trailing my fingers down to in between her legs, I grazed them along her clit and relinquished in the way her body responded.

"Kierian," she whimpered. I shushed her, withdrawing my hand.

"Sleep, you'll need your strength," I murmured, nestling her body closer to mine. She nodded against my chest, and it wasn't long until I heard her deep, even breaths as sleep overtook her body. I smiled down at my beautiful girl, enjoying the smell of her sex on my face.

My mind shifted, pulling me away from this moment. Tennyson's words lingered in my mind: *One day she'll be dust on the wind.* I didn't need these thoughts hampering my good mood. It was not something I could escape, but right now I only wanted to enjoy this time I could spend with Skyla.

Cash in your favors with the magic wielders. Mytilda jumped on the bed, her cerulean-blue eyes wide with anticipation.

Most of them, have gone crazy if they didn't die in the war three hundred years ago. I replied back, irritably. I hadn't seen any since that time and wouldn't have the faintest idea on who to seek out.

The twins are still sound of mind. The cat replied back eagerly.

Aerie and Al'Kede are still alive? They funneled their power into each other, acting as a conduit for one another. Of all the magic wielders, those two would be the ones I had trusted the most during the war. It was no surprise they would still be alive and of sound mind. The magic had not consumed them yet. I shook my head; I was beginning to toe the line far too close to those memories again.

If Skyla is agreeable to it, you could have a lifetime with her . . . Mytilda pushed.

Why do you care? I narrowed my eyes at the lavender cat. She blinked at me and then jumped off the bed.

Chapter Forty-Four

SKYLA

Kierian had me gathering more honey and combs from the Fae hives. I picked a few strawberries from the patch that had become overgrown. The pendant worked like a charm. The bees kept their distance when I came to collect from the hives. I fell into a routine of placing honeycombs into the bowl and then drizzled some onto a strawberry to pop into my mouth for a delicious, sweet snack.

The last two weeks of my life had become filled with orgasms from Kierian. Sometimes, he would stop working and take me right there in the kitchen. He loved leaving me as a sobbing, shaking puddle of a mess, the orgasms still coursing through me. That even the faintest touch would send me reeling over edge again. I was honestly the happiest I had ever been in my life.

I tried bringing up Tennyson's visit a couple of times, but he reacted the same way when I had wanted to tell him my feelings. I had not the faintest idea as to what they had talked about when

Kierian had gone outside. Sometimes, I believed he distracted me with sex to keep my mind from speculating.

Kierian's arms snared around my waist, pulling me close to him. I shrieked from the thrill it gave me.

"Someone is eating more than they are collecting, I see." He chuckled, nuzzling my neck. I moved my head to the side, giving him better access, loving the way he felt against me.

"Just a little mid-afternoon snack," I replied.

He kissed my neck, and a thrill coursed through my body, knowing exactly what would come next.

"I could think of the perfect afternoon snack . . ." he trailed off.

"And what would that be?" My heart raced excitedly.

"I don't think I could wait to get you inside." He breathed. His hands trailed down my hips as he gripped the bottom of my dress, slowly moving it upwards.

"Kierian, I have my hands full, and I'm sticky," I argued playfully.

His right hand moved to skim along my pantie line. I had to readjust my stance as he slipped within, and I gasped, bracing my free hand against the honey hive when his fingers slid along my clit. His free hand let go of my dress and came up to grab my left hand. He raised it up until he started licking the honey from it. He hummed in appreciation, and I moaned from the way his fingers played with my clit.

"Kierian, we can't do it here. There are dead Fae bees on the ground; we'll be stung on accident." I tried to rationalize. He hummed again in response, withdrawing his hand from my panties. One minute, I was standing there bracing a hive; the next, I was scooped up in his arms as he was striding us away from the hives. We barely made it to the privacy screen of the bathtub as he rolled us onto the ground, with me on top of him. My mind could not grasp that the bowl of honey and strawberries had not made a mess everywhere as it sat next to us.

I straddled his waist as he shimmed down the top part of his pants, exposing his hard cocked. Once it was free, his hands fell onto the base of my hips and moved upwards, taking my dress with it.

"Kierian, we're outside," I hissed.

"And?" His hands continuing to move upwards.

"What if someone sees?" I argued, glancing around nervously.

"You've lived here for months; no one is around to see," he countered. I bit my lip, mulling over his words. Giving in, I cringed from the stickiness as it touched my dress as I helped him remove my clothing. His hands came back down as he held my breasts in the palm of his hands.

"You are beautiful, Skyla," he murmured in awe. I preened under his compliment, and it almost masked my shyness from being on top. I placed my hands on his wrist, forgetting momentarily of their stickiness. Quickly, I pulled them away.

"Ah, sorry." I laughed nervously.

"Don't be. It gives me an idea," Kierian responded. Dropping his hand from my right breast he reached over and scooped two fingers into the bowl of honey and strawberries. The sticky strand of honey pulled taught between his hand and the rest of the contents in the bowl until it finally broke apart. He brought it closer to my body, and I started edging away, but I was not quick enough. He covered my nipples in honey, and his other hand trailed around to my back. He sat up, and I shivered as his lips kissed me where he had placed the honey.

"Kierian, you don't like sweet things," I whined from the pleasure.

"Who says?" He chuckled through the kisses.

"You do."

"Mmmh, maybe I lied."

"I thought the Fae couldn't lie?" I asked, becoming serious.

"Who said that?" Kierian continued his kisses.

"Everyone? Wait, you can lie?" I gripped his head, pushing him away from me. He looked up at me, annoyed.

"Yeah, can't everyone?" He went to make a move toward my breasts, but I held him in place.

"Um, I grew up being told that Fae couldn't lie," I argued. He grumbled to himself and flopped back on the ground, his arms landing outwards. I had to catch my balance when I lost the support of his arm. My hands landed on his chest, and I felt the rumble as he started laughing out loud.

"What is so funny?" I was confused by this response.

"That is a lie the Fae told humans when a truce to end the war was being negotiated. I had completely forgotten about it. I cannot believe humans have held onto the notion for three centuries." He continued laughing. I sat there on top of him, almost completely naked, aside from the panties I still wore, not seeing the humor in the matter. Were humans really this gullible the whole time?

"I don't find it that funny," I commented sourly. Kierian's body still slightly shook from his chuckles. I climbed off him, grabbing my dress. I glanced quickly at the privacy screen, concealing the tub, and down at my honey-slathered chest.

"Where are you going?" Kierian asked, amusement still lingering in his voice. I huffed, stalking towards the tub. I tossed my dress on the ground and slipped out of my panties. They barely touched the ground, and I was already sliding into the tub, lathering soaps and oils on my chest to remove the stickiness.

"Skyla?" His voice came from behind me.

I didn't even deign to acknowledge him.

"Skyla, what's wrong?" he pushed. I tensed as I felt his hands gently rest on my shoulders. I crinkled my nose feeling the honey still on his fingers.

I sunk lower into the tub until the water line hovered below my nose. It forced him to remove his sticky hands from my body.

"You are not dumb, Skyla if that is what you are thinking," His voice was low, and I felt his breath through my hair by my right ear. He must have crouched down behind me. "It is not your fault that something believed by your ancestors was passed down through the generations to you. I apologize if my laughing offended you. I just never thought I would hear about the negotiations from all those years ago again. Please don't be mad at me," he begged. His voice sounded earnest, and I felt my anger dissolving. I raised my head out of the water, missing the lingering warmth of water on my lips.

"I suppose I can forgive you," I grumbled. I was still a bit saucy about the ordeal, but offering him at minimal forgiveness was something I could do.

"Thank you," he trailed off, and I waited for what he would say or do next. "I will let you enjoy your bath."

Disappointment coursed through me that he was leaving. I didn't say anything to stop him and barely even heard the falls of his footsteps as he left. I was now mad at myself for letting him walk away. Prior to my upbringing beliefs once again being shattered by him, the moment we were sharing had become intimate. I sighed, lowering myself back into the water until the waterline was directly below my nose again.

Chapter Forty-Five

TENNYSON

I let out a breath of frustration, eyeing the red-haired lass in the bath below. Flapping my wings to keep myself a drift, I mulled over my life expectancy and being caught if I swooped down. Kierian hadn't noticed me way up here and he had already entered his cottage. The privacy screen completely concealed the tub. The chances of him looking out that confounded kitchen window when I swooped down would be minimal. They were chances I was willing to take.

It still weighed on my mind that Kierian should have told me. If he had been bottling his beast form up since the war and let his control slip, it could have ruined everything he had built. If his beast side took over, he would become a killing frenzy. When we fought together, side by side, I had only seen that uncontrolled side come out twice, and both times, I had feared for my own life. When he had looked at me each time, he no longer could recognize me as his brother, only as prey.

Glancing down at the pasture, I eyed the cottage and then where

Petal resided unprotected. I would need to stay on high alert in case Kierian did come after me. I didn't allow myself a moment longer to think about it as I swooped straight for the bathing area. I shifted into my human form; both my hands were pressed on the ground with one knee supporting me for balance. Looking up, I found Petal staring at me with startled green eyes. I could smell the instant fear rolling off her.

"Not one scream," I warned. "I'm not going to hurt you, Petal. If that is what you are thinking," I offered. While I wasn't overly fond of humans, they were born and dead in a blink of my lifetime. Their lives were far too short, and their bodies too frail. What would be a mild irritation to me could end up killing them.

Kierian had a soft side. My Petal had wormed her way into his heart. It wasn't hard to see why; he probably would never admit it, but she was the complete opposite of Erilea. He would never be able to handle being with someone who looked or even acted like Erilea. Skyla had a softness about her that Erilea would find offense to. The human girl's curly, long red hair was just shy of being a completely frizzled mess. Despite their thoughts, she didn't irk me. I gave her credit for the boldness she showed when standing up against me. Then again, when one found one's mate, one couldn't say no.

"Then what do you want?" She tried to muster boldness in her voice, but I could hear the undefining fear she felt. She tried to cover herself in the tub, not that I was interested in looking. I stayed solely focused on her face. Her eyes flickered for a second where the kitchen window lay behind the privacy screen. I perked my ears but did not hear my brother scrambling to come outside after me.

"Do you love my brother?" I asked. Shock crossed her face as she blinked rapidly. She adjusted herself in the tub, holding herself tightly. If she wasn't already claimed in more ways than one, the temptation to play with her naked body flashed through my mind, but I quickly dismissed the thought. I could never be here for that when it came to her.

"What's it to you?" She narrowed her eyes at me. There was the glimmer of boldness that I admired.

"There is a way for you to stay with him forever," I said, dropping the tidbit to see if she would latch on or not.

"How?" She didn't even pause to contemplate what I had said.

"Become Fae," I calmly stated. Dozens of emotions flashed across her face as she tried to sort through what my implication meant. What I said was simple, but the process to follow through would be far more complex.

"How?" She was like a child, repeating the same question.

"There are two magic-wielder twins that could do it." I needed to stack this deck. Kierian had too much honor in these matters. Petal would need to want this to convince him. My brother would sit and think on this conundrum far longer than his mate's life could grant him. Years would pass before he would even bring the notion up to her.

"Why are you telling me this?" she asked suspiciously. Her eyes narrowed more, trying to detect the game I was playing at.

"Because let's just say I like seeing my brother happy again, and I know he is a stubborn stag with his own moral code." I held back the eye roll I wanted to do. Kierian and his moral code had been a thorn in my side more than once in the past. An irritation in all honesty, but I suppose someone in the trio had to have morals because it certainly wasn't Erilea or myself. Knowing Kierian's luck, he would wait long enough that something irreparable would happen. Like an unfortunate death on her part, it wouldn't even have to be from old age.

"How do I know if I can trust you?" She challenged.

"You won't. However, my brother knows to trust the twins, and you trust him," I responded, meeting her challenge. I raised my eyebrow to see if she understood. She blinked and swallowed.

"Now, if we're done here, I would suggest agreeing to the change and I would also add that you should probably bring it up to him." I didn't even wait for her response as I shifted back into my raven form, needing to get away from the human before I did something reckless. Flapping my wings, I rose up into the sky away from the cottage. I would check in on them again —soon.

Chapter Forty-Six

SKYLA

I took longer in the bath than usual. By the time I got out, my body was pruny. I couldn't complain, though; the water stayed a lovely warm temperature the entire time. Tennyson's secret visit unnerved me. He caught me when I was completely exposed and then left me with heavy information to mull over. It didn't sit well with me; there was a small part of me that whispered to trust him.

My emerald dress was already cleaned of honey, and I thanked the magic, enjoying the feel of the breeze blow through my hair. Putting the dress and panties back on, I inhaled a deep breath and squared my shoulders to leave the privacy area of the bathtub. I would need to do another mental prep when I opened the cottage door with what I would be proposing to Kierian next.

As I walked around the house, I relayed everything I had thought about in the tub. Was I being silly in wanting to become Fae and stay with Kierian? Maybe. Could this all be a prank by Tennyson? Absolutely. The fear that Kierian would reject the notion bubbled at the forefront of my mind. Would the change from human to Fae hurt? The last one was my biggest fear. I could tolerate pain, but how much would there be?

My thoughts halted as I braced myself mentally, pushing open the cottage door. Kierian was not in his normal spot in the kitchen. Instead, I found him lounging on my reading bench with a book in his hand. He perked up when he heard me, looking over the pages of his book. Our eyes connected, and a thrill of excitement and fear ran through me.

"I want to ask you something," I blurted out before my nerves could get the best of me.

"What is it?" He didn't appear ruffled by my sudden abruptness. I took a deep breath.

"Can I become Fae?"

Silence filled the cottage. He barely moved a fraction, didn't even blink from my question. His eyes held mine, but they didn't search for an answer. He was waiting for what I would say next and how he should handle it. I chose not to fill the void as I stood there, my body feeling like warm pins and needles. I wanted to rock on the heels of my feet or fiddle with my still damp, dripping hair, but I withheld myself. Ever so slowly, he blinked and put the book off to the side. He changed positions from lounging to sitting.

"Where is this coming from?" He asked, testing the void growing between us.

"I want to know. Can I become Fae?" I pushed, choosing to ignore his question like he sometimes did mine.

"Yes, it is possible," Kierian replied very slowly, uncertainty in his voice. "I don't know where this is coming from though?"

"If you knew, then why did you never ask me?" I rushed out.

"Skyla, I think there is something you need to know first," he said quietly.

Tentatively, I took a shaky step toward him, nervous now about what he was going to tell me. When I stood in front of him, Kierian sat up and grabbed my wrist. He guided me to sit next to him. I noted the anguish that crossed his face as he looked down at the ground.

"As you know, I had been a warrior in the Fae wars when they had started three hundred years ago and continued through them for the twenty years they had raged. There have been some very unsavory things I have done during them." He swallowed, and I stayed still. "Tennyson, Er- Erilea," his voice breaking on the name. "And I had been a trio of warriors who fought together and were sent to do things most Fae did not have the stomach for. There's a side of me," he paused, and I watched as he struggled, trying to grasp for the words he needed.

"There's a side of me that when unleashed, I am unaware of what I am doing. You've seen me in my stag form, but there is a Fae monster past that form. It lingers beneath the surface. He has only escaped containment three times in my life, twice of which were during the war and one time as a child. When that side of me escapes, he slaughters everyone in his path. I don't recognize anyone or anything. When Tennyson visited the other week, I started to feel him slip again when my eyes changed to black. . . and if he appeared, I fear there would have been no saving you if you stood in his path."

My heart stilled as I listened to what he was telling me. I wondered what his other form looked like.

"The day at the market when you witnessed my eyes change to pure black was me losing control." He squeezed his eyes shut and I thought back to that night when his eyes had been black as well. I didn't believe he had been aware of his eyes.

"Skyla, you have become very dear to me and . . . and I want you to stay by my side." He looked down at his hands. I leaned forward, reaching out to rest my hand on his. I felt him tense beneath my grip and then relaxed. "Forever."

"What do you mean?" I breathed, my heart beating faster. I had taken the time to mull over Tennyson's words and already knew my answer.

"There is a possible way to make you Fae. If you would be interested despite my past and other self?" He replied, still not looking. "I know we haven't known each other long and only recently we have become intimate, but . . . but I feel something for you. I want to spend a life with you and see where this thing between us takes us. I want to be together." He took in a ragged breath. "I'm afraid if I wait and let this pass by, I will live in regret from the fear I have right now."

I watched him, my eyes looking back and forth over him. He was baring everything. I felt as if he was pouring his soul out to me. Happiness was coursing through me at how he felt. In all this time of living here, I would never have imagined I meant as much to him, as he did to me. My emotions swelled within me as I felt the warm rush of tears begin to fill my eyes.

"How?" I asked. I wanted to be certain the answer he gave me was the same as Tennyson's before I agreed to anything. I wanted to be with him, I wanted to spend a life with him. I only wanted to know that everything he was saying would be the same as his brothers.

"There are two magic-wielder twins who could change you. We would need to travel to them. It's not an easy trip, but if they change you . . . We could be together forever . . . Would you be interested in becoming a Fae?" He asked, and I could hear the hope in his voice. My hand flexed on his, and I shifted in my seat.

"What's the cost?" I asked. Tennyson had never mentioned what the payment would be, and it had made me wonder if it was a double-edged sword.

"The twins are the ones who decide the price," he replied.

"Will it hurt?" I swallowed.

"I honestly don't know. That would be a question for the twins." Kierian's voice started to sound defeated.

"Will I be able to shift, like you do as a stag or your other form?"

"I don't think so. Not all Fae have shifting abilities, and it's usually passed down through bloodlines."

I mulled it over. I was kind of hoping to be able to change into an animal like Kierian. Having another form that was uncontrollable scared me but didn't deter me. The fear of this change from human to Fae being painful still made me nervous, but I didn't see any other way around it.

"Can I ask you a question?" Kierian's voice broke my thoughts.

"Sure?" I shifted in my seat nervously.

"Why do you want to become Fae?" His eyes bore into mine, and I swallowed.

"Do you remember the initial reason I showed up at your doorstep?" I asked hesitantly and he nodded. We both avoid using the word 'wish' lest Mytilda was about. "You've already granted it."

"What was it?" Curiosity and hope filled his eyes.

"I wanted to get away from Piggs Burough, to live in a charming place with a life I could afford and a husband who adored me. I didn't need luxury; I only wanted happiness. I wanted a home." My face flushed from the implication of him becoming my husband. I felt there was something more between us, but I couldn't put my finger on it.

"You would want me to be your husband?" he asked hopeful. Kierian was not trying to mask his emotions and I was grateful for it.

"I mean, eventually, yes. Maybe someday? Um, I wasn't planning on having this talk now." I giggled nervously, tucking my hair behind my ear as I looked down to my lap.

"In the Fae world, there are marriages, but we use the term 'Mates'. There is something higher than overall all, and that is called a 'Fated Mate.'" Kierian was having trouble with his words as he said them. I thought maybe it was because this was an important topic.

"Then, let's see these twins. So we can become mates." I smiled. I would ask him later about the fated mates thing, but for now I was ready to take the next steps in my life with him.

Kierian's head whipped up to look at me, incredulous surprise on his face.

"Are you certain?" He asked, and I nodded, afraid to utter another word. He grabbed both of my hands, and leaning down, he kissed me softly.

Chapter Forty-Seven

SKYLA

The trip to the twins had not been the greatest, but I had spent most of the time riding on Kierian's back in his stag form. Even with his Fae speed, it had taken us nearly three weeks to arrive at the top of the mountain where the twins lived.

We stood on a flat ledge with a door placed into the side of the mountain. The door had even been painted to camouflage into its surroundings. If Kierian had not known where to look, I would have missed it completely. In our travels, Kierian had a difficult time answering any of my questions. All he could tell me was that many magic-wielders had almost ceased to exist because their conduits were not strong enough to withstand the power of their magic wielder.

Kierian didn't even knock; he simply opened the door and walked in as if he was home. I looked at him curiously. His boldness shocked me. He shrugged and led us down a path carved within the mountain, lit up by Fae light.

"Kierian, you are looking rather handsome these days, and you brought along your. . . do I detect *lover*?" A sultry, female voice laced with amusement echoed around the cavern, and I grabbed Kierian's arm, glancing about frantically as I tried to locate where the voice came from.

"Just stay close by." It was the only reassurance Kierian gave me. I tightened my grip on his arm. He continued to lead us through the carved mountain pass. Despite the amount of time we had traveled, I felt that we had not crossed any distance.

"Your lover is wise, Kierian." The female voice purred in approval, and I jumped again.

"Quit with your games, Aerie!" Kierian bellowed in annoyance. The sultry female voice laughed, and suddenly, we were walking into a luxurious room that I would never have imagined could be found inside a mountain.

The room we entered was light and airy, like the female's name. The walls reminded me of clouds that lazily moved around the room. It was when I noticed the floor beneath us, I gripped Kierian tightly. The floor was a swirling black hole, and I was certain we would be sucked in.

"Ignore it; it's an illusion to trick your mind," Kierian mumbled under his breath to me, but it did not comfort me enough to ease my grip from his arm.

"Kierian is *so* very right," the sultry female voice said in response. She emerged in a white-wrapped dress. Her skin sparkled gold with a long brown braid down the front. She had mismatched eyes; her right eye was a bright jade green, while the other was a lilac purple. She walked barefoot with a mesmerizing grace. Golden ankle bracelets chimed with each step; there was a matching pair of bracelets around her wrist and a single golden ring around her neck. Golden hoops adorned her ears, which I noted were round like my own. She wasn't Fae, but if she was a magic-wielder, what did that make her?

She stopped before us and gave a friendly smile; she did not look like she could be older than thirty. I knew she was hundreds of years old like Kierian, but she carried herself with the youthfulness of a girl in her twenties. She looked up at Kierian, batted her eyes with long lashes, and then they widened astonished.

"What a surprise, you want to turn her Fae?" She blinked multiple times, her gaze falling back onto me. I felt myself bristling from her reaction. "Nothing to fear from me dearie, Kierian and I are . . . old friends, are we not?" She flicked her gaze back up to him, but I did not miss the way she lingered on choosing her words carefully.

"What would be the cost?" Kierian asked, ignoring the magic-wielder's question. Aerie tilted her head to the side, and even I could tell she was only pretending to mull over the payment. She righted her head and gave him a feline predatory smile.

"She has to witness your memories and would still want to be with you after seeing your past." The words fell between us, and I felt Kierian stiffen within my grasp.

"Surely there has –" Kierian was cut off by a male voice that echoed from above.

"That is the payment requirement for the transformation. The Spellcaster, who gave you the protection enchantment, and we have agreed. Call it a two-for-one. The pendant and her transformation in exchange for her to witness your memories will be the payment. Take it or leave." I gripped the pendant hanging from my neck. Looking up I found a male resting on a cutout alcove in the wall. He dressed in midnight blue to black attire, but there was no mistake that he must have been Aerie's twin. His eyes tilted up like Aerie's, and his skin glittered a similar shade of gold. He leaped from his ledge, his cloak billowing out from behind him and gracefully landed beside his sister. Whereas Aerie's right eye was bright jade green, his was lilac purple, and his left was green. He had short, messy black hair and looked completely bored by the interaction. This must be Al'Kede.

Aerie giggled, and I realized what the payment would mean; I would have insight into everything Kierian had kept locked away from me. A small part of me was relieved the pendant would be paid off and not by means of sex with The Spellcaster, who was not present.

I glanced at Kierian, his jaw clenched as he glared at the twins. He understood the cost, and it wasn't me rifling through his past, it was the fear of whether I would stay after I witnessed everything he had done during the Fae Wars. Aerie's voice brought my attention back to her.

"Willing to play and stay or depart and lose your heart?" Aerie sang sweetly, tilting her head to the other side. She reminded me of a cat playing with its food. Kierian gave a low growl, and I peeked up at him through my lashes. He let go a sigh and looked down at me, his shoulders slumping.

"This is your decision, Skyla," he stated calmly, and I felt icy coldness run through me. Everything would be based on what I said next. I could have a chance to see Kierian's past and become Fae, or I could turn it down for his privacy and leave here to die a mortal life. I looked back to Aerie.

"Do it," I said with as much confidence as I could muster in my voice. I was selfish, I didn't want to give up my home. I was nervous about what I would witness, and would I still view Kierian to be the same male I had fallen in love with. I had never admitted it out loud, but I had fallen in love with the Fae male standing beside me.

Aerie started laughing, a glimmer entering her eyes. She grabbed her brother's hand, and then, reaching forward, she gripped my wrist, yanking me away from Kierian and into her soft, ample bosom. I looked back at Kierian, realizing I was falling into the twisting black vortex below our feet. Startlement showed on his face as he reached for me, and then a searing white light flashed in my vision as I felt sucked away from the world I resided in.

Chapter Forty-Eight

SKYLA

Pain laced through my head momentarily. Blinking my eyes open, I was blinded by the sunlight. Spots danced in my vision as confusion circulated around me. Screams and yelling mixed in with the sound of steel on steel surrounded me. I rubbed my eyes until the spots cleared; I was not anticipating what I found before me. I was standing on a bloodied battlefield. War was afoot between Fae and humans as they fought. *Where was I?* Panic coursed through me. Fear locked my feet into place; I was too afraid to move from this location. I was unsafe here. I needed to find a hiding spot, otherwise my life would be at risk. I whipped my head from left to right, but no matter which way I turned, someone was dying.

A screaming horse fell in front of me. Its rider already dead. Blood gurgled from his slashed throat, making me feel nauseous from the sight. Despite the hideous scene, it launched me into running towards a dead tree that had fallen. I could only hope that if I tucked myself into the hollowed-out part of it, no one would find me. I could not find anywhere else that was safe on the field. As I ran, a man came running at me with his sword raised. I skidded to a halt. My body locked up; I needed to move. The fear coursing through me kept me frozen in place again. I braced myself for the pain I knew would come from the sword that swung downwards at me.

This would be how my life ended. I watched in shock as the sword went through me, and I felt no pain. Is this what it was like to die? There would be no pain. But then, in my horror, I watched blood fly from my body, and a hand came through my chest with a sword, impaling the man before me. I whipped around and found myself face to face with a Fae male I didn't recognize, but he was not looking at me, his focus on the human he had gutted behind me.

It was then that I realized they couldn't see me. I looked down at my body and found I was perfectly fine. Neither blade had cut me. Somehow, I was merely existing here, but not actually physically here. I raised my hands, turning them this way and that to make certain I was really here.

"KIERIAN!" a male yelled, and my head whipped to where the shout came from. My eyes landed on Tennyson. I almost didn't recognize him. He was pure muscle, and his face was completely feral. I had thought Tennyson was intimidating before, but if he had looked like this when I first met him, I probably would have wet myself. The pain laced through my head again, and I remembered I was here to witness Kierian's memories.

Movement to the left caught my attention as a mound of human bodies went flying every which way. They were all dead before impact, taking out human and Fae alike in their path. Standing in the center where the mound had been stood the muscular backside of a Fae male. He was breathing heavily as he turned his head to Tennyson. I gasped when I recognized the blood-covered short brown hair with the white streak in it.

Blood streamed down Kierian's bare chest. His fangs, the longest I had ever seen, were coated in blood. His face was smeared with blood splatter, and I couldn't tell if it was from the battle or if he had just ripped someone's throat out. He held a sword in one hand, and the moment Tennyson made it to Kierian, they fought back-to-back to each other. My eyes couldn't track their movements as they weaved and blended with every blow. Their two forms blurred together as their speed increased.

Where they fought, it continued to rain blood, spraying every which direction as they moved around the battlefield, dropping their enemies with ease. It occurred to me then that these were humans like myself, and neither brother in arms showed a minuscule amount of mercy for my kind.

A white flash blinded my mind, and I felt the same sensation before as I was sucked and deposited into a new place. This time, I had been placed in what I assumed was a cave. Rock surrounded me everywhere. If I had to guess, I was in a tunnel. The path behind me was pitch dark, but in front of me, there was a light that danced on the walls. Following the source of the warm glow, I slipped into the hollowed-out part of the cave and stood with my back pressed against the stone wall, taking in the scene of the two Fae before me.

A beautiful Fae female sat on a stool with long black hair pooling on the ground at her feet. She had a small chin, flat cheekbones, and a straight, narrow nose. Her eyes were downcasted as she worked on bandaging a very battle-worn Kierian.

"Enough, Erilea. It'll heal on its own. You're wasting supplies on these surface cuts." Kierian yanked his arm away from her. She tsked at him. The realization struck me then: I had assumed Erilea was a male in the trio. It had never occurred to me that she was a female.

"When it's infected, don't come whining to me," she snarled. Erilea began packing up the medical supplies into a bag, shooting glares at Kierian. He wasn't paying attention to her. Instead, he was skewering raw meat onto a dagger. I relaxed a bit; they didn't appear to be on the friendliest of terms.

"Where's Crow Boy at?" Erilea asked, breaking their silence. It was interesting that I was not alone in calling Tennyson that. I wondered if I struck more than a nerve when I called him it, thanks to Erilea now.

"Rutting some virgin." Kierian rolled his eyes, holding the dagger with the raw meat over the fire.

"Fae or human?" Erilea's attention shifted to watching the fire flames flicker and lick at the meat.

"Both." He didn't even seem to be the slightest bit phased by this. It struck me odd that I had witnessed them murdering humans in the memory prior, but here, Kierian was stating that Tennyson was having sex with my kind. Tennyson made the disdain he felt towards humans evident, so why would he want to be intimate with them? Then again, he had offered multiple times to warm my bed.

"What, does he have a fetish for virgins or something?" Erilea growled.

"He likes the idea of being the best lay they've ever had. Doesn't want any other male to ever compare." snorted Kierian.

Erilea pursed her lips but didn't respond. They sat in silence until the meat was cooked. He ripped it in two with his bare hands, handing her a piece. They didn't even acknowledge the heat of the food on their skin.

I wondered why I was here witnessing this event. I found it odd that I was viewing them as a bystander and not through the eyes of Kierian. Maybe there was something that occurred that I was supposed to see that maybe through his eyes would have been missed? I looked around the cave and couldn't find anything marvelous about it. Just sand-colored walls with red veins in them.

I felt restlessness, and then the white light flashed again. I now stood in a busy tavern. The smell of barrel ale and sweat hit my senses, making me want to gag. It was a bit sweltering hot in the establishment with this many bodies. It took my eyes scanning the room twice until I finally found the trio nestled in a darkened black corner booth.

It was odd having people walk through my body as I made my way to the three. I noted how all the candles had been extinguished in this corner. All three had their hoods up, which was the reason I had missed them the first time while I searched the room. They were hunched over the table, talking to each other. Tennyson sat by himself while Erilea and Kierian resided in the other seat. I bristled slightly at Kierian's close proximity to Erilea.

Standing at the edge of their booth, I was disappointed; they weren't even talking to one another. There was nothing to glean from their silence. Tennyson surveyed the room, his eyes pausing on me, causing fear to slide through me, before he continued to scan, and I relaxed. He gave one curt nod, and the three slid out of the booth, unsheathing their weapons. Fear burned down my throat. I tried to swallow it, but the bitter taste made me scrunch up my face. I didn't have to move out of the way as they walked directly through me. I was one with Kierian, causing me to shiver.

I turned quickly, watching as Tennyson ran his sword through a human male's stomach. The male shrieked, and Tennyson yanked it out, bringing the bloody blade up to his lips. He smiled, showing off his fangs as he licked the blood from it.

The room filled with screams as humans stumbled over one another, trying to flee from the three Fae. Kierian and Erilea started to weave in and out of the tables, cutting down everyone in their way. Tennyson's cackling laugh brought my attention back to him. He stood with one foot on a chair and the other on top of the table. His sword raised as he watched with enjoyment at the scene unfolding before him.

Taking my eyes off him, I found the room around me becoming covered in blood. I clapped my hands over my ears, trying to block out the dying humans' groans and sobs. I wanted to squeeze my eyes shut and wish it all away, but I couldn't. Once again, another force was preventing me. There was something I needed to witness in this memory.

"Tennyson!" Erilea barked over her shoulder, they had cornered a female. She had long brown hair and hazel eyes. Her paisley clothing was splattered in blood, much like the rest of her skin. She was cowering as sobs racked her body. She begged for their mercy, and I could tell from here she had soiled herself. Tennyson jumped off the table and strode through me to the female. I gave his backside a look of disgust but followed him anyways. I was curious about what would happen next. He crouched down in front of her, and I mirrored him.

"You have been a very bad girl, Lorelei," he stated, lethally calm. The terror I felt made me want to get away from him. I feared for not only her life but my own as well. "You have been on the run from us for far too long. Give me what we came here for." Tennyson held out his hand, waiting patiently.

Lorelei sobbed harder, shaking her head. She couldn't manage to get a word out because of how hard she was crying. I felt pity for her, but I wasn't certain if I should. What had caused her to run from these three, and what did she have that they wanted?

Tennyson let out an irritated sigh. He stood back up and dusted off his knees. Feeling uneasy, I slowly stood up on wobbly legs. I looked between the four, trying to puzzle out what would happen next. Tennyson looked at Kierian and Erilea, who nodded at him in response. I didn't even blink, and Kierian had Lorelei by the throat, pressed up against the wall, high enough that her feet could no longer touch the floor. Her hands and feet grappled against the wall, trying to find support. Kierian's fangs elongated as he snarled in her face.

"You going to tell us now, Lorelei, or will I need to enlighten the mood?" Erilea asked, picking her nails with the bloody dagger in her hand.

The girl cried harder.

"I don't think she has it." Kierian tightened his grip on her neck. Lorelei began making a choking noise through her sobs.

"Such a pity," Tennyson replied. "Erilea." He turned, and I watched him take one step before the screams drew my attention back to Lorelei. Erilea's dagger went through Lorelei's palm and into the wooden wall. Kierian had released his chokehold on her enough to allow the screams and the ragged begging from her lips. The hairs on the back of my neck rose as I heard the dark chuckle of Tennyson walking away from me.

"Stop playing, Erilea," chided Kierian. Erilea huffed, and in one motion, she yanked the dagger out while simultaneously Kierian released his hold on the girl's neck. Lorelei's feet hadn't even touched the ground as Erilea's dagger sliced across the girl's throat. Blood sprayed everywhere, covering them. They didn't so much as flinch as I had tried to back away, forgetting it would go through me.

I felt my body shuddering as I tried to hold back the heaves. I didn't want to vomit here. One of my arms wrapped around my stomach as the other stayed pressed hard against my mouth, forcing myself to hold back everything that wanted to come up. Kierian turned his hood still up, blood spattered across his displeased face. His eyes were solid black. Erilea smiled wide while wiping her blade on the now dead Lorelei's dress.

Erilea followed Kierian as they trailed behind Tennyson. I had anticipated the white flash, but it didn't come. I scrambled after them, unsure if I could keep up if they traveled as fast as Fae could. Mid-stride, the white flash came, and the next thing I knew, I was tumbling and rolling across grassland.

The fresh, cool air, clean of blood, death, and sweltering heat, was a welcoming relief. I took in deep lung fulls of air, trying to rid myself of the tavern's massacre. One thing I was grateful for in this form was that despite the tumble I had just taken, I had no cuts or injuries from it. I pushed off the ground and dusted off imaginary dirt from my dress. It wasn't even wrinkled.

I looked up, and my eyes immediately settled on the trio amongst the rolling grass blades. They didn't have a fire lit, but they sat in a circle as if one was still burning. I walked, and then warmth hit me. They must have been heating their surrounding area with Fae magic. Erilea was braiding her long wet hair back while Kierian sharpened his sword.

Tennyson got to his feet; the other two didn't even look at him. He strolled away from the camp. I was conflicted about whether I should follow him or stay here. I blinked, and he was out of sight. I suppose that answered my question. Focusing back on the two remaining, they sat there silent. They acted as if the other one did not exist in the same space as them.

After the previous scene I had witnessed seconds prior, I was okay with a change of scenery. I shivered from the memory of Lorelei's throat slashed open with blood flowing out everywhere. Her lifeless eyes staring at the ceiling. I felt the world lurch under my feet, and then I was hurling into the grass, retching up everything in my stomach. I relived the smell of the tavern, the fresh blood, and the screams and cries of humans wouldn't leave my mind.

"It will be okay." Kierian's voice broke through my thoughts. My head jerked up, believing he could see me in this pitiful state, but instead, he was looking at Erilea. There was a tenderness upon his face, the same tenderness I had witnessed when he made love to me. My stomach knotted.

"What do you know?" Erilea questioned softly.

"I know you will do anything for his attention." Kierian paused in sharpening his sword. I could tell he wanted to say more but was holding back. Erilea's finger slowed from braiding; she glared at the ground. I got up from my hands and knees, walking around the upheaved contents of my stomach to stand in front of them.

"Like I said, what do you know?" She spat; venom laced her almost growl of a voice.

"I watch you become crueler than you want to be in your kills, and I watch how your eyes dim when either he didn't watch or isn't praising you for it," Kierian replied gently. Erilea's lip wobbled, and she ceased braiding her long hair altogether. I was curious why a warrior would keep her hair as long as she did. I would imagine it would be an inconvenience when fighting. Kierian put his sword down at his side and moved closer to Erilea. My breathing slowed.

He reached his right hand up to touch her face. She slapped it and looked away from him. Not being detered, he grabbed her chin and yanked it back to look at him. Her eyes filled with tears. His face softened, and he pulled her into his arms. Her body shook as she cried, clinging to him. He rocked her gently, trying to comfort her.

It was difficult to separate that this woman was the same one I had just witnessed play with a human life before brutally spilling blood everywhere. Was everything Erilea doing to obtain Tennyson's attention? I looked over my shoulder to where the male in question had disappeared to. Was she in love with him? I gathered that Tennyson was the leader of the trio. However, in the cottage, Kierian treated him as equals. The past version I was witnessing of these two terrified me with their cruelty. What had changed between the present and three hundred years ago?

The white flash happened, and now I was standing in a campground. Fae warriors were walking and lingering everywhere. I started my search for the trio, but the idea of peaking my head into tents made me a bit nervous. I didn't pay attention to the conversations as I passed the various groups of Fae warriors.

It was in my third row of tents when I spotted the trio. They were at a tent away from the rest, while everyone else had tents in colors of gray; theirs was a single large black tent. As I neared their campground, I realized it wasn't one large tent but two smaller ones next to each other. Shouldn't there be a third tent? Assuming that the trio owned the black tents, were two of them sharing one? I shook the idea from my head, figuring I would soon find out the answer.

I took a seat on an empty log across from them as a fire crackled between us. Tennyson was talking about their battle victories from the day. He sounded like the Fae male I had come to know. Kierian polished and sharpened his sword, barely acknowledging Tennyson's words. Erilea leaned back, picking her nails with a clean dagger. I noted how she had tiny braids weaved into her main braid. I wondered if she had done it herself or if another female had helped her.

"Did you see the way his intestines spilled out and how he held them, thinking he could put them back in? *Poof* just magically fixed himself. *All better*!" Tennyson laughed viciously. "Pathetic, weak humans. It'll be a sad day when the war against them ends, and I can no longer be covered in their blood."

"It's a good thing for you, they breed quickly and plentifully. If their numbers didn't outrank ours significantly as they do, the war would have already ended," Kierian stated dryly.

"I figure we have another five, maybe ten years to play with them." Tennyson leaned back and propped his feet on a log by the fire.

"I hope not. I am tired of war." Erilea spoke up wearily. Her attention shifted from picking her nails to staring into the fire. Fatigue plagued her as dark bruises formed under her eyes. Her skin held a dull pallor to it, and it was then I noticed her hair didn't shine as vibrantly as it had in past memories.

"Are you becoming like Kierian here? Never thought I would see the day, Erilea. *Disappointing really*. It's what I liked about you; your taste in bloodshed matched *mine*." Erilea stiffened, and I almost missed the twitch of her bottom lip. Tennyson didn't miss any of it. His pupils pulsed for a second as he noticed the way his words affected her.

"We've been at this for fifteen years. It was fun at first, but I would like to sleep in my own bed and not have to share my things with others constantly." Erilea sniffed.

Tennyson's lips pressed together as his eyes narrowed. He blinked, and his face was back to being good-natured. He kicked the log his feet were resting on into the fire and stood up.

"Speaking of sharing things, I think it's about time I figure out whose bed I will be occupying tonight." Kierian and Erilea didn't even look at Tennyson as he disappeared through the rows of tents. I had my answer as to why there were only two black tents for the trio. I had speculated, but now Tennyson confirmed it.

They had been fighting in the Fae wars. By my calculations, if they had been in it for fifteen years, they only had a few more years left to go. Erilea would have her wish of going home to her own bed soon.

I wondered where Erilea was in the present time. Unlike Tennyson, she had never dropped by. There had been no mention of her in any of the books I had read in the cottage; Tennyson had been in a few, but no Erilea. There wasn't even a drawing of her. From the few memories of Kierian's I had already witnessed, I was under a distinct impression these three were a tight-knit group of Fae warriors, especially with Tennyson still frequently visiting. What had happened to Erilea that she had been almost erased from history in Kierian's present life?

"Do you think he will ever change?" Erilea quietly asked.

"Someday, maybe, but in the near future?" Kierian paused to mull over his words. "Probably not."

Erilea sighed. My heart went out to Erilea with her unrequited love, even if it was to Tennyson.

"I didn't think so either." She stood, sheathing the dagger and dusting her hands. She bid Kierian a good night. He watched her slip into the black tent on the left. She never turned the light on.

Taking his attention off the tent, he stared into the fire. He may have sat a few feet in front of me, but his mind was miles away. Something I was familiar with after living with him for months. It always made me curious where his mind went. These memories didn't benefit me if I couldn't read his thoughts.

Chapter Forty-Nine

SKYLA

This time when the white flash happened, I found myself in a dimly lit bedroom. By the sounds I could hear outside the door, I assumed I had been dropped in a tavern with rooms upstairs. Groaning, I turned around to grab the door handle to go find my trio. A few memories, and I was claiming them as mine, apparently. I didn't even get a chance to touch the handle. It turned, and the door banged open with Erilea storming in.

"He can go drown for all I care!" She shouted; Kierian was a step behind her. He calmly shut the door behind them. "We've stood by his side for twenty years." Erilea threw her hands up in the air. She spied a vase on the stand, not hesitating as she grabbed it and threw it across the room. It shattered into hundreds of tiny shards, falling to the floor.

Kierian closed the distance until he stood behind Erilea. She whipped around, her fangs bared, as she glared up at him. Kierian didn't react. I took a step back, shaking my head. His left hand came up and caressed her cheek. She hissed at him, but it didn't stop him from tucking her loose strands back behind her pointed ears. Erilea tried to yank her face away from him, but his other hand came up and prevented her from looking away from him.

She tried to struggle out of his grip, and Kierian dropped his left hand. When Erilea thought she was free to escape, he wrapped his arm around her waist and yanked her body to him. She shoved her hands hard against his chest.

"Erilea," he said her name reverently as though any louder might cause the moment to vanish, the fight leaving her body. She sagged into him, tears filling her eyes. He didn't give her a moment to react as his lips crashed against hers, kissing her passionately. I stumbled backward until my back was pressed against the bedroom wall. I wanted to squeeze my eyes shut. I needed to escape, but I was forced to take in the scene.

Erilea's anger was replaced with lust as she wrapped her arms around his neck, welcoming the kiss. She pulled him closer to her while guiding them towards the bed. I couldn't get my body to run from here; I was forced to watch the Fae male I loved be intimate with another. Their muffled moans became loud when their kiss broke to begin undressing one another. The sound of buckles being undone and weapons falling to the floor filled the room.

His naked backside faced me, and my eyes roamed. I had become familiar with his body; I knew every scar and mark along the way. But this body was not the same as the one I knew; there were fewer scars, and the marks he had were fresh and still angry. I knew I was three hundred years in the past, but when he stepped to the side, I wanted to collapse. The moonlight cascaded down on Erilea's perfectly naked body.

Her black hair waved down in layers around her. Her breasts, which were always wrapped and hidden in leather, were now on full display. I didn't need to glance down at mine to know that they were half the size and not as perky as hers. Her stomach tapered inward as the faint lines of abs were outlined in shadows.

What could he see in me when he had been with her? Why couldn't I run away? I felt as if something or someone else had control of my body and was forcing me to watch. Whether it was for their own pleasure or my own good, I wasn't for certain. The only thing I did know was I hated everything about this.

They stood there in silence, quietly taking each other in, and in a blink of Fae speed, they were consuming each other. Tears ran down my cheeks as the couple rolled onto the bed. Kierian laid on his back with Erilea hovering above his hard cock. *No, no, no, no,* my head barely shook back and forth. The tears came harder, blurring my vision as she sank down on him. Kierian held his hands on her hips as they began to thrust in a rhythm together.

Erilea hissed at Kierian, and he growled back. In another blink, they were standing with Erilea's back pounded against the wall as he took her standing up. Erilea's moans came louder, and in my horror, I watched as his fangs sank into her neck. He was marking her, claiming her. My mind raced back to the day when he had come close to doing the same thing to me but had stopped himself. He didn't even hesitate with Erilea.

She snarled at him, and in the next blink, Kierian had her pinned to the floor on her stomach as he took her from behind. Her black hair wrapped around his fist; he kept her head pulled back. The sound of their flesh slapping against each other seared into my ears. My throat strained from the gasps my sobs brought from me.

Kierian pounded into Erilea three more hard times before groaning and collapsing onto her backside. She panted beneath him. Her cheek pressed into the floor, and I swore she was staring at me; her golden eyes became slitted like a cat's. She smiled seductively and closed her eyes in contentment. I swore I could hear her purring from where I sat.

The hold on my body broke, and I slid down the wall until I sat on the cold floor, sobs racking my body. I rested my head on my forearms, looking down into my lap as I cried harder. Of all the past events, why did I need to bear witness to this? Why did I need to see Kierian fuck another woman? *It was the past.* I repeatedly chanted that sentence in my head, trying to convince my mind that it meant nothing now. But what if Erilea returned one day if she walked back into his life? Would he discard me for her? Would she take away my home?

"We can't tell Tennyson," Erilea stated. I could hear the fear in her voice. I peeked up from my arms to watch how this conversation unfolded.

"He'll have already scented us, Erilea," Kierian replied, deathly calm. His honey-brown eyes were void of all warmth. He had shut down on her mentally, as he had done to me many times when I had first entered his life. She had hurt him.

"You shouldn't have marked me," Erilea said as she pushed off the ground and onto her knees, rubbing her neck where his bite mark was.

"Heat of the moment." Kierian coldly stated. He got off the ground and wordlessly started dressing again. Maybe if this was the way it had ended between them, I wouldn't need to worry about her coming back into his life.

"I didn't ask to be marked." She growled at him.

"How else could I make you mine?" He countered.

"By asking!" She shouted.

"You would never have said yes." Fully dressed, he glowered at her. Turning, he left Erilea still kneeling on the bedroom floor. He closed the door softly behind him. She glared at the space he had preoccupied, and then her gaze flicked to me. That predatory smile entered her face.

"Hope you enjoyed the show." Erilea purred. "Aerie."

I gasped as a voice within my mind simultaneously gasped.

"Let's see what memories you need to show whomever you're helping meddle." In a flash, Erilea grasped my arm, and then I fell into another memory, but this was different. There was not a flash of white light pain. It was gentle, almost soft, like being cradled against someone loving.

I blinked, and Erilea was still grasping my arm as we stood in another bedroom. This one was quite quaint, donned primarily in soft pink and white colors and decorated with pretty things. The pink bed had more ruffles on it than I had ever witnessed in my life, with a ruffled canopy top to match. I looked up at Erilea, who was still completely naked and wore a frown on her face. She glanced at me.

"I don't know who you are, human, but Aerie is using you to find something in the past. Let me borrow you for a moment to show you how dishonest the little magic-wielder is." She said, unhappy, as she glanced around the room, not letting go of my arm. "It scents as Aerie's room, and considering she was spying on me being marked by Kierian, the little witch always wanted his attention. She is obsessed with him." Erilea said bluntly with distaste.

I swallowed, afraid to speak. I only nodded as I wiped away my tears.

"Come along, Kierian," Aerie's sultry voice purred outside the bedroom door. I felt I was going to witness the same scene again, but this time with Aerie. It was set up the same, at the very minimum. Aerie led Kierian into the room we inhabited with their hands intertwined. Lust filled his eyes even with his fangs bared. She dragged him almost to the bed. Turning, she giggled up at him and started to help him unbuckle out of his leathers.

I felt Erilea's grip tighten on me, and I looked up at her, trying to look past her brazen nakedness. She glanced down at me and, raising a hand to her lips, motioned for me to keep silent. I wondered if all Fae had the power to go through memories like this or if only a certain few. I found it particularly odd that during my travels through the memories, I had not once had Aerie by my side, but now Erilea was gripping my arm tightly as I would be forced to watch another sex scene unfold involving Kierian.

Erilea motioned her head for me to look back at Aerie and Kierian. The magic-wielder leaned up on tiptoes to kiss Kierian, and he stiffly kissed her back, going through the motions. The passion he had given Erilea was clearly not present for Aerie.

We watched as the magic-wielder slid down on her knees and took Kierian's cock into her mouth. She purred and moaned as she looked up at him with sultry eyes. Erilea stiffened, and I looked back at her. Her nose wrinkled, and she wore an unamused expression on her face. She looked at me and rolled her eyes. I was at odds that I currently stood fully clothed in a room with three naked people, two of whom were females having sexual interactions with the man I loved.

Kierian let out a moan, and my attention fell back on the pair in front of us. Kierian's cock withdrew from Aerie's mouth, and she stood from kneeling to push him to sit on the bed. Standing between his knees she guided him until he was laying back on her bed. She crawled on top of him and did not even hesitate to sheath him within her. Her hand braced on his chest as she began a rhythm.

When he moaned, she picked up her speed and grinded down on top of him, causing him to hiss. I did not miss how she smiled gleefully. His hands came up to grip her hips, his nails drawing blood, and then he was groaning as he bucked up into her. She laughed in triumph, and Erilea shifted her weight next to me.

It didn't take long before Kierian was snoring, sound asleep under Aerie. He had never fallen asleep that quickly with me. His motions with Aerie had almost seemed mechanical. There had been minimal passion for the magic-wielder. I glanced at Erilea to gauge from her expression but found nothing as she surveyed the scene before us. I looked back to the couple in bed. Aerie laid herself on his chest, smiling down at Kierian as she trailed her finger along his chin.

"Our child will be marvelous," Aerie crooned. Coldness washed through me, and Erilea stiffened. I wasn't certain either of us had heard her correctly. Aerie laid her head on Kierian's chest, tucking her head under his neck as she looked at us smiling.

"Did you enjoy the show, Erilea? When he couldn't find solace in you, he came to me to mend his broken heart. I ought to thank you for rejecting him." Aerie smiled sweetly. She reached her hand down to her stomach and looked downward, serene like. "As I talk now, time has been set into motion for the unborn child of Kierian and I to be created." She looked back at Erilea with that feline smile, and then her gaze flicked to mine. "I will take over now, Erilea."

Erilea looked at me, and I barely heard her say mournfully, "Take care of him."

I was unprepared as the white flash occurred again, and I was deposited into the woods. I shook my head violently. Aerie had known we were there the whole time when she was fucking Kierian. She had wanted us to see that she too, had a claim on him. Did Kierian have a family with Aerie that he withheld from me? It made me wonder where the child currently was.

My arm stung; Erilea was no longer grasping it tightly. Instead, she and Tennyson were arguing at each other far ahead on the path. I scrambled to catch up to hear what they were saying. Kierian was not in sight anywhere, and for the moment, I was grateful. However, it worried me about where he could potentially be.

"Maybe Erilea, if you didn't go fuck another Fae, we wouldn't be in this situation." Snarled Tennyson.

"Like you're one to talk." Erilea hissed. "You rut every single female with two legs. It doesn't matter if it's human, Fae, or a half-breed." She shot daggers at his back.

"At least I don't do it while already marked." Tennyson fired back.

"I never agreed to it!" Erilea threw her arms up in exasperation. "Kierian did it without my permission!"

"Doesn't mean anything. You're still marked!" Tennyson halted, spinning around on his foot to glare down at her. "My best friend marked you, and you went and spread your legs for another!" He roared in her face.

"That is his problem!" She hissed back. "I am undoing what he did to me against my will!"

"Only a Fae higher ranked than him can undo that mark."

"Then you mark me!" Erilea challenged Tennyson.

He opened his mouth to speak but slammed it shut. His eyes narrowed at her, and then he threw his head back, laughing a dark laugh. Erilea gave him a puzzled look at his change in demeanor.

"What is ever *so* funny, Tennyson?" Erilea growled.

"You thought you could entrap me with that statement. I should have known all along it would come down to this. You played Kierian along just so you could hope to ensnare me." Tennyson laughed harder.

Erilea pursed her lips at him.

"Darling, you are not nearly as smart as you believe you are." He laughed again and turned to continue in the direction he had been heading.

Chapter Fifty

SKYLA

I was becoming familiar with the pain that accompanied the white flash. I stood in the middle of another campground with tents. I didn't even have time to take in my surroundings. My focus fell on Kierian and Erilea fumbling against a tree. A quick glance informed me this end of the camp was unoccupied. My gaze fell back on them as her fingers undid his pants while he yanked down hers. He turned her around as her hands wrapped around the tree, bracing herself for support. Just as the time before, I could not look away as I watched his cock sink into her.

"You shouldn't have gone to that magic-bitch," hissed Erilea as Kierian fucked her hard.

"You shouldn't have fucked another male," Kierian growled. Sinking his fangs into her neck to mark her again.

"Got your attention, didn't I? Made you want me more," she moaned. "But I didn't spend months pleasuring the little half-wit." Irritation laced Erilea's words.

Please, I don't want to watch this again. I whispered in my mind, a single tear rolling down my cheek. It was evident that Kierian had been with Aerie for quite some time. Why did Erilea take him back after the argument she had with Tennyson? Why was she playing games like this? The white flash happened, and I was on another battlefield.

Screaming and yelling surrounded me as the smell of blood hit my nose. My head whipped back and forth as I searched for the trio. Every time before I had been dropped close by them, where were they? I looked past the Fae stabbing humans, and the humans, in return, brought down horses with Fae on them. I walked through dying bodies and barely flinched as a sword sliced through my body to strike its intended target.

My gaze finally found them in the middle of everything. Of course, they would be in the middle. Even though I knew two of them were still alive in the present, I still feared for the worst. My stomach jumped into my throat as I ran to them. This invisible body came in handy as I did not trip over anything in my path, nor did I have to climb over the fallen warriors.

I made it to the trio, and they fought with their backs to each other as they circled and attacked any human that came within their reach. Their speed and fluidity were more than my normal human eyes could handle, and I felt dizzy trying to process it.

A shout from Kierian pulled my attention to him as a horse on fire came blazing toward them without a rider. In slow motion, I watched in horror as the horse knocked Tennyson off balance, and a human with a sword came and stabbed him in the stomach before jerking upwards. Erilea screamed, whirling her claws, and sliced the human to pieces. Kierian's eyes widened at the sight, and he bellowed.

Erilea grabbed both their hands, and the world shrunk and then enlarged as we landed in a small open room house. I felt like I was going to be sick from the feeling. Tennyson was coughing up blood, and I realized I was watching him die. I knew he was still alive in the present, but I was watching him die before my eyes, and I couldn't do anything about it. I didn't hate the Fae male, but I didn't want to watch someone I know die.

"Tennyson!" Kierian bellowed again. It was futile to even try to heal him. Too much blood was pouring from his body. Erilea bawled, holding Tennyson's hand while stroking his face. Tears rolled down my cheeks, following the dried tracks from the ones I had shed earlier. A cat's meow caught my attention, and I had to do a double-take. It was the same cat that resided in the cottage with Kierian and me. Mytilda. She was younger-looking, almost kitten-like.

My attention focused back on Tennyson. A cough turned into a gargled croak, and I watched as the light in his eyes faded, becoming glassy. Erilea sobbed harder, her gaze landing on the cat and back to Tennyson.

"I wish for the death gods to take my life in place of Tennyson. I wish for Tennyson's body to mend, and he live instead. Please, I beg. Take me instead of him!" Erilea pleaded.

"No!" Roared Kierian to Erilea as he spotted the lavender cat. Mytilda cocked her head to the side and meowed in response. A flash of yellow light that glistened exploded upon the room. Kierian kept raging as Erilea gasped and coughed. She smiled tenderly as she looked to Tennyson and fell to the floor dead.

Tennyson's body mended itself until the bleeding stopped, light returning to his eyes. He gasped, bolting upright. Kierian continued to rage, holding Erilea as he rocked back and forth.

I glanced at Mytilda, and she stared at me. She looked older, no longer a kitten. The wishing cat looked like she did in the present. Mytilda winked one eye at me and turned around, walking the way she had come from.

"Erilea gave her life for me?" Tennyson asked, unbelieving. Kierian didn't answer him as he continued to grieve. My heart broke for him. I had been hurt minutes earlier at the scenes I had witnessed unfold between the two, and now she was gone. She had given her life up for Tennyson. I didn't even believe she had thought about how it would affect Kierian.

Kierian's head whipped to Tennyson, his eyes pure black. In fear, I watched as his body started shifting. This was not the stag form I had come to know. Instead, in its place was some sort of stag with fangs and claws cloaked in blackness. Wings sprouted from its back, and it went to attack Tennyson.

Tennyson held up his hands, backing away. "Kierian, this isn't you. Don't let Erilea's wish be for naught," Tennyson tried to rationalize. The Fae beast that Kierian had transformed into didn't even react to that statement. He roared at Tennyson, trying for another swipe.

To save his life a second time for the day, Tennyson crashed through the window. Glass shards flew everywhere. I stood in the room, watching Kierian ravage the room to obliteration. Wood splintered every which way, and by the time he was done, the house crumbled in on itself. He heaved the wreckage from his body and stood still in that beast form, heaving deep breaths. I wanted to take a step toward him, but I knew my invisible body could do nothing. His legs shook under him, and then I watched as he collapsed. He turned back into his Fae male form, crying over Erilea's untouched body.

The white flash happened again. This time, it did not linger on a memory. Everything sped up in time as I watched Kierian. He found the cottage abandoned beyond recognition and began tidying it up.

He had become a husk of himself; he didn't speak a word as the time sped by. He barely slept. Some days, he lay there staring at nothing.

One day, the same wishing cat came to the cottage and decided never to leave. Kierian didn't even acknowledge its presence. Tennyson visited multiple times but never could elicit an emotion or reaction out of Kierian. I didn't recognize him. He was alive but didn't exist. The seasons began blurring together as the memory speed picked up. I couldn't keep track of how many years we were passing; each second was a new year gone. Random visitors would come to the door but never stay. I watched in a blink the oak tree, I had come to know, grow from a sapling to the massive beast it was today. I witnessed as other trees grew and died, new ones taking their place and repeating the process.

It slowed down when the meadow was clear of all trees but the oak, and then there I was bumbling from the woods how many months ago. I had been beyond starved, skinny, and frightened. I never realized how malnourished I had been. I wondered what Kierian had thought upon seeing this scrawny girl standing before him with newfound hope in her eyes.

I blinked, and the white flash happened, but this time when I looked around, I was in a white room with the twins. The room was void of all furniture. There wasn't even a door or windows.

Chapter Fifty-One

SKYLA

Aerie's eyes shifted back and forth, searching mine. I wasn't certain what kind of answer she was looking for. After Erilea had called her by name, I knew she had been the driver in this trip down Kierian's life. The question I had, though, was why she had lingered in spots? What had she been looking for, and did Kierian know what she had done?

"You saw everything," I stated.

"You saw everything," Al'Kede replied in turn.

"What does that even mean?" I turned my attention to him.

"If you want to become full Fae for the male waiting for you, can you handle knowing his past?" Aerie asked. I stared at her.

And the child? I raised an eyebrow.

Never happened. Her eyes shifted to coldness.

Then why say it?

To piss Erilea off. Her face hardened more, almost daring me to keep pushing and see what she had in store for me if I did.

"It's in the past," I replied as calmly and steadily as I could to the male twin. Neither twin turned their head as they flicked a glance at each other.

"We have turned humans before who claimed they could handle the past but had not been honest. It did not end well for either party involved." Al'Kede informed.

"Giving up being human to live a Fae life can feel like an imprisonment if you cannot look past Kierian's history," Aerie added on gently, but I could hear the threat in her voice. She was still very protective of the Fae male, and I wondered why she was willing to help me turn Fae to spend my life with him. Why she had fixated on his intimate scenes with another female. I felt it had not been for my benefit but hers instead, as she forced us to watch intently.

Some answers are best left unknown, human it was Al'Kede's voice in my head this time. It should be bothering me that my thoughts were currently not private, but it also made it easy to communicate about things that were difficult to say out loud.

I closed my eyes, going over everything I had witnessed from Kierian's past and what Erilea had helped show me. It made me wonder who she was to have been able to see me. Did she know we were there the whole time but didn't acknowledge us until that one moment? I had too many questions that would remain unanswered when it came to Erilea.

"What were the trio searching for that they killed that girl in the first tavern?" I asked the twins. They glanced at each other, and I got the sense they were having a private telepathic conversation. I waited for them to conclude their decision. I felt if I became impatient or rude, I wouldn't receive an answer.

"The trio were a special unit of warriors," began Al'Kede, "there were many missions they were sent out to find various items and –"

"Sometimes they made things up to kill for sport," finished

Aerie. I knew they weren't going to tell me, and even what they were telling me didn't scratch the surface of the truth.

"You're wise to not meddle in things that do not concern you," Aerie stated.

"Like you spying on Kierian's sex with Erilea?" I raised an eyebrow, despite the sting in my chest from the memory.

Aerie narrowed her eyes at me.

"I could say no to your change," Al'Kede threatened. I gulped. I had thought Aerie was running the show, but for some reason, I felt that had been a front. Was Al'Kede the real master here? He smiled at me slightly.

"What was Erilea?" I asked, changing topics. It lingered in my thoughts that she saw us and took control.

"A special kind of Fae," Al'Kede answered.

"No concern for you." Aerie chirped.

"Dead now." Al'Kede finished.

I found it odd how quickly they answered me. There was so much about the Fae world that I did not understand. Despite all the reading I had been doing with the books Kierian had bought me, I continuously learned new things. Similar to the human world, there were unsolved mysteries in the Fae world. Erilea would probably stay one of those for me.

"What is your choice, stay human or become Fae?" Al'Kede asked. I looked between the twins, trying to find my answer. I had witnessed only a tiny bit of Kierian's memories, and I wasn't even sure if they were the worst he had done or if there were more horrors from his past. Seeing him being intimate with others gutted me, and the fear of pain to become Fae weighed heavily in my mind now. I would be giving up my human life, Kierian had centuries of life on me. How much life did he have left, and then would I be living as a Fae alone? I let out a breath. I needed to make a decision.

Chapter Fifty-Two

KIERIAN

Two minutes passed by since the twins had taken Skyla from my grasp. I stood there waiting, knowing I could tear this place apart and still not find her. The twins were too powerful, and I knew they would not be on this plane anyway. I worried about what memories they were showing Skyla and if she would even be able to look at me afterward.

Was she witnessing my childhood and all the fights I had picked or all the humans I had murdered? There were too many centuries of wrongdoings. I would never be able to repent enough to receive forgiveness from her. I should cut my loss now; accept she will choose to stay a human and then leave me. I would give her whatever she needed to be successful in a human village. I had enough gold to put her up nicely. Whatever she desired, and then she would never have to hear from me again if she chose it.

I had been selfless in not telling her about our mating bond. I had never wanted her strapped to me out of guilt. Maybe I was in the wrong, keeping that information from her, but I didn't want to take her freedom. I never wanted to cage her or take away her light. I wanted Skyla to be happy. I had done so many horrible things in my past that if she no longer wanted me, I would cut my losses.

My heart ached from the thought. I would probably beg the twins and The Spellcaster to make me forget Skyla just so I could make it through each day without her. If The Spellcaster or Aerie demanded my body as payment, I would become their sex toy; I didn't care. As long as Skyla was happy with her choice, I would figure out a way to live without her. I didn't want to forget her, but if she didn't choose me, I didn't think I could live without the memory of her being wiped from my mind.

The room flashed a bright white light, and I had to shield my eyes from it. I didn't even feel the pain as my knees cracked against the marble flooring. A female Fae walked from it with feline grace toward me. She wore a beautiful silk-wrapped white dress. Her red hair floated around her as if levitating. I would recognize those green eyes anywhere, and I felt myself choking up. She chose me. She chose to be with me.

The white light faded as her hair fell back down to her waist. She nervously tucked it behind her new delicately pointed ear, looking down at the ground and then back at me through her lashes.

"Do I look ridiculous?" she asked, biting her lip. She looked back at the ground, and a flush graced her face. I rose from kneeling and took the few steps needed, wrapping my arms around her waist and pulling her close to me.

"No, you look like mine."

She looked up at me, searching my eyes, trying to detect the lie.

"You're crying," she commented.

"Do you always state the obvious?" I laughed, thinking back to the first day she had shown up at my doorstep. She joined in my laughter, wrapping her arms around my neck.

"Enjoy a lifetime of happiness, Kierian," Aerie's soft voice surrounded us. I didn't take my eyes off my mate. I only nodded and moved with ease to pick Skyla up. I intended to carry her out of this cave and bring her back to our home.

"As a gift from me, I will transport you home to prevent any... casualties," Al'Kede's voice echoed off the walls. There was a soft pop noise, and then I smelled the cottage herbs.

Chapter Fifty-Three

SKYLA

I relaxed into Kierian's arms as I felt the familiarness of the cottage. I was grateful that we did not need to travel another three weeks to come home. I glanced up at Kierian to find him smiling down at me. I blushed, ducking my head slightly.

"How do you feel?" His warm voice caressed my ears. I mentally did a check all over my body; it may no longer be human, but it felt the same. Pulling away from him, I glanced down at myself. When the twins changed me, I barely had a moment to inspect the changes. Reaching up slowly, I felt my newly pointed ears and inhaled sharply. I knew they were no longer rounded, but the pointedness startled me. Tilting my head to the side, I met Kierian's eyes.

"I think I feel fine? What do I look like, though?" I shrugged, uncertain if I looked better or worse. Upon hearing my request, the cottage chimed a melody, and a deluxe mirror from floor to ceiling appeared in the room by my reading bench. I didn't wait for Kierian to reply as I untangled myself from his arms and sped to the other side of the room. I tried to stop but tripped over my own two feet.

"Oof!" I let out as I crashed into Kierian's bed. How did that happen? I looked back at Kierian, who was trying to hide his laughter behind his hand. I raised an eyebrow at him. "What is *so* funny?"

"You're not used to your Fae speed yet. We'll need to do some Fae training outside." He glanced around the cottage, eyeing some of the more fragile items. Things such as the wooden furniture. Untangling myself from his bed, I carefully made my way over to the mirror.

"Are you trying to sneak up on it?" He laughed, this time not bothering to hide his amusement.

"What do you mean?" I stopped and cocked my head to the other side.

"You're tiptoeing to the mirror." He nodded his head at my feet. Following his gaze, I glanced down and realized the muscle strain I felt in my calves. I had been walking on my tiptoes. Gingerly, I lowered both of my feet down on the ground and took a step forward. I glanced up at him and he smiled, biting his lip. I narrowed my eyes slightly at him, and then proceeded to the mirror.

I held my breath, bracing myself for what I would find in the reflection. I let the breath out slowly, in awe. I looked the same but there were noticeable differences, aside from my pointed ears.

"Have my eyes always been this green?" I asked Kierian, without looking away. He crossed the short distance and wrapped his arms around my waist, pulling me into him.

"Mmh-hmm." He kissed my neck, and a zing running through me. I inhaled sharply from the feeling and then tried to dismiss it.

"Why have I never noticed before? They seem brighter and more colorful," I commented, nuzzling my cheek against his head.

"It's your Fae sight; you are seeing what I have always seen." He rested his head on my shoulder and met my eyes in the mirror.

"Do you think I'm pretty as a Fae?" I nibbled my lip. If he hadn't been holding me tightly, I would have rocked on my feet.

"I find you gorgeous regardless of if you are a Fae or human," he murmured.

A thought crossed my mind, and it made me more nervous. I knew what I was planning on saying next could ruin this moment, but I didn't want to put off the inevitable. I was newly Fae, and I could already be putting a wrench into everything.

"Do you want to know what I saw?" I asked quietly.

He stilled, knowing what I meant, and I felt the temperature drop in the room. I shivered, finding it odd, considering I had never noticed it happening before. His jaw moved back and forth on my shoulder as his eyes were downcasted. I patiently waited quietly as he mulled over his decision. He tilted his cheek into my neck and squeezed me a bit tighter.

"Yes," he breathed.

I undid Kierian's arms from my waist and led us to sit on his bed. When we were comfortable, I took a deep breath and began telling him from start to finish of the memories I witnessed. A few times, he looked ashamed from what I had witnessed, and other times, we were both blushing as I fumbled over my words. It didn't go unnoticed the way he still grieved silently for Erilea. I left out my small interaction with Erilea and Aerie's secret. I was too nervous how far the twins reach would be if I did tell Kierian.

When I finished, tears brimmed his eyes, and I reached up to cradle his cheek with my hand. I rubbed my thumb to catch the first tear that fell. My heart broke for him, knowing it had to be difficult listening to me retell Erilea's sacrificial wish.

"Thank you for telling me." His voice came out hoarse, his body trembling.

"You're welcome." I wasn't certain how much more I should say, so instead, I chose to remain quiet. When Kierian was ready, we could go from there.

"Would it . . . would it be inconsiderate to ask you to hold me?" He choked out. I didn't even reply as I wrapped my arms around him tightly. He cried into my shoulder, and I rocked our bodies together. Aside from the day Erilea had died, no other time had Kierian cried from what I had witnessed in his memories. This was three hundred years of grief being finally released.

Even in grieving, Kierian had considered my feelings by asking my permission to hold him. Somehow, I had the sneaking suspicion that I would have gotten along with Erilea if she were still alive. I would like to believe somehow, my life would have ended up with Kierian and myself still together, even if Erilea were here. It may have been more rocky and more difficult, but there was a knowing feeling for Kierian since becoming Fae. I simply didn't know what to call this feeling, though; it tugged, needed, and knew him. It was the best way I could describe it as it hummed throughout my whole senses.

Cradling Kierian, I leaned us back until we were curled up on his bed. I snuggled him close to me, staying like that for hours. Giving him what he needed as his heart shattered in grief and mended back together in my arms.

"I need to tell you something," Kierian's low voice said as he held me in his arms. We were still in his bed, with me nestled into him. There was a reassuring humming through me that what he was about to tell me would be good and that I shouldn't fret.

"What is it?" I asked, not moving from my spot.

"Remember how before we made the trek, I had told you in the Fae world our spouses are mates, and that above mates are 'Fated Mates'?" his voice was a bit gruff as he spoke.

"Yeah?" I was hopefully he was going to ask me to be his mate. I knew our previous conversation had not been an outright marriage proposal, but it danced around the thought.

"We are fated mates."

I shifted my body so I could look at him, trying to understand what he was telling me. By the Fae world standards, did that mean we were already married? I gave him a confused look, trying to understand what he was saying.

"Fated mates," he began, "are not uncommon in our world, but they can be difficult to find due to a Fae's long lifespan."

"How long have you known we were fated mates?" I interrupted him.

"The Spellcaster told me right after she enchanted your necklace." He closed his eyes, concentrating. "The bond didn't snap into place until the first time we had sex."

My mind raced back to how it felt like a rubber band had snapped within me. I had felt the bond and didn't realize what it had been. I looked at him wide-eyed.

"Is that why you put off having sex with me for so long? You didn't want the bond?" Icy fear slid through me. Had I made a mistake in becoming Fae? Day one and already the twins' warning of turning humans Fae not going over well could be coming true. He opened his eyes, and they were filled with sadness and worry.

"No, I was afraid you would not want to be chained to me for life if the bond snapped into the place."

"Kierian," my voice broke as I wrapped my arm around him. "I want you. Don't you see, I want you."

Kierian continued to explain to me about fated mates and how things didn't always go well. While fated mates weren't uncommon among his kind – our kind. Kierian witnessed that sometimes fated mates were more of an inconvenience and heartbreak for Fae. Due to the longevity lifespan of a Fae and the size of our world, fated mates weren't a rarity. However, finding each other before falling in love with another is where the inconvenience came in. I had been confused until he explained that usually a Fae would choose a mate to wed. Then, some time afterward, they would stumble upon their fated mate. It caused a difficultly to stay with the spouse they had chosen when their whole being yearned for their fated mate.

Then there was the other spectrum, the Fae who longed to know who their fated mate was. Some would go a whole lifetime of never meeting them and would die alone. These Fae lived the opposite of the inconvenienced ones. They yearned for their other half, but never gave themselves a chance to love anyone else. My heart broke from the thought of them never finding what I had.

A twisted cruelty Kierian mentioned was that even though two Fae were fated mates, it didn't mean they would always get along. Every fiber of their being would call for one another, and the fight to not give in to temptation would drive them crazy. They would come together in a violent, passionate whirlwind to then separate, loathing each other. The process would continually repeat. I wrinkled my nose from the thought of being with someone I despised intimately for the rest of my life.

Somehow, through it all, Kierian and I had found each other. We had been strangers, complete opposites, but yet here we were, fated mates nestled in each other's arms.

Chapter Fifty-Four

SKYLA

A month had passed by since I became Fae. I picked wildflowers, enjoying their delicate scent to my nose. Today, we were taking it easy because, almost daily, Kierian had me doing Fae training. This ranged anywhere from learning my speed, how to stop, and using all my senses. If I had thought I disliked the smell of lavender before, I was wildly wrong. Now, even on the completely opposite side of the clearing, I could smell it. At first, I wore a constant face of disgust from the smell. I learned to block it out as other scents became more apparent and noticeable. Although, when lavender was drying in the cottage, Kierian would find me continuously glaring at the offending herb.

My Fae speed was not as fast as Kierian's, but I was working on it. The worst was stopping. I still hadn't built the correct muscles and coordination to help me. More than a few times, I ended up removing multiple slivers from my body after taking out some trees. I winced as I glanced at their splintered stumps along the clearing's edge. Kierian only joked that he had planted them not knowing the reason, until now. I didn't find his joke hilarious, as I felt it physically painful from each tree I had taken out from failure to stop properly.

Unfortunately, my protection necklace did not prevent my injuries from unsuspecting trees. Even with my change, I still wore the pendant. I may no longer scent as human, but as a Fae, I was weak like a child. Until I was a more skilled fighter, I promised to continue to wear it. Reaching up, I touched the necklace; I knew I probably would never take it off. The metal antlers were a reminder of my mate.

Warmth spread throughout me. Our bond was another thing I was learning as well; there was always a tug for Kierian. When I was human the draw had been minimal and not noticeable even when the bond had snapped into place. However, as a Fae, it was a pleasant, welcomed hum in my body. We had discovered with the bond that we could feel if the other became injured. Which meant every time I crashed into a tree, Kierian felt a wave of pain. It wasn't as strong as what I felt, and the best way to describe it was like a numb pain.

I glanced over my shoulder at Kierian, smiling as our eyes connected. I was lucky the man I loved was my fated mate. I watched as he stood up and crossed the distance between us.

Chapter Fifty-Five

KIERIAN

Instead of mixing salves today, I chose to enjoy a moment's peace outside as the wind rolled over the grassy knolls. I sat underneath the old oak tree, taking in the serenity of my surroundings. I had cultivated this space and made it my own.

My gaze settled on Skyla, picking wildflowers that were scattered throughout the hills. The wind softly blew her red hair in tilting waves as I caught glimpses of her pointed ears. My chest swelled with happiness. Her head moved back and forth, trying to choose which flowers to add to the growing bouquet she held in her hands. I would need to dig out a vase in my cupboards for her to place them in. Our home was already filled with the scent of various plants. A few more of the sweet-smelling kind would be no harm.

Skyla turned to look at me, and there was my happiness. My beautiful mate smiled. I stood up from where I sat, traveling the distance of the hills until I was wrapping her in my arms.

"What were you thinking?" She asked, smiling up at me. I grabbed Skyla from under her thighs, hiking her up until I had to look up at my mate. She wrapped her legs and arms around me, not letting go of the bouquet of flowers as she continued to smile down at me, waiting for my response.

"I love you, Skyla." Her smile widened as she leaned down and kissed me deeply.

"I love you too, Kierian," she said softly. The gentle breeze picked up around us as the flowers swayed in the breeze. I had been lost for far too long, unfeeling for the last three-hundred years. Then one day, this red-haired girl showed up at my doorstep wanting a wish granted. Little did she know, she had been my wish come true.

CHAPTER 56

Bonus Chapter

TENNYSON

In the distance on a hidden branch, the couple were unaware of me watching them. I let one leg swing lazily from the branch as I leaned back against the tree. Tilting my head to the side, I took in the scene of their lovey-doveyness. I had considered stopping by multiple times to see how Petal was fairing as one of our kind. Every time, I withheld myself, knowing it would cause more harm than good. I had endured witnessing Petal not being able to control her Fae abilities too well. I didn't fear handling a clumsy new Fae stumbling about, but Kierian made me rethink my thoughts. My brother would still be too overprotective of his mate.

Everything went as predicted. Mytilda's voice drifted into my head. The lavender fluffy cat dropped down in between my legs from the branch above. She sat with her back to me as we watched the couple in the distance. I did not even stir from her sudden appearance. Mytilda's tail lazily swished along my leg that swung.

He needed her. I replied mentally to the cat.

One could argue, she needed him too.

I huffed, rolling my eyes as I glared into the distance. My irritation wasn't directed to Kierian and Petal; it was deeper, but I was not about to delve into that issue currently.

She would have been proud . . . At first, I believed Mytilda had been talking about Petal until she continued with . . . *to know that everything she had done with her wish had led to this.*

Mytilda looked back at me over her shoulder, her eyes flashing ever so slightly before her pupils expanded until there was only a sliver of cerulean-blue to be seen. I pressed my back slightly into the tree. An eerie sensation passed over me. Fear didn't find me easily, but the wishing cat unnerved me.

It would have made her happy to know you helped bring them together.

I narrowed my eyes at the cat; she knew far too much. A meddling Fae creature is what she was.

You meddle the same as me, if not more. She snipped. I hadn't even projected the thoughts in her mind. Her tail swished as she blinked.

You believe you hide your thoughts so well, but as a wishing cat . . . there are so many wonders I have access to. Mytilda twisted her body backwards over my leg, abandoning the branch we occupied. I leaned over the edge to find she had disappeared without a trace.

Tennyson, just know the wish you made long ago has not gone unforgotten. Erilea remembers.

I shuddered from a centuries-old memory. My eyes widened at the implications, and I shook my head. Distracting myself, I looked back to my brother and Petal. Yes, I meddled to bring them together. I helped speed up the process as best as possible without ruining everything. I worked side by side with Mytilda to make it happen. Her paws were equally dirty in the matter; mine may just be a bit more tainted.

I only wanted to make up for the error I had wished for all those years ago. My brother had been lost for far too long, and the red-haired lass needed someone who wasn't heartless. Someone who believed she was the air they needed to breathe. Kierian was everything that fitted that description. No other human or Fae could give her that, and no one else could have brought Kierian back to the light.

They would never know what I had sacrificed to bring the two of them together. No, the truth is, they would never have an idea how many sacrifices were made to lead up to this moment. Nor would they know that I would do everything in my abilities to never allow harm to come between them. I vowed to protect Kierian and Petal at all costs for the rest of my life, even if it destroyed me.

Author's Note

Hello Reader! Thank you for reading my book! It means so much to me that you took the time to pick my book and read it out of all the other amazing books in the world! Let me give you a little insight on *Kierian*. The idea for his book came to me while I was still in the process of writing, *A Kingdom of Promises and Lies*. It nagged and lingered in the back of my mind relentlessly and wouldn't stop bugging me until it was written.

Kierian's character came easy to me. He is this silent, broody, former warrior. He's done horrible things, had his heart ripped to shreds, and only wants to live a simple, quiet life. He needed a little shaking up, which is where our leading lady comes into play.

Skyla, on the other hand, I had to figure how I wanted to really capture this fiery girl. I knew I wanted her to have anxiety. I know it's not stated in the book, but I gave her traits that aligned with anyone who battles anxiety, such as myself. She has worries and fears, the girl has nothing to lose in life, but has so much to live for.

As I was writing *Kierian* I probably received more second-hand embarrassment and giggles from what Kierian and Skyla went through to get to know each other. Poor Skyla had to go through some major slow-burn when it came to Kierian; even I felt sorry for the girl. Alas, it all worked out in the end.

Like my other series, *The Courting Seasons*, which was supposed to be a standalone, this too was going to be. However, I fell in love with the backstory I created for Tennyson and whelp; now he needs a book, too. The bonus chapter at the end will definitely elude to some major things happening in his book. Erilea's story I am still fleshing out in my mind, but her book has some good bones for a base structure.

If you didn't know, I enjoy giving my character's, no matter how minor a good background. Even Rhoda, the waitress in the cafe, has a whole little mini backstory created. She may even receive a novella. I like knowing what makes my characters them and what quirks they have. However, because I enjoy giving them a whole backstory, it also means I want to write their story as well. Alas, why we may never receive a standalone novel out of me. Lol.

Now, you may be wondering about the series name, *FaeVille*. Well, until I had a name picked out for *Kierian* that is what I had been calling this story, "FaeVille" which my book wifey, Amy, kept thinking of FarmVille so there's that, lol (I do love playing a good farm simulator game on the Nintendo consoles). Anyway, after being called "FaeVille" for so long it only fitted to make it the series name.

I want to say thank you once again for taking the time to read my book, you will never know how much it means to me to have another individual know about the world and characters I have created
-N. F. Schmitt

Acknowledgments

Thank you, everyone, for reading Kierian, part of the *FaeVille* series. I hope you fell in love with Kierian and Skyla as much as I have fallen in love writing their story.

Cody: Thank you as always for being my super supportive spouse! You never know what my neurospicy brain will throw your way, but you always come along for the ride with your unconditional support and love. I cannot wait to see what the future brings with us as I keep writing more books.

My Parents: This book is dedicated to you. If it were not for your support and encouragement of my love for reading as a child, I would not be here publishing books! Hope you enjoy reading this one too Mom!

Amy: Thank you for being my wifey and always being super supportive in helping me navigate some of the behind-the-scenes waters in the book world! I know there has been so many times you shook your head at me and went, "Dear God Woman!" from my lack of modern technology knowledge, all said with love of course. Thank you again for giving me feedback when I was creating my book cover; it would be nowhere near as bomb-ass if you didn't tell me what needed tweaking.

Alisha: Thank you for being my Iowa Book bestie! You are the extrovert to my introvert side of a coin, and I wouldn't want to have it any other way! You are there for me every step of the way and I cannot wait to see what the future brings for us as we do midwest book signings together! Starting *Iowa & Midwest Book Lovers* was an amazing idea to help connect us to other locals! I am so happy BookTok brought us together!

Bookish Sirens: Thank you to my fellow Modmin team (Dana, Maggie, and Hannah) for always supporting and helping me with my Author career! The support team this group has, not only as Modmins but also as group members is phenomenal!

My Alpha Readers: Thank you for being my first set of eyes with this book! I know *Kierian* would not be in its strongest form if my alpha readers hadn't given me feedback on how to improve it. Thank you: Amy, Heather, Erica & Kyle

Beta Readers: Thank you for being my second set of eyes! My beta readers are what helped me tweak a few more areas and make *Kierian* become extra special. My Beta Readers helped me know I was on the right track before I did my final rounds of editing. Thank you: Alisha, Andrea, Cristina & Courtney

My Amazing Street Team: My hype team! You help me stay motivated every day with the love you show me and each other in our chat! You are so dang supportive, and you will never have any idea how much I appreciate you all! My author career would not be nearly as far without each and every single one of you helping me along the way!!!

Social Media

Keep in Touch with N.F. Schmitt

Website: www.NFSchmitt.com
Add me on Facebook: www.facebook.com/n.f.schmitt
Facebook Page: www.facebook.com/NFSchmittAuthor
Tiktok: www.tiktok.com/@n.f.schmitt
Instagram: www.instagram.com/n.f.schmitt
Threads: www.threads.net/@n.f.schmitt
E-Mail: NFSchmittAuthor@gmail.com

Want to discuss my books and other fun shenanigans with like-minded readers? Join my reader group:

www.facebook.com/groups/nfschmitt

About the Author

N.F. Schmitt is a born and raised Iowa girl, living in the country with her husband and all their pets. When she doesn't have her nose in a book or head in the clouds, you can find her ATVing most weekends on a dirt bike or sports quad, video gaming, drawing or planting a new tree in her yard (the local plant nursery know her & hubby on a first name base from all the indoor/outdoor plants they buy).

www.ingramcontent.com/pod-product-compliance
Lightning Source LLC
Chambersburg PA
CBHW070443300726
48975CB00007B/2026